Mike

MW01599538

The Hopeless Cases

by

Mike Bowerbank

© October, 2023

Thursday, 2:06 a.m.

Abby Lunay sat on the side edge of the woman's bed in the darkness and sighed. "So, that's when I decided to give up my life of crime and become a private detective." She exhaled sharply. "I have to say, though, I've discovered that being a detective is way more involved than I ever imagined it would be. Being a criminal was so much easier, that's for sure. No licenses required, no need for certification, and no paying taxes. I never knew how many taxes there were until I started paying them. Oh, and I hate filling out all those boring tax documents, especially since I have the attention span of ice cream in a blast furnace. It's no wonder so many people choose crime, because it's so much more work to be legal. But I've got my first client now, and it looks as if my very first case is going to be a big one."

She looked at the woman; or rather, she looked at the shape in the darkness where the woman was. Abby could only see she was sitting up, and seemed to have the blankets wrapped tightly around her.

Abby beamed. "I can't wait to get started, so I can see how it all works out in the end. Anyway, like I said, I've recently started out as a private detective, and things have really moved quickly. If I'm being honest, I'm not sure how any of this whole chain of events unfolded, at least not quite the way it did, but, somehow, my very first case looks like it's going to have murders, an actual demon, and other cool stuff."

Abby chuckled. "It's kind of funny. My best friend Alyssa? She's nineteen now, and she'll never, ever believe there's a demon in my case, and that's okay, aside from the fact it means she'll be completely wrong. Anyway, this all started a year or so ago when I first told Alyssa I was going to begin the process to open my own detective agency. I don't know if she believed I would actually go through with it, but now that I have my first case, I can't wait to tell her all about it, but I'll need to get the timing right, because I don't think she'll believe me. You see, I was asked by my client to look into the mysterious deaths of two people who died in a fire a little over a year ago, so it's going to keep me busy."

In the ensuing silence, the woman in the bed cleared her throat and finally spoke. Her voice was soft and hesitant. "Is it okay if I ask you a question now?"

"Yeah, sure. Go ahead."

"Who are you, and how did you get into my apartment?"

Abby blinked in the darkness. "Wait, aren't you Gina?"

"No."

"Isn't this apartment twelve-oh-two?"

"No, this is twelve-oh-*three*."

"Oh, I'm in the wrong room." Abby stood up and headed toward the window. "I must have miscounted the windows out there, but I have to say, you're a really good listener." She climbed onto the window sill. "Have a good night."

"You're leaving through the window?"

"That's how I came in, so yeah."

"But this is the twelfth floor."

"Thanks, but I already knew that. My sense of up and down was perfect; it was my side-to-side senses that were off by one window."

"Wait a second," the woman called out. "Seriously, who are you?"

"My name is Abby, and I'm twenty-six-years old, and if I'm really, *really* lucky, I'll live to be twenty-seven in another two months. Bye."

The woman watched Abby climb out through the bedroom window and then close it behind her. The woman was wrestling with whether she should scream, call the police, go to the window and watch, or some combination of those options. The one thing she was certain about was her sudden urge to get to know her neighbour Gina in 1203, so she could find out what kind of person would have a guest at two in the morning who enters through the bedroom window.

Thursday, 8:39 p.m.

Alyssa Bristol stared at Abby, mouth agape. "You're *seriously* ready to open your detective agency? As in right now?"

Abby stood nodding in the doorway of Alyssa's bedroom. Abby didn't grow up with friends, so her social interactions were mainly with accomplices. As such, she didn't have any expectations for what a teenager's room would typically look like; yet when she first saw Alyssa's room, it still came as a surprise. Abby had heard about the walls of teenagers' rooms being adorned with pop stars, boy bands, and heartthrobs, but Alyssa's walls were sparsely decorated. The wall which her desk was up against had a poster of the Periodic Table of Elements, and the only other decoration, if it could be called that, was her framed high school diploma.

"Yeah, I did the licensing course, submitted my criminal records check, and did the PI license course. I got my beginner's license in the mail, so now I have to obtain two thousand, four hundred hours of experience in order to get my full license."

Alyssa stood up from her desk, walked over to Abby, and then hugged her. "I'm so proud of you for seeing this idea through. I really am."

When the hug ended, Abby flashed a crooked smile. "Thanks, I've been busy looking for clients so I can get some hours logged." She wasn't yet ready to disclose she already had a client, as the nature of the case would be difficult to explain, and she certainly didn't yet have the right words to explain it to someone who was so rooted in logic that she tended to insist on trivial things, such as evidence and believability.

"That's womderful." Alyssa returned to her chair. "What kind of cases are you looking for?"

Abby shrugged. "Right now, I'll take anything, just to get the hours and experience I need. Maybe I'll take the cases other detectives decline because they thought they were hopeless." Abby's face lit up. "There's an idea. I could call my agency *The Hopeless Cases*."

"You may want to keep working on the name," Alyssa grimaced. "You know, now that I've taken a few moments to think about it, I can picture you doing well as a detective. You're certainly clever and resourceful, so it should be a good fit for you."

Abby swayed back and forth where she was standing. "And you'll help me, right?"

"No, I don't think I can, Abby." Alyssa gestured to the pile of books on her desk. "My classes are keeping me so busy right now."

"Right, your classes, I keep forgetting." Abby smacked her forehead. "You're doing that lab technician… *thing,* right?"

"Yes, even though I have some aunts and uncles who are trying to gently nudge me toward getting a law degree instead." She rolled her eyes. "Well, I say *gently nudge,* but it's more of a *passive-aggressive shove,* but you get the idea."

"You know," Abby walked across the room and sat on the edge of Alyssa's bed, "I can work around your studies. You could be my junior partner, if that makes it easier for you."

"Abby, I'm neither qualified nor interested in that field, whether junior partner or any other position.

My studies were in biology and chemistry, not criminology. I'm a science nerd, not Sherlock Holmes."

"No, of course you're not," Abby adjusted her position on the bed. "You'd be *Dr. Watson* in your example, not Sherlock Holmes. I'd be the one doing the sleuthing, and you'd just be my trusty helper. You and Watson both look at stuff differently than the detectives you help, so I need you to be involved."

"I'll tell you what," Alyssa sighed. "If you ever need to bounce ideas off of someone, then let me know and I'll be your sounding board."

"Great," Abby beamed. "I'd love your help on my cases."

"Whoa, hold on a second." Alyssa's eyes grew wide. "I didn't say I'd help on your cases, I said I'd be your sounding board."

Abby folded her arms. "Alyssa, think about it for a minute. If you're my sounding board, then it means I'm telling you about my cases and you're offering me feedback, insight, and advice, right?"

"Sure."

"Well, hello?" Abby chuckled. "You'd be Dr. Watson, except female. And I'd be *exactly* like Sherlock Holmes, aside from my gender, experience, age, location, name, criminal background, lack of drug habit, and…" Abby waved her hands. "Never mind, I wouldn't be *anything* like Sherlock Holmes, except for the detective part. Anyway, now that we've established our working relationship, it's time to come up with an online ad."

Alyssa blinked. "An ad? You mean for your detective agency?"

"You mean for *our* detective agency." Abby rubbed her hands together. "So, what do you want your part of the online ad to say?"

"No, Abby. I need you to listen to this because I want to be sure you fully understand." Alyssa paused to let what she said sink in. "This is *your* venture, not mine. I don't need or want to have any part of an ad whatsoever."

"Yes, you do, so that people will know about our arrangement."

"Our…?" Alyssa's mouth hung agape for a moment before she could manage to form some words. "What do you mean *our arrangement?* Wait, do you think we need to create an ad stating that you're the detective and not me?" Alyssa rubbed her face with her hands. "I'm also not a professional hockey player or an astronaut, but I don't go around placing ads stating that."

Abby waved her left hand in a dismissive gesture. "Of course not. We won't be playing hockey or doing space travel."

"Then what's the point of placing an ad pointing out that I'm not a detective? Seriously, what *exactly* do you see as the point of that?"

"I thought it would be great marketing to run an ad explaining how you're not a detective and don't want cases."

"Ugh." Alyssa closed her eyes and massaged her temples. "You're making my brain hurt."

"No, think about it." Abby stood up and paced around the room. "The purpose of advertising is to get noticed, right? And I'm competing against so many other detectives who are already out there and established, right?" She stopped pacing and locked eyes with Alyssa. "All of these other detectives have ads that look pretty much the same. An ad like mine would stand out from the others and would definitely get noticed. I think it's a clever angle which will generate calls."

"But you're missing the point." Alyssa stood up. "I don't want to generate calls, especially for something I don't want to do. If I make an ad saying I don't want calls, then people will call me just to ask why I don't want them. Plus, any message I post will automatically be responded to by a handful of men telling me what I'm doing wrong, and another handful who will make gross comments. Placing an ad saying *don't call* defeats its own purpose, and it only gets more absurd the longer you think about it."

"But you not wanting calls could be a selling point for people who would like someone to help them with their problems, but who also don't want or trust conventional detectives."

Alyssa exhaled sharply. "Setting aside the point about my not wanting people to come to me with their problems in the first place, there's a huge flaw in your marketing idea. Can you imagine how ridiculous the ad campaign's slogan would sound? *We'll take your case, no matter how much we don't want to have anything to do with it.* It just sounds completely ludicrous."

"No, it's brilliant." Abby hopped up and down. "We can say *you'd prefer it if you didn't need a detective, and we'd prefer it if you didn't bring us your case, but here we are.* And we could call ourselves *The Reluctant Detectives.* We can get business cards with that printed on them."

Alyssa shook her head. "Don't get me wrong, I can see the humour in the idea, but as a business plan, it's terrible. I mean, if we were going for ludicrous, then we could just say *if we're forced to work your case, I guess we will, even though we'd rather pull our own fingernails off with pliers.*"

"That's not bad, but it's a bit clunky and doesn't flow well."

"I'm not being serious, Abby."

"I know, but I *am* being serious." Abby waved a finger in the air. "How about this: *when you've tried everyone else and they ignore you, come to us and we'll get on your case.*"

"No."

"But why not?"

"Because there is so much wrong with every single aspect of this terrible idea." Alyssa cast a weary look at Abby. "And, by the way, I don't know if the wordplay there was accidental or deliberate, but either way, it doesn't work."

"You're not getting it. This detective thing I'm doing represents a huge change in my life's direction, okay?"

"I know it's a big change for you."

"Do you really? Because I don't think you do." Abby sat back on the bed and put her arms around herself. "For the past eight months, I've been working in the local hospital, and I'm really hating it. I mean, sure, the job itself is good and the people there are great, but I hate hospitals in general. As you know, I spent years in a hospital in the United States, wasting half of my childhood there, being force-fed pills, being told I'm broken, that I needed to be fixed, that I wasn't a complete person, and that kind of thing." Abby scowled. "They never used those *exact* words, of course, but that's what they were saying, except in sugar-coated medical babble. I don't have good memories of those years. I only work there because you don't want me breaking into places and stealing things anymore, so my primary money-earning skills are off the table. I couldn't go back to work for my former employer even if I wanted to anyway, because he still has another twenty-three years to serve in prison. Needless to say, I won't be getting my old job back any time soon. I need to earn money, and I thought maybe you and I could work together to solve the problems people bring us."

Alyssa responded in a soft voice. "I really do admire your enthusiasm, Abby, and I'm honestly flattered you want to work with me, but you'll need to come up with another idea for a career if you want me to be involved. I have no interest in detective work, as I keep telling you. If you want to pursue this on your own, completely and totally without me, then go for it. I'd be happy to cheer you on and maybe – *maybe* – help you get set up, as long as I'm not involved in your actual sleuthing."

"I can probably work the actual cases on my own once I get going, but I don't know how to set up, organize, and run a business, so I'll need your help in those areas." Abby looked at Alyssa. "I'm great at *doing* things, but I'm terrible at documenting and organization."

Alyssa walked over to the bed and sat beside Abby. "I'm happy to help with those areas from time to time, as long as you leave me out of the actual detective parts."

"That's fine, I'll be the sleuth, and I'll hire you to help me when I need it."

"I don't mind you *consulting* with me if you need an opinion, sure, but that's it."

"So, I'll be the detective, and you can be the non-detective." Abby grinned. "That's perfect. Next, I need to design an ad for us."

"Again," Alyssa groaned, "there is no *us;* there's only you."

"No matter which it is, I still need your help coming up with an ad idea for either *The Reluctant Detectives* or *The Hopeless Cases.* I'm still deciding which of those two names to use."

Alyssa shut her eyes, hoping it would help to avert the inevitable headache. "If I play along with this, do you promise to stop asking me for ad ideas and let me get back to my school project?"

"Absolutely. One hundred percent."

"Okay, then here's an idea." Alyssa took a deep breath. "A full-page ad, in a large, bold, sans-serif font, with a headline screaming *I have no interest in your case, and would rather be trampled by a herd of rampaging, mood-disordered dromedaries than work on it.* Then the body of the ad could read: *For the love of God, don't call me, because my interest in your case couldn't be seen if you placed it under a microscope and shone a spotlight on it. If there is a way for me to care any less about your case or about being a detective, then I haven't yet discovered it, but will gladly embrace it the moment I do.* Then the ad can end with our bios. Yours, so they can see who they should be calling, and then mine, so they can see who they should *not* be calling due to my having zero interest in anything they might want to tell me. Then a line can run under our bios which states anyone who has read that far should make an appointment with a licensed therapist, and then ask their doctor about which medications may be right for them, because anyone who still wants to bring me a case after everything they've just read is clearly in need of immediate professional intervention. Now, Abby, do you *finally* understand just how much I don't want anything to do with being a detective?"

"Yes, I think I do now." Abby nodded. "It was so clear, the way you phrased that."

"Thank God for that. You finally understand."

"Yeah, the way you outlined our mission statement in the ad… it was brilliant."

"That's not –"

Abby stood up. "I want to go back to my room and give this some more thought."

"You know what?" Alyssa tossed her hands into the air. "That's fine. You go right ahead and do that, Abby, and knock yourself out. Just leave me completely out of it."

Friday, 7:02 a.m.

The buzzing of her phone on the bedside table woke Alyssa with a start. Her bleary eyes squinted as she fumbled for the phone. She answered the video call and put it on speakerphone.

"Yes?" her voice croaked.

Abby's face appeared on the screen. "Have you seen it yet?"

Alyssa simply blinked, hoping the mental cobwebs would soon clear, so she could make some sense out of the question. She could only manage one syllable in response: "Um?"

"You really need to see it right away." Abby gushed. "It looks great."

"See what?" Alyssa rubbed her eyes. "What looks great? What are you talking about?"

"Our ad."

Alyssa froze, and her eyes sprang wide open in a sudden panic. "Our *ad? Our* ad? *Our ad?* Nope, no matter how I say it, the two of those words put together are filling me with a profound sense of dread." Alyssa let out an exasperated sigh. "Oh my God, Abby, what have you done?"

"I just texted you a link to the ad I posted on some online message boards." Abby looked up from her phone and smiled. "Check your messages, open the link, and take a look. It turned out brilliant, and I couldn't have done it without you. I'm so happy with it."

She sat up. "Did you seriously place an ad? Like, an actual ad?" Alyssa and her wide eyes saw Abby nodding onscreen. "You placed an actual, real-life ad without talking to me first?"

Abby wrinkled her face. "Well, yeah, you told me to go right ahead, and leave you completely out of it."

"And did you leave me completely out of it?"

"Of course."

"So, just to be clear," Alyssa decided it was important to clarify, "I'm not in the ad?"

"Oh, you're definitely in the ad."

Alyssa flashed an angry look. "Then you and I appear to have contrary views on what *leaving me completely out of it* means. In what universe does *leave me out of it* also mean *go ahead and include me?* Who on earth would think those two things have the same meaning?"

"I didn't bother you with the process, and I let you study, which was exactly what you asked me to do for you."

"No, it's not," Alyssa snapped. "Look, I was okay with helping with your idea-generating, stream-of-consciousness thing, but not actually, you know, being placed in your ad for a job I don't want any part of."

"Well, you can relax, because I'll be doing all the actual detective work, and the ad is out in the world now, so you might as well have a look at it. I couldn't remember all of the ad ideas you said, so I filled it in based on what I could remember, and then made up the rest. A couple of messages have already come in, so I've got to run. Bye."

Alyssa slammed her phone down on the pillow and let out a groan. There was no way she was going to give Abby the satisfaction of looking at the ad. She had been very clear that she wanted no part of it at all, so, if she looked at the ad, she'd be encouraging her, and that was not in the cards. She glared at her phone, as though daring it to argue with her.

Alyssa felt fully justified in her anger. The entire turn of events which had unfolded was outrageous. No, it was outrageous *and* completely unacceptable. And maybe even egregious. Alyssa considered getting her phone to look up the word *egregious,* just to make sure it was the right word she was looking for, but then decided if she picked up the phone Abby would win, and that would never do. No, she would focus on her fully-justified fury at the betrayal of her trust. Yes. *Fury.* That was a good word. It was the root word of *furious,* and she was feeling every letter of that word, especially the first two.

How furious should she be? Well, on a scale of one to a hundred, she'd be… well, how much would depend entirely on how horrible the ad was. Regardless, it would be an easy seventy. Maybe a seventy-five. Then again, if the ad was completely outlandish, she'd be short-changing herself with a seventy-five, when this could very well be an incident worthy of a solid ninety or more.

She should probably look at the ad, if only to find out her proper level of outrage. And, she said to herself, it would not at all be for Abby's benefit. No, if she looked, it would only be to determine that appropriate level of fury she should be justifiably experiencing.

Alyssa muttered under her breath as she picked up her phone and went into her text messages. She opened Abby's message and opened the link. It took a few seconds to load and open, but there it was in front of her. The ad Abby placed, in black and white on the message board.

The headline read *"Need a detective, but nobody wants to help you? I'll get on your case."* The sub-heading elaborated: *"I'm not a fully-licensed detective yet, and my associate wants nothing to do with any of this, but if you're desperate, then we're probably as good as you're going to get."*

Alyssa rubbed her face and sighed. She wanted to stop reading, but couldn't help herself. She began to read the text in the body of the ad out of sheer, morbid curiosity.

"We know you'd rather not hire us. People don't hire a detective because they want to, it's usually because they have to. If we're being completely honest, we'd rather not be working on your case either. In fact, here is a partial list of a few things we would rather do than have to work your case:

- *Parasail over a crocodile pond.*

- *Drive fast over a dirt road with a trunk filled with nitroglycerine.*

- *Eat sushi that had been left out in the sun.*

You still want to hire us? Wow, you really must need help. Fine, we'll listen to your case, and if the help you need is psychological, we'll try to recommend a nice doctor for you."

"No," Alyssa groaned. "That is wrong on so many levels. This is a complete nightmare."

Alyssa continued to read, and felt the knot in her stomach twist tighter with each line.

"Anyway, if you've read this far, then you might as well meet our team who are not – I repeat, not – fully-licensed detectives. In fact, one of them isn't a detective at all."

Alyssa prepared herself for the worst.

"Abby Lunay: Born and partially raised in a mental health facility, Abby is new to the whole detective thing, so she won't charge as much as other detectives, but that also means you shouldn't get your hopes up. She's happy to listen to you, but she won't remember anything you say if it's boring, and in most cases, it's likely to be exactly that."

Alyssa's eyes all but popped out of her head when she saw her name in the ad.

"Alyssa Bristol: Definitely not a detective, and she is completely disinterested in your case, and would probably rather be attacked by a pack of concussed wildebeests than talk to you. Unless the wildebeests had a case for her, of course, in which case she'd avoid them too."

She saw Abby's phone number and email address on the bottom, and took some slight solace in not seeing any of her own contact information listed. Okay, so perhaps her fury would have to be capped at a strong eighty-five, but she was still unhappy about it all.

Alyssa grunted with disgust and got out of bed. She had a lot of work to do in order to complete her school project, so she shuffled down the stairs and went to the kitchen to make herself some breakfast.

Friday: 8:41 p.m.

When Abby knocked on the frame of the open doorway of Alyssa's bedroom, Alyssa looked up from her laptop and textbook to Abby, who was still dressed in her light blue work scrubs. Alyssa then looked at the time.

"Wow, it's nearly nine already," Alyssa put her pen down and rubbed her eyes. "Time flies when you're not having fun. Are you just getting home from work?"

"Yeah," Abby yawned. "It was a long day. Hey, where are your parents?"

"They're still in London."

"Oh," Abby frowned. "I thought they said they'd be home by now."

"They did say that, but Mom called, and whatever they're working on over there is taking them longer to wrap up than they anticipated. Dad is coming home mid-day tomorrow, and Mom doesn't know which day next week she'll be back. Why? Do you need something?"

"That depends." Abby tried to study Alyssa's face. "Are you still mad at me?"

Alyssa sighed. "I was furious this morning, but it got downgraded at lunch to *peeved,* then to *a bit miffed* by dinner, and now I'm just too tired to be angry. I'm still upset, but I'm choosing to believe you meant well, so I'm trying to focus on that detail and not the rest of it. What do you need my parents for?"

"I was hoping to get their advice." Abby stepped inside Alyssa's room and sat on the edge of the bed. "Can I ask you instead? I'm stuck, and really need some help."

"Sure thing." Alyssa closed the lid of her laptop. "I could use a short break from doing this homework project anyway. I'll help, as long as you promise to let me work uninterrupted for the rest of the evening. My paper is due first thing tomorrow morning."

Abby nodded. "Deal."

"Okay, then what's on your mind?"

"So, like, you know how I've been looking for some detective jobs, right?"

Alyssa squeezed her eyes shut. "Yes, please don't remind me."

"I have a new client."

"The ad worked? That's terrific news, Abby." Alyssa beamed. "I'm so proud of you right now."

"I'm really excited, too, but I need help with one particular aspect of my case."

"Which aspect?"

"The details."

"I'll need a bit more to work with than just that. Which details do you need help with?"

"All of them, to the point where I need you to come with me to meet my client tomorrow."

"Please tell me you're kidding."

"No, I'm being serious, and it's weird you didn't know that. Anyway, I was going to ask your dad to go with me, but you just told me he won't be home until mid-day tomorrow. The thing is, I start work tomorrow at eight, so I'll need help hours before he's home. This is my first case, and I need to make sure I'm asking all of the right questions."

"I don't know why you think I'd know what to ask them, but… how about after my class tomorrow, you bring your client to the little coffee place at the corner near us, and we can all meet there instead?"

"Um, that's not going to work, because she's not going to be able to meet us anywhere around here."

"Oh, does she live out of town?"

"No, she's just eight blocks from here."

"Oh, then is she physically disabled?"

"No, but due to her circumstances, we need to go to her."

"What kind of client isn't willing to come and meet us halfway?"

"She'd be very willing to meet us if she wasn't locked up all day. Then again, if she wasn't locked up, she wouldn't have hired me in the first place, so we wouldn't need to meet her at all."

"Wait, just back up a little there. Are you telling me your client is in prison?"

"No, of course not. Well, she's not there *yet,* anyway, but she is in a secure room at a mental health clinic being evaluated. *Later* she might go to prison."

"I'm too busy to be playing guessing games with you, Abby, so can you jump ahead to the part where you tell me *specifically* what you need from me?"

"It's quite straight forward. I have my first *actual* case, with an *actual* client, so I need your *actual* help with it."

"But I can't help you with any sort of detective work, you know that. I'm not the least bit qualified to even begin to help you with any part of your case."

"That's why I wanted to talk to your parents. They have experience with weird things."

"I'm fine with you saying that, as long as raising me doesn't count as one of those weird things they have experience with." Alyssa exhaled sharply. "I'm really sorry, Abby, but you'll need to take your actual case and actual client to someone who is an *actual* detective."

"I can't. No detective would take a case like this. They'd avoid it the way they'd avoid a hippopotamus sneezing plutonium."

Alyssa made a sour face. "That was unnecessarily graphic. Okay then, fine. I know I'll regret saying this, but why don't you go ahead and tell me why you think no other detective would want to take this case."

"Okay, so like, a year ago, two people died under suspicious circumstances, and my client wants me to investigate it."

"So far, it's sounding *exactly* like something a detective would take on. A police detective might be your best bet, so your client should call them."

"No, the cops already looked into the case, and that's how my client got arrested, tried, convicted, and then sent to my workplace for evaluation."

"She was convicted of the murders *and* she's a patient at the mental health clinic you work at?"

"Yes, well, she's *one* of the patients I look after there. Anyway, Zee and I got to talking and she told me everything."

"Your client's name is *Zee?* As in the letter zed?"

"No, her birth name is Suzanne, but she hates that name. She also hates the shortened *Suzy,* but when I only used the last syllable of Suzy, she liked it. So now we all call her *Zee*."

"So, if this *Zee* person was tried, convicted, and sentenced, then there's not much you can do for her. Did she launch an appeal?"

"She tried, but her application for the appeal was rejected due to insufficient grounds, which I think means the judge denied her appeal because he found it unappealing."

"Then I'm sorry to have to be the one to tell you this, Abby, but I don't think there's anything you can do at this stage."

"There must be *something* I can do. I mean, sure, yes, she was convicted for the deaths, and yes, they found evidence at the scene linking her to the event, and yeah, they established a *borderline* motive, but she says she didn't do it, so that should count for something."

"What was the borderline motive?"

"Zee told the court if they sent her to a hospital get a psych review done, she'd burn the place down."

"And let me guess. The hospital mysteriously caught fire."

"Yup, and it burned like a marshmallow thrown into a campfire. And the two people who died in the incident were killed due to smoke inhalation."

"And that's your criteria for a *borderline* motive, is it?" Alyssa smirked. "To me, it sounds like the motive didn't stop at the borderline at all, and instead rammed through the gates, drove across the entire country, and then took up residence in a small, coastal town called *Guilty Village*."

"I know it all sounds bad, but she told me she's innocent."

"I don't know how to break this to you, Abby, but around ninety-five percent of every prison's population is filled with people who say they didn't do it."

"If that's true, then I'll be able to get my twenty-four-hundred hours done in no time by helping them all. Well, now that I think about it, I really mean to say I'll be able to get my twenty-four-hundred hours in twenty-four-hundred hours, which is still a lot more than no time."

"Do you realize that works out to a hundred straight days-worth of hours?"

"No, so I guess I'll need lots of energy drinks to keep me awake."

"Quick question for you." Alyssa raised her hand. "Why did you want to ask my parents about this?"

"You were busy with school stuff, and I thought maybe your dad could help me."

"What you're talking about doesn't sound like a national security issue, so I doubt he'd be much help to you."

"But he's the guy with the reputation as a problem-solver. I thought you said the government always calls him whenever there's a big problem."

"Yes, but Mom says it's only because they want to ask him if he caused it."

"Can I phone your mom and get her opinion?"

"Not a good idea." Alyssa stretched her arms. "When she's on an assignment, she works best with no distractions, or she'll overthink everything."

"What about your dad?"

"He won't be much use, because he'll *under-*think everything."

Abby made a face. "If your mom overthinks and your dad under-thinks, then what about me? What am I?"

"Lucky, because you're not related to us."

"And you?"

Alyssa sighed. "I'm the worst of all, because I'll both overthink *and* under-think all the wrong things."

"But you'll help me anyway, right?"

"I'll certainly try, Abby. You're my friend."

"So, can we go together to the clinic tomorrow morning?"

"Tell you what. Come with me to campus so I can drop off my assignment, and then we'll head over to your facility, and I'll help you as best as I can."

"Thanks."

Alyssa picked up her phone and checked the time. "My dad's going to phone me at ten tonight, so I'll get to bed right after that, so I'm fresh in the morning."

"Okay. Good night."

Friday, 10:04 p.m.

Alyssa was sitting at the desk in her bedroom, thoroughly engrossed in the chemistry book she was reading, when she was startled by the sound of her phone buzzing. She closed her book, picked up her phone, and then smiled as she answered it. "Hey Dad."

"Hey, kiddo."

"Are you still coming home tomorrow?"

"Yeah, I'm supposed to be at Heathrow for my flight in five hours, and it's scheduled to take off about an hour after that. All going well, I should land in Vancouver around eleven in the morning your time, and then at the house by around twelve-thirty or so. Anything going on over there?"

"Actually, yes." She stood up and leaned against her desk. "Do you remember when Abby mentioned awhile back how she was interested in becoming a detective, but we weren't sure whether or not we should take her seriously?"

"Yeah, of course. And she started taking some courses and stuff."

"Right," Alyssa chuckled, "and we never know when she's saying something on a whim, or when she's serious about going ahead with it."

"Yeah, because that same day, she also mentioned possibly being a medical test subject or a rodeo clown, among other things."

"Exactly. Anyway, last night, Abby came into my room and said she was ready to open her detective agency."

"Seriously? I didn't even know she'd finished the detective course."

"Same here."

"Jesus. Well, then, I'm happy for her."

"I'm so proud of her." Alyssa beamed. "And because of my complete surprise at the news, I needed some more details, so I started by asking her if she was seriously ready to open her detective agency."

"Tell me the whole story."

Saturday, 7:42 a.m.

As Alyssa walked along the sidewalk toward the temporary clinic with Abby, Alyssa glanced up at the grey clouds dominating the sky. It smelled as though it might rain later. As a child, Alyssa used to find it odd when people said it smelled like rain, but then she experienced it for herself soon enough. There was a certain aroma of general dampness in the air, and one could feel the humidity in the cool, autumn air as it blew around one's skin. Alyssa was about to ask about the weather, but noticed Abby was fussing with her straight, blonde hair.

"What's the matter?"

"Nothing." Abby grunted. "Well, not a complete nothing, more like a minor nothing with a side of a little something."

"And what's the little something which is mostly nothing?"

"It's been more than a year, and I'm still not used to my hair being like this."

"Your hair's gorgeous, Abby." Alyssa ran her fingers through Abby's smooth hair. "It's so much better now than when you used to cut it with a hunting knife and it was all different lengths. What do you think's wrong with it?"

"That was what I liked, though." Abby frowned. "It was so practical. When my hair got long, I would just *swish, swish* and it was nice and short again."

"And completely uneven."

Abby shrugged. "Maybe, but cutting it my way was quick. It was efficient."

"It was a *disaster*." Alyssa looped elbows with her friend. "Sorry, Abby, but your hair always looked like you'd been arguing politics with a blind hairstylist."

Abby gestured with a nod of her head. "The clinic is just one more block this way."

"By the way, I appreciate you being so patient while we were at the college." Alyssa glanced at Abby with a smile. "My professor was busy helping another student, so turning in my paper took a lot longer than I anticipated."

Abby cast a sidelong glance at Alyssa and smirked. "Was that the real reason, or was it because of him?"

"Him?" Alyssa wrinkled her brow. "Him who?"

"Him, he, the guy." Abby chuckled. "You know, the dude in one of your classes who you'd been crushing on. I think you said his name was Elias."

"Yes, his name is Elias, but no, I am not crushing on him." Alyssa cleared her throat. "Or, at least, I'm not anymore."

"I thought you liked him."

Alyssa exhaled sharply. "I did like him, and the key thing to note is how I used the past tense there."

"Why didn't you ask him out?"

Alyssa scoffed. "You mean aside from terror, panic, anxiety, and a crippling fear of rejection?"

"Yeah."

She shrugged. "Aside from those things, I didn't ask him out because he lacked the most important quality I look for in a man."

"What quality was he lacking?"

"Having any sort of interest in me." Alyssa turned her head toward Abby. "That's an automatic deal-breaker in my books."

"I guess that is an important quality." Abby and Alyssa both stepped down from the curb and began to cross the street. "I know you want a relationship, and I want you to be happy. How about you tell me what sort of man you're looking for, and maybe I can help to find you someone suitable."

"Thanks, but…" Alyssa looked down at the pavement. "I don't think anyone can help me."

"Why not?"

"Because in my head, I know exactly what I want, but my head and reality don't seem to be on speaking terms." The street was crossed, and they stepped back on the sidewalk. "I want someone reliable, intelligent, and supportive. And they also have to be secure."

Abby thought for a moment. "Yeah, money is important."

"I suppose it is, but that isn't what I meant by secure. I mean *emotionally* secure, like someone who will help me achieve my goals without jealousy of any progress I make. And I want someone who will let me help them achieve their goals without them feeling threatened or emasculated."

Abby laughed.

"Why is that funny?"

Abby looked at her friend. "Because you're not exactly setting the bar very high."

"I know," Alyssa kicked at a pebble on the sidewalk. "But let's be honest here, there's no lineup of people waiting to go out with me. I'm a hopeless case, so I can't be too picky."

"You can't be a hopeless case, because that's going to be the name of my detective agency. Besides, what you're asking for sounds reasonable, in my opinion."

"I think so, too, except for one huge flaw."

"What's the flaw?"

"My criteria resides in the same part of my head as my social anxieties, which means they both live inside the same brain that stops working the minute I'm attracted to someone."

Abby pointed to the building just ahead and to their left. "We're here."

"Seriously?" Alyssa stopped walking and stared in disbelief at the edifice. "This place?"

It was an old, two-story building, with a foundation of large, bright, square granite blocks, on top of which was a dark red brick façade. The front door frame and second-level window frames were outlined in white stone, set within the brick, and the colour contrast was striking. The stairs leading up to the door had clearly been replaced, as they were made of smooth, modern concrete.

"Yup. "Abby approached the steps. "This is the clinic."

Alyssa gestured at it with her hand. "But this is a police station."

Abby shook her head. "No, it *used to* be a police station, but it closed down three or four years ago. The owner of the clinic needed space to put the long-term patients who were in the damaged section of the hospital, so he leased this space for eighteen months, until the repairs are done."

Alyssa blinked hard. "He's seriously keeping patients in a former police station?"

"Yeah, but it's been renovated, to be more health-ish and less cop-ish, so it's cool." Abby waved for Alyssa to follow her. "Come on."

Alyssa walked behind Abby. When they were halfway up the eight steps, Abby turned to face Alyssa. "Listen, when we get inside the front door, there's something I need to do."

"What?"

"Rob the security guard…"

"No, stop right there." Alyssa held up her hands. "I'm *not* going to let you rob anyone."

"You didn't let me finish." Abby smirked. "Rob is the security guard's name."

"Oh, sorry." Alyssa blushed. "My bad."

"Anyway, *Robert,* the security guard, is a bit of a hard-ass when it comes to security, so let me do the talking, and just roll with whatever I say."

"Why do I suddenly feel the onset of a deep sense of dread?"

"You've been my friend for two years, so my guess is experience." Abby went up and opened the ornate oak door. "You shouldn't worry, though, because I've arranged for an access card to be waiting at the security desk for you."

"That's great." Alyssa playfully tapped her finger against the side of Abby's head. "You were thinking ahead. Well done, Miss Detective."

The two stepped inside and let the heavy door close behind them. The foyer was small and smelled of old books, despite there being no books in sight.

There was a large security desk ahead of them, and to the right of that desk was a narrow pathway, where anyone coming and going had to pass through. The front and side of the desk had a four-foot-high wall, topped with a narrow counter.

"Now," Abby whispered, "just relax, say nothing unless spoken to, and follow my lead." She walked across the black-and-white checkered floor toward the desk, with Alyssa directly behind her. The guard looked up at her, and she flashed her crooked smile. "Hey, Rob. How's it going?"

The guard tilted his head back and looked over at her. "Same shit, different day, just like always, Abby."

"That bad, huh?"

"You betcha." Rob looked to be in his late forties, with a square jaw, stocky build, and eyes which seemed to be stuck in a permanent squint. He was already a sizable man, yet he wore a white dress shirt, which was at least a size larger than he needed. He had a black tie, but the knot lay slack, a few inches below his throat. "Life only has one dish on the menu, and it's a shit sandwich, and there's plenty of 'em to go around.

The best you can do is never let anyone serve you seconds."

"Yeah, that's great life advice." Abby pointed over her own shoulder. "Anyway, this is Alyssa Bristol. I understand there's an access card here for her to pick up."

"Yeah, sure." He pushed a clipboard on the counter toward Alyssa. "Sign in first."

Alyssa took the clipboard, wrote her name on the next available line, and then handed it back to the guard. Robert grabbed the card and handed it to Alyssa. "Make sure I get this back when you've done whatever bullshit you need to do here."

"Um, I will. Thanks."

Abby and Alyssa turned and strode past the security desk and then turned right to go down one of the darker hallways.

As they walked, Alyssa squinted in the dim light at the access card she'd been given and frowned. "Hey, Abby, I think they gave me the wrong pass. This one says *government* on it."

"I know. That's the right one."

Alyssa held up the card. "But I was expecting to get a *visitor* pass."

"Meh." Abby sniffed. "Procedurally, yes, that would have been more accurate, but on a practical level, no."

"I'm not sure I understand what you mean."

"Well, in truth, you *are* a visitor, but a visitor pass won't get you access to the places you'll need to go, the files you'll need to see, and the patients you'll need to talk to in order to help me, so I arranged for you to have a pass with unlimited access in order to get around all the privacy laws."

Alyssa's mouth fell agape. "You're able to get me a pass with that level of access?"

"Sure." Abby wore a triumphant look. "Once I cracked the security computer's password, I was able to get any type of pass I wanted."

Alyssa squeezed her eyes shut. "You know what? That one's on me for asking the question in the first place. It's better if I don't know any more than that or my stomach will start to hurt."

"Oh, by the way," Abby put her hand on Alyssa's shoulder, "you're a government investigator doing a follow-up report on the events of a year ago."

Alyssa stopped walking. "I am?"

"Yup." Abby pulled her forward. "Like I said, just roll with it."

"My stomach just started to roll, does that count?" Alyssa exhaled sharply. "Look, I'm not comfortable impersonating a government official. I mean, it has to be some kind of a felony to do that, right?"

"No, you don't need to worry."

"Really?"

"Yeah, it's only a felony if you get found out *and* arrested, and I won't let both of those things happen."

"Both?" Alyssa groaned. "We need to talk about what constitutes reassurance, because that was far from it."

Saturday, 8:11 a.m.

Abby led Alyssa down the long, narrow hallway. Their footsteps echoed as they walked, and they approached a large, locked door at the end. There were no windows, neither in the wall nor in the door, just a small metal hatch built into the upper part of the heavy-looking door.

Alyssa made a face. "Where are we going?"

"It's time for you to meet my client, Zee."

Alyssa pointed toward the door, which was just twenty feet away. "And she's in there, behind that huge door?"

"Yup." Abby lowered her voice. "Let me talk to Zee first, to make sure she's still willing to speak with you."

Alyssa nodded. "That's probably a good idea."

"She can be confrontational, volatile, and temperamental, but aside from that, she's a total sweetheart."

"Once again, that's not even close to being reassuring, but I do appreciate you making the effort. I should start taking notes so we can review your language skills each night." Alyssa stopped walking and turned to face Abby. "Wait a second."

"What?"

"How come she's way down here in a separate section away from the other wing, where you said the other patients are?"

"Oh," Abby nodded in a knowing manner. "Yeah, don't worry, this isn't her regular room. This room is only used for solitary confinement."

Alyssa blinked as her jaw dropped. "Are you serious? Why is she in solitary confinement?"

"Relax, it was just a minor thing."

"Exactly how minor a thing was it?"

"Really minor." Abby waved her hand in a dismissive fashion. "It was almost nothing."

"Allow me to seize upon the word *almost* and get you to tell me *exactly* what happened, so I can decide for myself how minor it was."

Abby grunted in frustration. "Okay, look, last week, she stabbed someone with a fork. Don't worry, the injuries weren't fatal, and she missed the artery, so there was surprisingly little blood."

Alyssa rubbed her face. "Reassurance just doesn't come naturally to you at all, does it?"

"I guess not." Abby stepped toward the door. "You'd better make yourself comfortable, because I might be a few minutes."

"Not a problem." Alyssa pointed to where she was standing. "If you need me, I'll be right here, rethinking every one of my life choices."

Abby placed her access card on the reader and the door clicked. She opened the door, stepped inside, and then pushed the door closed behind her. She looked at the room's occupant and smiled.

"Morning, Zee."

Before the renovations, the room had been a ten-by-twelve jail cell. After the renovations, it was a ten-by-twelve jail cell with a fresh coat of paint and a white plastic chair for visitors.

"Hey, Abby." Zee was sitting on the floor, her back against the side of the bed. Her straight, black hair was long at the front and back, but was close-cropped on the sides. Her dark brown eyes were almost completely covered by her bangs. The pale skin on her thin arms sported several tattoos of varying sizes and subject matter, from a black rose with a thorny stem and a skull, to a dagger set within a stylized coil of barbed wire.

Abby approached Zee. "My friend Alyssa's outside, ready to talk with you. I told you about her yesterday."

"Yeah, and I've been thinking about your suggestion. I don't know if I want to talk to her now."

Abby made a face. "How come?"

"Because I think it's going to be a waste of time, and get my hopes up for nothing." Zee looked up through her long bangs. "I have to accept the reality that you're the only friend I have, both in here and on the outside. There's no knight in shining armour out there who's going to come to my rescue."

"To be honest, I wouldn't put my trust in a knight in shining armour. I'd be way happier seeing a knight in scuffed and dented armour, so at least I'd know it wasn't just being worn for show."

"Okay, listen, I really kind of like the way you think, but none of what you said was even slightly helpful right now."

"Sorry."

"You're the only person I completely trust, Abby, and I don't even know you that well." Zee scowled. "I'm being evaluated by an allegedly professional and experienced doctor who *should* understand me, but he really doesn't, so you're all I have."

"Well, yeah, I like to think I understand you."

"You do, but that's only because," Zee tapped the side of her own head with her finger, "you're not right in the head yourself."

Abby shrugged. "I've heard people say birds of a feather flock together."

"If you're anything like me, then you're the one who's flocked." Zee shook her head. "As whacked as I am, you take neurodivergence to a whole new level. So, how about you finally tell me your story?"

"No, my story's not important right now."

"Yes, it is." Zee raised herself enough so she could sit on the side of her bed. "I tell you everything about me, but you never want to tell me anything about yourself. You're always so secretive, and when I ask about your life, you change the subject." Zee paused for a moment. "Tell you what, Abby. I'll make you a promise. I'll agree to meet with your friend and answer all of her questions, but first you've finally got to share with me, and it has to be right now."

"Okay, if that's what it takes, then I'm cool with it." Abby went over to the bed and sat beside Zee. "What do you want to know?"

"Let's start with my biggest question. What kinds of neurodivergence do you have?"

"I'm dyslexic, but aside from that, none at all. My head's just completely wonky due to being badly-wired from birth, that's all. I was born with a damaged brain and it left me mostly catatonic, because my mind always felt like it was wading through glue. And it's not just my head that's screwed up, either. My internal organs are damaged, too, because I did too many years of heavy drinking in order to be coherent."

"You drank to be coherent?" Zee looked at Abby with a sour face. "That's messed up, Abs."

"I didn't want to tell you this, but my brain is broken, and it has been since I was born." Abby looked at the floor. "You know, as much as you hate this place, I spent nearly half of my childhood drunk, in and out of a place way worse than this."

"Sounds like it was a better place, if they regularly got you drunk."

"They didn't give me alcohol on purpose, at least not at first." Abby's eyes met Zee's. "When I was around six years old, my nurse at the time was a nasty piece of work. She was also a total alcoholic, and she kept vodka in a water bottle, so she could get away with drinking on duty. If she sneezed near an open flame, her breath would probably have been a decent flame-thrower. Anyway, one time she accidentally left her special bottle behind, and the other nurse gave me my neural stimulants with what she thought was water to wash it down with."

"You downed your stims with vodka?"

"Yup," Abby nodded, "and about an hour later, I was reasonably coherent for the first time in ages, and the second nurse eventually figured out what happened. After that, instead of giving me pills, she'd slip me alcohol and then sell my stims out in the alley after work."

"You've been drinking vodka since you were six?" Zee's eyes were wide. "Holy shit."

Abby made a face. "What's so sacred about poop?"

"Nothing, I'm just saying that's *seriously* messed up."

"I know, but if my choice was to be drinking and coherent, or not drinking and vegetative, it was an easy choice, and all *bottoms-up* after that."

"That really sucks."

"Yeah," Abby sighed, "but my best friend Alyssa is a chemistry ace, and she made some kind of root-based medicine that keeps my brain working, so now I don't have to drink in order to be functioning. I've been taking it for nearly two years now, and I've healed quite a bit, but the damage to my internal organs is probably permanent. I'll be twenty-seven in a couple of months, and the last doctor I saw told me that chances were good I wouldn't live to see thirty, so I know I'm living on borrowed time."

"That totally sucks for you, Abs," Zee scoffed, "but we're all living on borrowed time, and then Death comes along, demanding it back with interest. And speaking of interest, I have none at all in being locked up here for the next few decades. I don't suppose you and your friend could convince the doctor I didn't set the fires in the old place, and that I never killed anyone, because nobody except you believes me."

"You have some family in town, I mean some of them must believe you, right? How about your parents?"

"Ha!" Zee laced the word with derision. "Those evangelical hypocrites? I've already told you how useless they are. Sure, they'll pray for me, but not give me any actual or useful help, so I'm on my own. I need to get out of here, so I can prove my innocence."

"And I'd really like to help you prove that innocence, Zee, but are you willing to help me to do that?"

"Yeah, of course."

"Then talk to Alyssa."

Zee shook her head. "I don't know how that will help, but I'll keep my promise and talk with her."

Abby stood up. "You might want to be a bit more optimistic than that."

"There's no point, so I'm not going to get my hopes up. Nobody except you takes me seriously anyway. They see my tattoos and hair, and then decide what kind of person I am. They don't even bother listening to me after that."

"I can relate to that." Abby walked backwards toward the door. "Just because I don't have great social skills, people think I'm stupid. But Alyssa doesn't. She treats me like a person and as if I matter. Just give her a chance, okay?"

"Fine, I'll try to keep an open mind."

"And talk to her nicely. She's my best friend and she wants to help you, so politely answer whatever she asks you without any attitude."

"Okay, fine, I get it. I'll be nice."

Abby opened the door, leaned out, and waved Alyssa over. Alyssa walked to the door and Abby held it open for her. Alyssa stepped into the room and stood beside the door frame. She wasn't sure if she would wave, approach, say hello, or just stand there, so she opted for a posture of awkward fidgeting which she instantly regretted.

Abby pointed at Alyssa. "Zee, this is Alyssa." She then pointed at Zee. "Alyssa, this is Zee."

Alyssa raised her hand and waved, then realized it wasn't a helpful thing to do, so put her hand down again. "Er, hello."

Zee did a quick nod in Alyssa's direction. "Hey."

"Well," Abby clapped her hands and rubbed them together. "I've got work to do, so I'll leave you two alone. Later."

Abby left and closed the door behind her.

Alyssa began to smile then decided against it, causing her face to twitch and briefly contort. She shuffled closer to Zee. "Hello."

"Yeah, so you said earlier."

"Oh, that's right, I did."

Zee cracked a faint smile. "You're not good in social situations, are you?"

"No, sorry." Alyssa exhaled in relief. "They're my biggest nightmare."

"Yeah, same. You want to sit down so you can be less fidgety and awkward? Just seeing you all uptight like that is stressing me out."

"Sorry. Yes, that's probably a good idea."

Zee waved her hand in the direction of the plastic lawn chair which was against the opposite wall. "You might as well use the cheap, plastic visitor chair I have, or you can sit on the toilet seat if you're feeling really brave."

"No, I think the chair sounds perfect." Alyssa nodded and stepped over to the chair. She picked it up and brought it closer to Zee, set it down, and sat in it. She stopped herself from saying hello a third time.

"Um," Alyssa took a deep breath. "Listen, sorry, but I just want to talk with you to see if there's something I can do to help you."

"Yeah, sure."

"I'm not yet sure what I need to know, so I'm going to ask you a wide variety of questions to feel things out. I'm not exactly sure where to start, so I'll just take a shot in the dark."

"Wise move." Zee nodded with appreciation. "Shooting in daylight results in too many witnesses." Zee exhaled and made a disgusted sound. "Stop doing that wide-eyed thing, okay? It was just a joke."

"Sorry."

"And stop apologizing all the time." Zee stared at Alyssa. "Christ! I'll bet the whole time Abby was in here with me, you were out there rehearsing what you were going to say, and then you forgot everything as soon as you walked in here."

"It's way too embarrassing for me to admit how accurate that was."

"Look, tell you what." Zee shook her head. "Just close your eyes, and think about what you were going to say and then say it as though you're still outside rehearsing."

"Okay." Alyssa took in a deep breath and closed her eyes. "My name is Alyssa Bristol, and I am a nineteen-year-old college student, studying to become a lab technician, which I should point out has nothing at all to do with being a detective. To be even more emphatic on this topic, I'm *not* a detective, and I have zero interest in ever becoming one. I wanted nothing to do with Abby's detective career, except to maybe help her get started, but I should have known better. Whenever Abby's involved in something, the craziness comes stampeding my way, no matter how much I try to avoid it."

Zee smirked. "That's seriously what you were going to say to me?"

"Aside from *maybe* half of the first sentence, no, not even close. The thing is, when I'm nervous, the words just pour out on their own, and I can't stop them."

"Now that the awkward introduction is done with, you can get to the real stuff you want to talk about."

"Right. Um, so, you ended up getting blamed for a fire which killed two people."

"Which I didn't do."

"The court ruled differently."

"Well, what can I say?" Zee shrugged. "The court was wrong, and I ended up convicted based on bullshit evidence."

"Both sides in court will make claims about innocence and guilt, but the Devil's in the details."

"No, the Devil's in the people." Raised her index finger. "The details are everything else. The real problem was that nobody would listen to me."

"What about your doctor? Is he listening to you?"

"Listening isn't Dr. Friesen's problem." Zee looked down. "If I'm being honest, I have to admit he's a pretty good listener, but... when it comes to believing me and understanding me? No. He's hopeless in those areas, so I'm not interested in anything he has to say."

"Sounds like the doctor is in your bad books."

Zee shrugged. "I have no other kind, so he shouldn't take it personally. Look, no matter what happens, he's going to be like everyone else and do what's most expedient for himself. He'll go through the motions so he can milk as many billings out of the clinic as he can, and then he'll submit his report stating what he would have said on day one."

"Which is--?"

"That I'm a nutcase who needs to be locked up for the good of society, as well as my own, of course, so this is hopeless."

Alyssa nodded. "Maybe that's how you feel about it now, but tomorrow's another day."

"Yes, another day closer to the end of my life."

"You really feel like a fish out of water in here, don't you?"

"If you mean suffocating and feeling as though I'm close to death, then yes."

"I meant more like you feel as though you're different from other people."

"Everyone feels different." Zee shrugged. "Or so I'm told. I want to ask you something now, are you cool with that?"

"Sure, go ahead."

"You and Abby." Zee gestured toward the door. "How is it possible the two of you are friends when you're so radically different?"

"I suppose I can't blame you for asking that, and you're completely right." Alyssa thought for a moment. "Most times, Abby and I are so extremely different, but then there's those rare times, when we're somehow like two peas in a pod."

"You mean trapped in a suffocating shell and treated like a vegetable? That's the first thing you've said so far that I can relate to. And you know what?" Zee glanced up at Alyssa. "She thinks the world of you, you know. She says you have a calming influence on her."

"You know, it's hard for me to believe it now, but I used to lead a dull, quiet existence." Alyssa shook her head. "I'd complain about how my life was so dull, and I'd yearn for some excitement. Then around two years ago, I met Abby for the first time, and that first year ended up containing an entire lifetime's worth of excitement. I was kidnapped, chased, attacked, and even had a ghost encounter, leading me to yearn instead for the dull, quiet life I had completely failed to appreciate. I have been trying to re-establish a sense of normalcy in my life, and am hoping it can once again be dull and uneventful. If there's one thing I've learned over the past couple of years, it's that excitement is definitely overrated."

"Maybe, but because of that, you now have a best friend."

"It's like they say," Alyssa smiled. "Every cloud has a silver lining."

"Then the inverse must also be true, which means every silver lining has a cloud."

"I suppose that's the more cynical way to look at things, sure."

"So, based on what you told me, you led a sheltered and comfortable life, and didn't experience anything close to reality until Abby came into your life."

Alyssa considered this for a moment. "I hadn't thought about it like that, but I suppose one could argue that."

"If you have so little life experience, what makes you think you can help me?"

"I'm not in any way qualified or experienced enough to help you with your actual life, but I'm also not here to do that. I'm here to look into the circumstances surrounding why you were sent here to see if you were wrongly convicted. Look, maybe I was sheltered from the real world in your opinion, but the main thing is I'm here now. As the saying goes, better late than never."

"A saying which is completely wrong when it comes to antidotes, wars, and birth control."

Alyssa paused to mull over what Zee had said. "Okay, I'll give you that one, but despite your negative outlook on life, I'm going to look at the facts and see if you were wrongly prosecuted."

"And if you find something, what then?"

Alyssa shrugged. "We'll cross that bridge when we get to it."

"We can't exactly cross the bridge before we get to it, can we?"

"I think that's the whole point of the expression."

"Then it's a ridiculous saying." Zee glowered. "You might as well say you'll wake up when you stop sleeping."

"This might very well be the most difficult conversation I've ever had with another human being, and, if you knew my dad, you'd know that's saying something. All I'm asking you for is information, and some patience."

"Patience?"

"Yes." Alyssa smiled. "Good things come to those that wait."

"Only if you're waiting for death, rot, or decay. If you want good things, you have to go out and get them. Waiting gets you nothing except old age and bitter disappointment."

"Well, that was bleak. There must be *something* positive about things here. How about the food? I'm sure at least the food is decent here."

"Decent? Not even close." Zee folded her arms. "The doctor says the lasagna here is a dish fit for the gods, but if that's true, then it may explain the recent uptick in atheism."

Alyssa looked around the dimly-lit room and shivered. "You wouldn't normally be here for murder and arson charges; you'd be placed in a correctional facility. Why did they specifically send you to a mental health clinic instead?"

"I'm here because I have the acronym trifecta: ADHD, ASD, and PTSD, and am currently being tested for BPD, to see if we can make it an even four. When they serve alphabet soup here, I have good odds of spooning up at least one of my disorders during the meal."

"But none of those disorders would be reason enough to keep you in a place like this."

"No, but the two murder charges would be, which happens to be why I'm in this lovely cell with no windows."

"I'm not understanding the chronology." Alyssa paused to organize her thoughts. "You're in this facility because of a fire you allegedly set at another facility, which killed two people. But logically, you would have had to have been there already for you to have set the fire in the first place, so how does that work?"

"Easy. I was already there, but on an unrelated matter."

"What was it?"

Zee was ready to assert her firm belief that it was none of Alyssa's business, but then she remembered her promise to Abby. She glanced at the door, wishing Alyssa was on the other side of it, and then finally answered. "I was arrested for aggravated assault, and was undergoing a six-week psych evaluation there."

"And I'm guessing the fire ended that particular evaluation."

"Yup." Zee's scorn was evident. "Both the facility and my chances of release went up in smoke on the same day."

"So, what's the prognosis? Any estimates on when you might be officially cured?"

"It's not possible for me to be cured, because I'm being treated for a series of disorders that aren't really disorders in the first place."

"Sorry, but I don't understand what you mean by that."

"Here's an example that should clear it up." Zee's eyes met Alyssa's. "I'm left-handed. Now, imagine I was able to design everything in the world, and I made it all to suit left-handed people. You, being a right-handed person, would be considered disabled, because you weren't born or wired for the world I created. They'd come up with some stupid term, like *left-hand deficiency disorder,* or something. You with me so far?"

"Yes."

"Okay, so there's nothing in my brain that needs to be cured. Some supposedly-normal people designed our society with rules that suited *them,* assuming everyone should follow *their* lead. Anyone like me with a neurodivergent brain struggles to live within their neurotypical structure, so we get labeled as freaks and outcasts, and get the *disorder* label."

Alyssa nodded. "But instead, you've just got a different operating system installed in your brain. It works perfectly fine, but isn't compatible with people who have a different operating system inside theirs."

"Yeah. Something like that, yeah."

"But your violent outbursts and other symptoms can be managed, either through medication or therapy."

Zee scoffed. "Yeah, easy to say, but a lot harder to do."

"The medications themselves are easy, but yes, sometimes the therapy can be difficult, but at least try one or both. They'll probably be hard to adjust to at first, but it'll get easier as you go."

"There's no point. Aside from Abby, I'm completely on my own. Nobody cares if I rot in here."

"I'm glad you have Abby on your side, at least."

Zee gave a conciliatory nod. "Yeah, it's made a huge difference to me. She lives in the same house as you, right?"

"Yes, Abby's been staying at my parents' place for the past year, so we live under the same roof. She rents a furnished room in our basement."

"How's that going?"

"Mixed, if I'm being honest." Alyssa took a deep breath and let it out. "It's great having my best friend there; but, at the same time, it's also difficult when I have to study, or have school projects I need to do and she's upstairs distracting me."

Zee rolled her eyes. "I bet you're an only child, aren't you?"

"Yes." Alyssa's eyes widened. "How did you know?"

"Because you don't know how to get things done when there's other people around, and, if you had siblings, you'd have needed to learn how to do that."

"I hate that you're right about that." Alyssa frowned. "Do you have siblings?"

"Yeah, one older brother."

"Do you get along?"

"No, we're not close. At all. Like, you could travel at the speed of light for several years and still not reach the distance between him and I."

"I'm sorry to hear that." Alyssa shifted her weight in the chair. "It's rough when families fall out."

"It was more of a shove than a fall." Zee shrugged. "On a bad day, I see it as being rejected by my parents and brother, but on a good day, I see it as losing four-hundred-and-fifty unhealthy pounds in a single day. Any other questions?"

"No, but thank you." Alyssa stood up. "It was nice to meet you."

Zee scoffed. "If it really was nice meeting me, then your life must really suck."

Saturday: 9:22 a.m.

Abby noticed Alyssa coming out of Zee's room, so she hopped toward her.

"So?" Abby put her arm around Alyssa's shoulders. "Did you find out what you needed to find out?"

"I think I have enough to get started with, at any rate." Alyssa glanced at Abby. "She's got a lot of things to work through. I can understand why she needs to be here."

"I'm just glad she cooperated with you."

Alyssa nodded as she walked. "Yes, Zee is certainly a character."

Alyssa wrung her hands as she walked with Abby down the echoing hallway, and let out a loud groan. "Listen, Abby, I'm so uncomfortable doing this."

Abby wore a confused look. "You are? It's just walking, and you've been doing it for years. If you're not comfortable, then maybe try different shoes."

"No, it's not the walking part that bothers me." Alyssa groaned again. "I'm uncomfortable pretending to be someone and something I'm not."

"That kind of goes with being a teenager, doesn't it?"

"No. Well, yes, actually, but not like this. I'm pretending to be a big-wig government authority, but I'm just some nobody college kid playing make-believe."

Abby shrugged. "I don't see what the big deal is."

"It's illegal, immoral, and unethical."

Abby waved her hand as though shooing a fly. "Oh, that."

"That? This is a lot more than simply a *that.* This particular *that* could have serious consequences for me."

"Stop worrying."

"Did you seriously just tell me to stop worrying? You obviously haven't met me." Alyssa extended her hand. "Hello, my name is Alyssa Bristol, and I'm a chronic stress case."

"There's nothing to stress over, even for you." Abby patted Alyssa's shoulder. "Everything's going to be fine."

"Fine? Really?" Alyssa scoffed. "What if the security guard looks me up?"

Abby chuckled. "Oh, Rob will *definitely* look you up, if he hasn't already, and when he does, he'll see the fake profile I put up on the government's website."

"He'll see the *what* you put up on the *where?*"

"Relax, or at least make some sort of attempt at it." Abby gently squeezed Alyssa's shoulder. "Your credentials will check out. I've got you covered."

"Abby, you know how I feel about this sort of thing. I don't even jaywalk, yet you have me impersonating a government official."

"You're going to need to meet me halfway, okay?" Abby let out an exasperated breath. "You won't let me hack into corporate databases, break into shady businesses, or rob criminals anymore. It really feels as though you don't want me to succeed."

"I definitely do want you to succeed, but I'm stressing out over the number of laws I'm breaking today."

"Maybe I can help you with that part."

Alyssa blinked hard. "At the risk of being exposed to another one of your ill-fated attempts at reassurance, how do you think you can help me to not stress?"

"Let me ask you something." Abby paused to organize her thoughts. "What happens when a person is caught parking illegally?"

"They get a ticket."

"Right, and they have to pay a fine." Abby pressed onward. "And what happens when a person gets caught dumping their old sofa out in an alley?"

"They also get fined."

"Exactly, which means everything is legal for the right price. People with money look at fines as the cost of doing business or of getting what they want. You can always get the best parking spot, as long as you're willing to risk the ticket. If you've got money, you can commit any number of misdemeanors and never have to worry about the consequences, as long as you pay up when the fines are due."

"Where are you going with this disturbing set of statements?"

"If your parents were injured, and it was up to you to get them to the hospital, and every delay meant they were more likely to die, would you come to a complete stop at every stop sign?" Abby saw the discomfort on Alyssa's face. "Would you drive the speed limit? Would you wait at a red light if there were no cars around?"

Alyssa fidgeted. "Well, no, I'd do whatever I could to get them to the hospital quickly."

"Right, so there are scenarios where even a total goody-two-shoes like you is willing to break laws in order to achieve something you want. Now, Zee is about to spend twenty to forty years of her life locked up because of something she didn't do."

"Something you *believe* she didn't do."

"Yeah, so if there is even a reasonable chance an innocent person was convicted, isn't that worth a second look, even if the justice system says no? If somebody was falsely accused of a serious crime and they've exhausted their legal means of defending themselves, then anyone wanting to help them out would have to step outside of the usual processes in order to see justice done." Abby shrugged. "It's the way we have to do business in order to get what we want."

"But not to this extent." Alyssa went back to wringing her hands. "It's one thing to block a road to prevent a chemical truck from dumping its load of toxic sludge into the river, but this is fraudulent representation."

"No, this is the same as blocking the road, except the chemical truck is injustice, the toxic chemicals are misplaced criminal charges, and we're the ones looking to block the road. I thought you were all in favour of fighting injustice."

"I am, but…"

"But what?"

"Abby, around a year ago you were given a blanket pardon for everything you'd done, and I don't want you to waste this opportunity by going back to a life which will likely lead to prison." Alyssa put her arm around Abby's shoulders. "You have a fresh start. You have a clean slate."

"What I have are no employment prospects."

"You're making decent money working at the clinic."

Abby clucked her tongue. "One-tenth of what I used to make when my slate wasn't so clean."

"How much you made is irrelevant, because your former employer kept everything you ever stole on his behalf. For your efforts, you slept on an old cot in a small, smelly storage room above his bar. He took advantage of your skills, and he didn't properly compensate you at all."

"You're right, he did take advantage of me and my skills, but at least then I had a purpose. When I stepped out of that small, smelly storage room, my life had meaning, what I did mattered, and only I could do it. But in this job?" Abby scoffed. "If I don't show up, somebody else gets called in, and they do it just as well, or even better."

"Wait, I think I might finally understand what's going on with you. The problem is that you no longer feel unique and valued."

"Yeah, I guess I am saying that. I don't matter anymore. Or at least, I don't *feel* like I matter. But when I started the process to become a detective… it felt so good. I felt alive for the first time in over a year. I felt as though I'd finally be able to become whoever and whatever I was meant to be." Abby turned her head to look at Alyssa. "So, if I need to bend a few rules, or get around a law or two in order to help my client, then that's what I'm going to do."

"What you're going to do is time."

"Only if I get caught."

"It's times like this when I can actually feel myself aging."

Abby turned as the front door opened and a man in his early fifties walked in and approached the security desk.

"Oh, hey, the doctor's here." Abby tugged at Alyssa's wrist. "Come on. I want you to meet him."

The two women walked briskly over to the man, who had just put his access card away. He was a taller man, who looked to be in his late forties or early fifties, with greying temples. He wore a brown blazer over a simple white golf shirt.

"Hey, Doc, hold up." Abby called to him.

"Good morning, Abby." The doctor smiled. "Can I assist you with something?"

"No, I just wanted you to meet my best friend, Alyssa Bristol." Abby pointed to her. "Alyssa, this is the awesome Dr. Friesen."

Friesen beamed and held out his hand. "Delighted to meet you, young lady."

"It's nice to meet you, too." Alyssa shook his hand. "Abby speaks very highly of you."

He chuckled. "I assure you that she's simply being unreasonably kind to the cantankerous old coot standing before you. All right, then." Friesen gestured toward Alyssa's access card. "So, Abby, why is someone from the government visiting us today?"

"There's a follow-up investigation going on, and Alyssa would like to ask you about the fire a year ago."

He began to walk and the two women followed him. "As long as it can wait for a few moments, then certainly."

"I hope it's okay that I ask you questions."

Friesen grinned. "Either way, I get paid for my time here, so ask away, and feel free to speak slowly, to take as much time as possible." He winked. "It'll help with my month-end billings."

"Is that a Norwich accent I hear?"

Friesen's eyebrows raised. "Oh, aren't you the clever one. Yes, you're more or less correct. I'm originally from Long Stratton, just down the road from there. Bit of a linguist, are you?"

"My mother's a polyglot, so I picked up quite a bit from her. Your accent is still quite distinct, so I'm guessing you moved here as an adult."

"I did, indeed."

"What brought you to Canada?"

"Well, money, if I'm being honest." Friesen winked. "Britain's National Health Service doesn't pay me as well as consulting for a private clinic over here. I'm a life-long bachelor with no deep roots, so there was nothing holding me there, so I simply up and left one day. After a long and tedious immigration process, I was finally allowed to stay. So, here I am, boring you with my life story."

"Do you miss the UK?"

"I do a bit, yes." Friesen shrugged. "I mean, I can't get a decent football match over here on the telly. And ask people here about football, and they start prattling on about that silly American game of *'throw the ball and fall down'*. When I want people to understand real sports, I have to use the term *soccer,* which offends me to no end. And don't get me started on cricket. Ask anyone over here about cricket, and you'll hear, well, *crickets*."

"I can understand why." Alyssa shook her head. "I have no idea how the game works, or how people can watch a single cricket match for an entire day."

"Perhaps another time, I shall attempt to explain it to you." Friesen flashed a brief smile. "Right now, I have to see Suzanne, or, rather, *Zee.* I shall answer any questions you have as soon as I can."

Saturday: 9:28 a.m.

The door to Zee's room opened and Dr. Friesen stepped inside, wearing a wide smile. "Good morning to you."

"Ugh," Zee made a sour face. "I didn't know you were back from your time off already."

"And here I thought you'd be delighted to see me, being the pleasant little ray of sunshine that you are. You know, I haven't seen you in three days, and there's an old saying about how absence is supposed to make the heart grow fonder."

"Let's test that theory." Zee folded her arms. "You play the part of the absent person, and I'll contact you if any fondness develops."

"Now, now, I was only teasing you." Friesen sat down. "I thought a little levity might break the ice."

"You'd need something harder than levity to break ice. Your skull might do the trick, as it's solid cement. Your jokes aren't funny. In fact, I'm kind of surprised people don't assault you constantly. The fact that you've lived this long is as surprising as it is disappointing."

"There's no need for that sort of response and attitude." He pulled out a pen, put on his reading glasses, and then looked at the clipboard in his lap. "I'm aware my humour is not to everyone's taste, but I don't do it as a therapeutic exercise. If, indeed, laughter is the best medicine, then I dare say my face could cure much of the world. But I'm equally aware my humour is not why you make such sour comments, Zee. I know inside you're deeply unhappy, but I continue to believe it's better to light a single candle than to curse the darkness."

"Really?" Zee cast a pained look in his direction. "By that logic, if a candle is good, then a blowtorch is better, and a three-alarm blaze is best of all, yet when I was eight years old, I spent a year in juvenile detention for arson."

"Is there a particular problem on your mind today, or is this just how you are daily, and I somehow forgot in my brief absence?"

"I just don't feel like having a session with you, that's all."

"Well, just in case you forgot, we have a minimum number of court-ordered hours per week we need to maintain, so you'll just have to persevere, I'm afraid."

"Maybe I do, but I don't have to like it."

Friesen looked at her over his glasses. "No, you certainly do not have to like it, and to be clear, I'm not saying you do. I'm just your doctor and therapist. I have my own set of personal problems, yet here I am treating you instead of myself. It's like they say: those who can, do, and those who cannot, teach."

"And those who can do neither apparently end up being selected to serve as my court-appointed defense lawyer."

"Indeed." Friesen chuckled. "Just to satisfy my own curiosity this morning, are your negative feelings today somehow related to me? Do you have a particular bone to pick with me this morning?"

"If you're asking if I've selected a particular number of your bones which I'd like to break, then yes. Just say the word and I'll get snapping."

Friesen smiled. "I'm quite certain you're very capable of doing that, but I'm willing to bet my limbs you won't, because deep down – and I do mean *very* deep down – there's a microscopic part of you which hopes I can help you. After all, no person is an island."

"No person is a mountain range either, but topography has nothing to do with my well-being."

"Fair enough." Friesen clicked his pen. "Right, then, let's start today's discussion by addressing the elephant in the room."

"Are you calling me fat?"

"Heavens no."

"Are you calling yourself fat?"

Friesen patted his stomach with his free hand. "I could skip a dessert or two, but otherwise no."

"Then if you're seeing an actual pachyderm in here, perhaps I should be the doctor and you the patient."

"It's not a *literal* elephant in the room, and I suspect you know that, but I'm referring to the fact that, after ten months of you threatening me with permanent incapacitation or worse, you haven't followed through with anything more injurious than assault and cutlery. So, if you're done with the verbal warnings, I'd like to touch base, so we can make sure our expectations are aligned."

Zee cast her eyes toward the ceiling. "Then this will be a really short conversation."

"If that's how you feel, then let me skip ahead to the bottom line. Is there any part of you that hopes my upcoming evaluation will lead to a fairy-tale ending for you?"

"Yes, but not in a good way." She looked at him. "My expectations are more like the fairy-tale ending that every wolf, giant, and witch in those stories got, and they were most often torture, death, or both. Why are you asking me this?"

"Because another month is about to go by, and I thought this would be a good opportunity to compare what we each hope to get out of these sessions." Friesen made a note on the page on his clipboard. "Let's start by looking ahead to the report I'll be writing later this week. What would you like to see as the result of my evaluation?"

"You mean aside from you losing your medical license and then jumping off a bridge?"

"I'm serious. What would you say is the ideal outcome of our sessions?"

"Fine. I'll play along." Zee stood up and leaned against the wall. "I want your report to read, *I hereby conclude that Suzanne Alicia Dawson isn't crazy. She just needs a little help, patience, and understanding for once, and oh, by the way, she didn't kill anybody, so everyone's been completely wrong about her this whole time.* That's what I'd want from your evaluation."

"Those are some tough nuts to crack."

"Are you really going to give me that expression to pick apart? Sometimes, you make this way too easy."

"Yes, and I realized it was a mistake the moment the phrase left my mouth." Friesen tapped his pen against the clipboard. "What I'm saying is the very results you're seeking may be difficult to obtain, but they're far from being impossible. Establishing your state of mind and what happened the day of that terrible fire are certainly possible, but only if you work with me."

"I have been working with you, but I gave up."

Friesen raised his eyebrows. "And why did you give up?"

"Because *you* weren't working with *me*."

"I see."

"Do you really?"

"I don't know, as it's still too early for me to say anything definitively."

"Too early?" Zee sat on the bed. "We've been working together for nearly ten months, so how can it be too early for you to know?"

"My goodness, Zee, I may *sound* like a pretentious know-it-all, but I assure you I'm only pretentious. The only reason I seem to have all the answers is because I'm the only doctor here."

"If you don't have the answers, then what good are you?"

"Because I have something far more valuable than the answers, Zee." Friesen looked triumphant. "I have the questions."

"How is that better?"

"Because I wasn't there when the fire broke out, but you were, along with Gina, Celia, Wing Zhen, Cenk Vollack, and Robert." Friesen made eye contact with Zee. "Only each of you know what you saw and experienced that day, so I can't possibly have any answers pertaining to what actually happened with any of you. However, I do know what questions I need to ask in order to discover those answers. When I conclude my evaluation of you, it will only be a fair and accurate assessment if I go into it with an open mind and listen carefully to whatever you tell me."

Zee looked away. "Even though I stabbed you with my fork?"

"Yes, despite even that." Friesen winked. "And, by the way, I forgot to thank you for stabbing me, as it allowed me to cancel my acupuncture appointment for my stiff shoulder."

Zee stared at the floor for a moment before speaking. "Listen, I'm... I'm really sorry I stabbed you."

"Yes, I know you are, and that's the only reason we're still having these sessions." He flashed a quick smile. "If I believed, even for a moment, you weren't sorry, we'd have ended right things right then and there."

"If I hadn't made a point of making sure I missed your artery, *you* would've ended right then and there."

"I know you hate it when I bring this subject up, but if you'd take your medications, you'd be more able to control such impulses."

"No pills." Zee's eyes flared. "I need to do this on my own. I know the fork attack seemed like a crazy thing to do, but I'm not really a crazy person."

"After all these months of getting to know you, I can safely say that I don't believe you're crazy at all, unlike your initial doctor, who was of the opinion you weren't playing with a full deck."

"She was partially right, because I don't think anyone's playing with a full deck. Everyone has a few cards missing. Though between her and you, at least I know where both of the jokers are."

"And to think you don't believe you have a sense of humour." Friesen stood up. "The medication would help, but as you refuse it, I have a little bit of homework for you."

"What homework?"

"When you have violent thoughts, I want you to try writing them down instead of lashing out. Writing things out can be very powerful and therapeutic." He looked at his pen and held it up. "It's likely where the expression *the pen is mightier than the sword* came from."

"And you believe that about pens?"

"Yes, I do."

"In that case, if I'm ever in a life and death duel, I'll be sure to choose you as my opponent."

"Mock me if you will, and I know you will, but here's your immediate problem. If you're not willing to try the medication, homework, and exercises I give you, then your chances of leaving this facility decrease exponentially with each refusal."

Zee groaned. "Fine, I'll try your stupid homework assignment, but only because I don't want to spend the rest of my life living in this dump.

"I'm delighted to hear you'll try it. That said, is it really so terrible here?" He raised an eyebrow. "After all, home is where the heart is."

"By that logic, my home is inside a police evidence locker, because that's where my collection of hearts was most recently stored."

Saturday: 9:35 a.m.

Alyssa walked with Abby down the corridor, their footsteps echoing off the concrete walls. "Who's next?"

"The next room is Jeff's, and he's such an interesting guy." Abby gently nudged Alyssa with her elbow as they walked. "He's doing both too much and too little at the same time, which is kind of fascinating."

Alyssa's walking pace slowed as she flipped through the pages of his file. "It says here they ran an MRI and a half-dozen other tests on Jeff. You're right, this is interesting. He isn't unresponsive due to a lack of neural activity, as there's an abundance of it going on in his head. In fact, he's charting high above normal to the point where they had to adjust the chart in order for his readings to fit inside it."

"See what I mean?" Abby hopped up and down. "So, what do you think is blocking his brain?"

"Abby, I'm not here to diagnose anyone. I'm not even remotely qualified to do that. I'm just here to ask him some questions."

"Ah," Abby raised a triumphant finger, "but unless you can figure out what's happening in his head, he can't give you answers."

"To an extent sure, but without the foundational knowledge I'd need to figure him out, I'd have about as much success as a concussed moose who'd been asked to design a cold fusion reactor."

Abby tapped her finger on the page Alyssa was looking at. "You have his file right there. And I mean Jeff's file, not the moose's, so, what do you think? Is there, like, a disconnection between his mind and body or something?"

Alyssa read some more. "The problem doesn't seem to be any sort of disconnect, per se, it appears there are too many thoughts and stimuli overwhelming his brain, rendering him largely immobile."

Abby drew circles with her hand, prompting Alyssa to continue.

Alyssa looked at Abby. "Everyone receives more information than they're aware, but our brains filter out the vast majority of it so we can focus on the things which most require our immediate attention. As far as the doctors can tell, Jeff's brain isn't as able to triage, so it doesn't filter or block effectively, so he seems frozen due to neural overload. I'll know more once I meet him."

"Cool." Abby tapped her access card to the reader beside the door. "Because we're meeting him right now."

Abby pushed open the door, and the two women walked into Jeff's room. Alyssa wrinkled her nose, as the room had an unpleasant, musty odor. The room appeared no different from the other patient rooms she'd seen, but it somehow felt eerily different.

Jeff was sitting in a plastic chair, and due to his tall, thin body, it was a sight which might be seen in a geometry book when the lesson is sharp angles. His right knee was parallel with his ribs and his left knee was at a wide angle, as that leg was extended further out. Jeff's long hair was unkempt and matted. His eyes appeared to be focusing intently on something invisible ten inches in front of his nose.

"Good morning, Jeffrey." Abby put her arm around Alyssa's shoulder. "Jeff, this is my friend Alyssa. She's going to talk to you while I make your bed and tidy up."

"Hi," Alyssa smiled and waved. Jeff sat motionless. "It's nice to meet you, Jeff. Do you prefer Jeff or Jeffrey?"

There was the slightest of movements in his shoulders, which appeared to Alyssa as being a half-hearted shrug.

"I'd like to ask you about the fire last year."

Jeff didn't respond, move, or even blink.

Alyssa pressed onward. "A lot of people were negatively impacted by the fire, Jeff, so it's really important that we learn anything we can about what you may have seen. Do you think you can help me?"

Alyssa studied him for any signs of cogitation or acknowledgment, and then lowered her standards to accept any sort of indication he was even conscious. She looked at Abby, who shrugged. Alyssa returned the shrug, and the two women left Jeff's room.

"That poor young man." Alyssa felt her heart ache. "Does he get groomed or washed at all?"

"Yeah, every second day, so he'll get cleaned up when Gina arrives." Abby tapped at the file folder in Alyssa's hand. "What's his proposed treatment? It should say near the bottom of the page under therapies."

Alyssa opened the folder and read the summary page. "It looks like Dr. Friesen recommended sensory deprivation therapy, to see if it allows him to respond, but it hasn't been scheduled."

"Why not?"

"The administrator indicated he didn't want to go forward with it, because it would cost an arm and a leg."

"Give Zee five minutes in the morgue with a bone saw, and she could get him both of those things."

Alyssa flipped the next few pages, skimming each document. "I've noticed a pattern in many of the reports I've read. When the administrator's choice is to spend money to fix things, or ignore them, he prefers to bury his head in the sand."

"Suffocation?" Abby raised an eyebrow. "I approve of his choice, and volunteer to help him do it."

"This place is so badly run. There's no communication between the owner, the managers, and the medical personnel." Alyssa closed the file and shook her head. "The left hand clearly doesn't know what the right hand is doing."

"Zee once tried using that left-hand, right-hand thing in her defense during an assault trial, but the court didn't accept it as plausible deniability."

"So, the bottom line is Jeffrey is unlikely to ever get his sensory deprivation treatment."

"That really sucks." Abby thought for a moment. "Maybe we can do it ourselves."

"That's completely out of the question. We're not qualified to treat him."

"But we need to know what, if anything, he saw the day of the fire."

"How do you propose we get the equipment to do his testing?" Alyssa closed her eyes. "Please don't say you'll steal it."

"No, I wouldn't steal it. It's too big and heavy, and I'd have no way to transport it. No, I was thinking we could move him into the janitor closet."

"How will that help?"

"I'll clear out the closet and put him in there. Then we can put a blindfold on Jeff and use some earphones, so we can talk to him."

"I don't know if that'll work."

"Me neither." Abby grinned. "Which is exactly why we should try it."

"That was quite the leap you took there. How does doing that make sense?"

"Because I'm a detective and you're a science nerd." Abby beamed. "We're both curious and want answers, so this is the way to do that."

"I suppose it's possible it could work, and it shouldn't cause him any harm or distress." Alyssa pondered this, and then looked at Abby. "How long would it take you to set that up?"

"I can get my hands on the headphones by tomorrow, and I have a blindfold by my bedside."

"I don't want to know why you have a blindfold at your bedside."

"Silly." Abby gave Alyssa a playful punch in the arm. "I wear it in summer when it gets so bright so early in the morning. I don't like seeing any light when I'm trying to sleep."

"Oh, thank goodness, I thought you were going to say –"

"And it's also good for sex games."

Alyssa pinched the bridge of her nose. "And there it is."

"I can spend part of tomorrow moving the stuff out of the janitor closet."

"Fine, but I'll only go through with this if Jeff agrees to try it."

Abby shrugged. "He won't object."

"That's not the same as consenting."

"He's mostly unresponsive." Abby rolled her eyes. "If he could give you verbal consent, he probably wouldn't be in here getting treated in the first place."

"You're probably right, but I'm going to try and ask him anyway."

"Before you do that, there's one more patient for you to meet." Abby pointed to the next door down the hall. "We're coming up to Cenk Vollack's room. He's particularly interesting."

"How so?"

Abby smiled. "He claims to be five-hundred years old, possessed by a demon, and believes mankind is doomed."

Alyssa found Cenk Vollack's file folder and opened it. "He doesn't sound like someone we'll be able to get credible information from."

"He's actually quite smart, especially for a demon." Abby retrieved her access card from her pocket. "And he's interesting to listen to, which is a good thing, because he talks all the time. If he was one of those boring ramblers, it'd be torture."

"You know, just for the record, when I said I'd be your sounding board, I imagined it happening in my bedroom, not outside the door of a hospital patient who believes he's been demonically-possessed for centuries."

"You see?" Abby beamed as she swiped her card on the door lock. "You'd have missed out on all this fun you've been having."

"Not at all where I was going with that, but here we are."

Alyssa stepped inside the room and saw a man lying in his bed.

He tilted his head up just enough to peek at who had entered, and then lay his head back down on the pillow.

"Morning." Abby walked over to the bed and patted the man's feet. "I need you to meet someone, Mr. Vollack."

With some effort and a grunt, he sat himself up in the bed, and then looked down his nose at Alyssa. "Bah."

Alyssa figured the man to at least be in his late sixties. He maneuvered himself into a sitting position and continued looking down his nose at her.

"Alyssa's going to chat with you." Abby wagged a finger at him. "I have to get back to work, so be nice and answer her questions."

She turned and left the room.

Vollack swiveled himself around so his legs could be set down upon the floor. He rested his elbows on his knees and looked at Alyssa. He was an odd sight to behold. His torso was the same shape as a butternut squash. If you added four strands of linguini in the right places, you'd have his arms and legs well-represented. A strategically-placed ripe tomato on top would not only make for an accurate description of his head's shape, but you'd now also have enough ingredients to start making a potentially interesting pasta lunch. Vollack's uncombed salt-and-pepper hair only served to draw more attention to his annoyed expression. "What questions?"

"It's nice to meet you." Alyssa pulled the plastic visitor chair close and sat down. "I'm here to look into the fire last year at the other facility."

"A boring subject," Vollack grumped. "I have no interest in discussing such tedious matters. What could you possibly want to know about it?"

"I'd like to know how the fire made you."

He scoffed. "Warm."

"Were you upset that your section of the hospital was destroyed?"

"Why would I be upset over some useless building being ablaze? Useless things should burn."

"Useless?"

"Yes, useless." He repeated. "Completely useless. Institutions like that serve no useful purpose to anyone. If anything, they're hurting our society."

"How can you say such a thing?" Alyssa shook her head in disbelief. "People are in medical facilities because they're troubled and need to heal. Don't you want people to have a safe place where they can get as much healing as is available?"

"Healing?" He recoiled in horror. "Don't be daft, child. If every tormented person was permitted to heal, it would be a travesty, a tragedy, and other words starting with *tra* and ending in a *y*. No, they should be housed here and given art supplies instead of getting counseling and therapy."

"Sorry," Alyssa blinked, "did you say art supplies?"

"Absolutely," he roared. "Art supplies, musical instruments, pens, pencils, paper, canvases and oils, whatever they want, and then just let them get on with it."

Alyssa rubbed her face. "Wait, just so I'm clear… you think therapy and drugs don't work, but art supplies do?"

Vollack sneered at her. "No, you're not understanding what I'm saying at all. They *do* work, and it's a complete travesty."

"You've completely lost me, unless you're a sadist. If counseling works, then where's the travesty?"

"Let me simplify this, so even you can understand it. Do you know what kills great art? *Healing.* There's no great art without great pain, great suffering, and great misery. Their misery is everyone else's salvation, so when you cure the artist, you rob the world of the joy and meaning behind their suffering."

"I think we can all be relieved you don't write horoscopes."

"And we give the wrong kinds of drugs to these people. We give them anti-psychotics and relaxants, when we should be giving them LSD, pot, or whatever recreational substance they desire."

"That is beyond absurd." Alyssa stood up and put her hands on her hips. "Most people with mental health challenges have brain chemistry which would quite often react dangerously with hallucinogenic drugs and other mind-altering substances. If you give them all drugs, then you'll be amplifying their illnesses and miseries, instead of giving them ways to cope and providing them some relief from what ails them."

"It appears you finally understand, as that is precisely what I'm saying. They should take one for the team and allow their lives to be absolute hell, so the rest of us can have something beautiful to live for." He saw her horrified expression, so softened his voice. "Listen to me, child. Can you imagine the literature we'd have missed if they had healed Edgar Allan Poe and Ernest Hemingway? What if they gave Salvadore Dali and Vincent Van Gogh antipsychotic medications, or sent Brian Wilson and Roger Waters to the best therapists? We'd have so much less worthwhile art and music in the world. And let's face it: once an artist is no longer in pain, he's also no longer making anything good. All the best art comes from dysfunction and pain. All of it.

Every scrap of art worth hearing, seeing, touching, and reading is borne out of pain, trauma, and sheer misery. There's so much wretchedness in life, so the best you can do is get numb to it, and hope it comes with a half-decent soundtrack."

"Well, that just might have been the most bleak and depressing thing I've ever heard."

"I'd be disappointed if it wasn't." Vollack stared at her for a moment. "You know, the Victorian era was filled with misery, suffering, and hopelessness, yet out of those times, we got Austen, Dickens, and both Charlotte and Emily Brontë. Oh, and Lewis Carroll and Lord Byron. And I can't believe I almost forgot to name Oscar Wilde, one of the most charming and clever fellows I ever met. And Edgar Degas, the most amazing painter in history, in my view. I wasn't a huge fan of Burns and Blake, but that was more due to personal reasons. I'm not a sadist; I'm a pragmatist. Those artists were only great because of their suffering."

"So, you're saying none of them would have done what they did if they'd been happy?"

"Absolutely." Vollack added an emphatic nod. "A couple of them were *reasonably* happy, but they were surrounded by misery, and that fueled their art instead. And it wasn't just then. Do you know why so many great artists came out of Britain in the 1960's and 70's? Because the whole country felt miserable. There was a malaise, a sense of hopelessness, and it was a positive boon to the arts, giving some of the greatest theatre and music during that period. Oh, and then there's Russia. Their entire culture is steeped in hopelessness, suffering, and despair, which is why they gave the world some of the greatest artists in history, from Kandinsky and Dostoevsky, to Chekhov and

Tolstoy. Oh, and my two favourite musicians of all time were Russians, Tchaikovsky and Rachmaninoff. They don't make music like that anymore."

"Yes, the dead are notoriously bad at composing new music. *Decomposing,* sure. Oh no. Don't tell me I'm starting to turn into my dad with jokes like that." Alyssa winced.

"It's no coincidence that New York City gave the world some of its best music, art, literature, and theatre in the 70's, at the same time New York was a chaotic, slum-filled, crime-infested pit of misery and despair. Commercialism didn't kill great art, but hope certainly did. Human beings should be miserable – that's when all the best stuff emerges."

"Maybe you can argue that, but I still think healing is better."

Vollack scoffed. "What do you have against people making great art?"

"Nothing. I love art, literature, and music, but not if it means there has to be so much suffering in order to get it." Alyssa thought for a moment. "Well, let me clarify. I love *some* art, literature, and music. So much of it is too shocking and offensive."

"But that's the good stuff," Vollack roared.

"You think *that's* the good stuff?"

"Yes, it's definitely the good stuff. I'd argue it's even the best stuff. Art is nothing more than a mirror. It reflects the times we live in and who we are. If art offends you, it's because society is offensive. If you want art to change, then you need to change society first. The art will change by itself to mirror the new reality. If there's one thing today's art tells us, it's that we're doomed."

"What is it about art that makes you so pessimistic about mankind's survival?"

Vollack cast his eyes toward the ceiling and was quiet for a few seconds. "If I'm being completely transparent with you, it wasn't art that made me give up on humanity, it was toaster pastries."

"Toaster pastries?" Alyssa blinked hard. "You mean like *Pop-Tarts,* and that sort of thing?"

"Yes, exactly like that sort of thing."

"Okay, then you'll need to explain that to me."

"There's nothing to explain. The box has instructions on it."

"And…?"

"They're *toaster pastries.*" Vollack's face reddened. "Pastries you put into a toaster. Their very name has the directions in it. You take them out of the box, remove the wrapper, and put them into a toaster. This does not require heavy thinking, so instructions are ludicrous."

"Somebody buying them for the first time might—"

"No, wait, let me stop you right there, child. Anyone stupid enough to need instructions on how to put a pastry into a toaster when it's called a toaster pastry is also too stupid to be the sort of person who would read the directions in the first place. Society now caters to the ignorant, and, when that happens, it's the beginning of society's imminent demise."

"You should meet my dad sometime. The two of you hold an alarming number of views in common."

Saturday: 10:18 a.m.

"Doctor Friesen?" Alyssa scurried over to him, as he walked along the corridor.

"Yes?" When he recognized Alyssa, he smiled. "Oh, hello again."

She walked alongside him. "Is this a good time for us to speak?"

"Certainly." He pointed to the door up ahead and to his left. "I'm just heading into my office. Do join me."

"Thank you." She followed him to the door.

He used his access card to unlock it and held the door open for her. "After you, miss."

She went inside and sat in the chair which was in front of his wooden desk. The room was on the small side. Had there been three desks in the room, the only way to reach the opposite wall would have been to walk on top of the desks. Friesen went around the desk, pulled out a puffy leather chair, and then sat down, letting out a loud sigh.

"Amazing," he said. "The older I get, the more noise I make while standing up and sitting down. Now," he looked at her, "what are your questions?"

"I'd like to start with this one." Alyssa locked eyes with him. "What do you think about Mr. Vollack?"

"You mean the fellow who thinks he's a five-hundred-year-old demon, insists that he met King George the Fifth, and believes lawns are a sign of humanity's impending doom?" He chuckled. "What would you guess I think about him?"

"That he has mental health issues."

Friesen's eyes twinkled. "He's either a compulsive liar or a delusional loon. This clinic is his current residence, so I think you'll agree that would tilt the scales toward the latter option."

"But couldn't he be both?

"Indeed, he could, as the two are not mutually exclusive." He leaned back in his chair. "However, even if that were the case, it wouldn't be a fifty-fifty proposition. Whatever the split may be, he's mostly on the side of being mentally unwell, so that's where I'm focusing my treatments for the time being."

"That makes sense, now that I think about it."

"I'm sorry, I've forgotten your name."

"Alyssa."

"Thank you. Well, you see, Alyssa, the patients in here are, in some ways, just like everyone else." Friesen studied Alyssa's face for a reaction. "Everyone has some level of darkness, it's simply a case of how much, and how well they can manage it. Those who can manage it well enough simply continue on with their lives. Those who can't get the upper hand on their dark sides will hopefully end up in a place like this, where they can get some help."

"You mean *literally everyone* has darkness?"

"Yes, everyone. Why does that surprise you?"

"Well, it only surprises me a little." Alyssa shrugged. "I mean, you, for example, seem far too cheerful to have a dark side."

"Then it would appear I have you fooled." Friesen laughed. "Every human being who has made it to kindergarten has had a dark side, milady, and I'm as human as the next fellow. We all have the darkness; therefore, we need to learn to manage it. It's a large part of being human."

"What's your darkness?" Alyssa held up her hands as she winced. "I'm sorry, I shouldn't have asked that. It's none of my business."

"I don't mind telling you, but you may regret hearing it."

"No, please, I'm curious and I'd like to know."

"Very well, then." He sat forward in his chair. "The truth is, I genuinely despise the overwhelming majority of people, and I very much loathe needing to be upbeat, friendly, and polite to everyone. It's bloody exhausting having to do that every day, let me tell you. When I go home, I turn off my phone, lock the doors, pour myself some unbelievably strong drinks, and then watch the darkest, most unpleasantly violent movies I can find. After an evening of inebriation and watching fictional people being tortured and hacked to death, I'm ready by morning to once again pretend I'm all pleasant and cheerful. Are you sorry you asked?"

"Not really, actually. You sound a lot like my dad, except he doesn't bother pretending to be pleasant. He views humanity as the only plague able to wear pants."

"A bit of a cynic, I take it."

"He's *a bit* of a cynic in the same way the Swiss Alps are *a bit* of a bump in the autobahn." Alyssa furrowed her brow. "I only just met Mr. Vollack, but my first impression isn't that he's a cynic. At least not in the literal sense. I get a sense that he's much more bitter than cynical."

"I rather suspect it's a blend of both bitterness *and* cynicism, as my work with him seems to be pointing rather emphatically in that direction."

"Is any of his behaviour caused by his medications?"

Friesen shook his head. "Absolutely not, as I haven't had to give him medication in a few years now."

"Really?"

"Oh yes, indeed, and I'm delighted he no longer seems to need it." Friesen looked pleased. "You see, I'm a bit of a history buff, and Mr. Vollack has such interesting stories, so I wouldn't dream of medicating him unless it was absolutely necessary."

"But is he telling you stories or just fantasies?"

"It hardly matters, as some of the best stories are fueled by fantasies, and many fantasies are fueled by stories. The two go hand-in-hand. Human beings are innately wired to love a good story."

"I suppose that's true."

"And whether stories or delusions, either way, there isn't an appropriate medication to treat it." Friesen's eyes met Alyssa's. "And I must say how much I enjoy all the intricate details he provides in his gripping tales. Regardless of whether he's lying or delusional, you have to admit he's a gifted story teller. If he wrote historical fiction, he'd be a rather rich author, in my opinion."

"And then he'd be seen as eccentric instead of needing help."

"Indeed." Friesen's eyes twinkled. "That's one of the many benefits of having an abundance of money. People are willing to overlook all sorts of odd and eccentric behavior, as long as they believe there's a chance some of that cash could end up in their pockets."

Saturday: 11:09 a.m.

Alyssa walked toward the security desk. Robert glanced at her and rolled his eyes. "What?"

"Can I talk to you?"

He gestured toward her with his hand. "Much to my annoyance, you already are talking to me, so that should answer your time-wasting question."

"I want to talk to you about the fire a year ago."

"Yeah, well, I want to be in Vegas with a pair of showgirls in a hotel penthouse counting my millions, but that's not going to happen, either."

"If you were rich enough to have millions to count, then you'd also be rich enough to hire someone to count it for you."

Robert narrowed his eyes. "Who are you, anyway? And I mean for real, because I'm not buying that bullshit story about the government sending someone here to double-check what they already know."

"What Abby told you is true. I'm a friend of hers, so I'm here as a favour to her to take a fresh look at what really happened in the hospital on the day of the fire."

Robert studied Alyssa's face. "Huh."

"And what is that response supposed to mean?"

"It's just I never imagined any of Abby's friends being able to speak coherently."

Alyssa frowned. "Abby's not dumb, you know."

"Dumb?" Robert guffawed. "No, she isn't dumb at all. In fact, she's clever as shit, and she's got more street smarts than most people. That said, there's more than a few lights burned out upstairs, if you catch my drift. Now, I'm busy at the moment, so kindly piss off."

"There's no need to be rude."

"I know, which is why I said to *kindly* piss off, because I'm polite like that."

"Meaning you're not at all polite."

"Deal with it, kid, because that's as good as you're going to get from me." Robert wore a sour expression. "If you want me to talk, then serve me with a subpoena and we'll do everything on the record in court."

"Why in court?"

"So that any accusations you make about me will be on the record, which will make it easier for me to personally sue you if I don't like what you're asking me."

Alyssa rested her elbows on the counter. "I just want to help the patients here, is that wrong of me?"

"Help Jeff and Zee all you like." Robert waved his hand. "If you want to wear your bleeding heart on your sleeve and get all misty-eyed with them, then go ahead and knock yourself out. I don't give a shit. But Vollack? No, he's different. Stay the hell away from him."

"Why just him? What is it about him you object to?"

"Listen closely, girlie," Robert held up his index finger, "because I'll only say this once. Cenk Vollack is no ordinary whack job."

"Call me girlie again and I'll stop being so polite. While we're at it, you shouldn't use the term *whack job* either. It's extremely offensive."

"Yeah? Then what term should I use?" He scoffed. "Nut-job? Looney Tunes? Head-case? Cray-

cray? Fruitcake? Insane in the membrane? Screwball? Unglued, unhinged, unbalanced?"

"I'm not sure any of those are –"

"Bonkers? Nitwit, batshit, apeshit? Cuckoo for cocoa puffs? Three quarters short of a dollar? Five cans short of a six-pack? A few sandwiches short of a picnic?"

"You can stop now."

"Listen, gir...*young lady,* instead of focusing on the words that offended you so much, how about being offended by the demon possessing that lunatic's body?"

Alyssa's mouth dropped open. "Wait, do you think he's seriously possessed by a demon?"

"No, I *know* he's seriously possessed by a demon."

"Come on. There's no demon possession involved in this whatsoever. Now I know who Abby got the demon theory from, but you're both just being astonishingly ignorant of his condition."

"I'm not ignorant of anything. Well, except maybe the federal tax code, but that thing is a total gong show. But I'm serious about that whack-job having an actual demon living inside of him, whether you and the cops want to believe me or not."

"You told the police he was possessed by a demon?"

"Of course. It's the truth, so why wouldn't I tell them?"

"And they somehow disregarded everything you told them. Wow, what a shock. Sorry, but there's no demon; he's just unwell."

"He can be both of those things, you know."

"No, he can't, because demons don't exist."

Robert pointed at her. "You mean you don't *believe* they exist. On those rare occasions demons do possess a person, they keep a low profile, so they can just watch humans and learn about evil directly from them."

Alyssa pinched the bridge of her nose. "Thank goodness you're a security guard and not his doctor, or you'd be prescribing an exorcism."

"He'd be cured if I were his doctor, but it wouldn't be from no hokey ceremonial bullshit. When it comes to getting rid of demons, I'm the only one in this building who knows what works and what doesn't, you got that? And I'll tell you what doesn't work, and that's holy water, exorcisms, and prayers."

"I know I'll regret asking this, but what *does* work?"

"Demons have one main weakness: they can't manifest themselves in our world without a human host, and while they're occupying the meat suit, they're as vulnerable as anyone else."

"So, you're saying," Alyssa was having difficulty forming the words to what she viewed as a ludicrous sentence, "the only way to beat a demon is to kill the person who is hosting it?"

"You got it."

"Which means the only way to save Mr. Vollack is to murder him, is that really what you're saying to me right now?"

"That's what it boils down to, yeah." Robert shrugged. "Sure, one person dies, boo-hoo, how sad, but you end up saving the lives of so many other people who would have been possessed later."

"You mean kill one host today to save the lives of other potential hosts tomorrow?"

"Exactly."

"Just so I'm fully understanding how this all works, when the host dies, does the demon die, too?"

"No, but he's banished back to his own realm until he's summoned again."

"But how do you know when a person is possessed by a demon?"

"Oh, you'll know." He nodded, knowingly. "They're temperamental, irrational, confrontational, and openly hostile."

"You've just described yourself."

"No, amplify those traits until they're at an extreme level. That's what I'm talking about."

Alyssa bit her lip. "Still sounds like you."

"No, *way* worse than you seem to think I am."

"Now I'm really confused. What if you think they're possessed by a demon, but they're actually just a complete jerk? Or the Governor of Florida?"

"Who cares?" Robert shrugged. "At the end of the day, the world either has one less demon or one less asshole, so no matter which it turns out to be, there's no down side."

Alyssa covered her face with her hands and groaned louder than she had planned. She lowered her hands and cast a weary look in his direction. "So, you're saying demons are real, some people are just jerks, but demons are what make people evil?"

"You're mostly wrong." Robert glared at her. "I got news for you, lady, people don't need demons in order to be evil. Human beings are naturally capable of the worst shit you can imagine all on their own. The main reason you don't normally see demons on earth is because human beings scare the shit out of them."

Alyssa shook her head. "I've noticed that you don't have a wide variety of descriptive words in your vocabulary, do you?"

"Don't need 'em." Robert waved dismissively. "The word *shit* is pretty versatile, so it much covers pretty much everything I need to say."

"It really does cover the things you say, in more ways than one, so I'll agree with that much. From now on, whenever I hear that word, I'll be sure to think of you." She backed away from the desk. "Thank you for sort of answering my questions. I'd give you a nasty look, but you've already got one."

He waved her away.

Abby, who was eavesdropping nearby, watched Alyssa storm away. Abby then approached Robert. "I caught the tail end of that discussion, and you were really rude to my friend."

He turned in his swivel chair to face Abby. "It's nothing personal, Abby, and you should know that by now. I don't discriminate, because I hate everyone equally."

"Yeah, but I would've hoped you'd be a good colleague, and act a bit nicer to someone who's important to me."

Robert scoffed. "I don't know how to break this to you, Abby, but I'm not a nice person, and I'm certainly not a good one either."

"Maybe not, but you're not an evil person either."

"Do you even know what evil is?" Robert leaned back in his chair. "Because most people don't."

"I think I do." Abby reflected on the question. "I mean, I've seen a lot of people getting their thrills through their own cruelty. That's pretty evil, if you ask me."

"Sure, but there's the more subtle forms of evil, which can be found printed in things like cell phone contracts and home-owners' association minutes. The worst evil isn't always obvious. It's layer after layer of petty, little things put in place by petty, little people, which we don't notice right away until it's too late. Did you ever read Orwell's *1984?*"

"No."

"Why not?"

"I'm dyslexic, and don't have the attention span for novels."

"Well, you should find a way read that one." Robert nodded. "We're currently living in the very dystopian nightmare the author warned us about, and it all started through small, subtle advances in evil and the collective stupidity of people."

Abby wasn't sure what to say, so she shrugged, turned around, and went down the nearest corridor.

Saturday: 11:50 a.m.

Doctor Friesen looked up as Abby knocked and then opened his door.

"Got a sec?"

Friesen nodded and pointed toward the empty chair in front of his desk. "Certainly."

"Thanks." She walked in and sat down.

"What can I do for you?"

"I'd like to talk to you about Zee."

Friesen nodded. "Is there something wrong?"

"Yes, but also no. I just want your opinion on something."

"Ask away."

"Zee says she's innocent, but my friend told me somewhere around ninety-five percent of all convicted people say the same. I don't know if I believe that."

"Your friend may seem cynical to you, but she is basically correct." Friesen put down his pen and leaned forward. "Regardless, Zee's guilt or innocence is irrelevant to me, as I'm merely focused on completing her evaluation."

"So, you're open to the possibility of her being innocent, despite the court saying she's guilty?"

"Yes, of course I am. The justice system deals with all of that nonsense, but it's irrelevant to me."

"Why?"

"Because it makes no difference to me." Friesen tapped his finger against his desk. "Guilty or not, either way, she still needs an assessment coupled with psychological help from me. All going well, I'll treat her until she's fully able to manage herself, and then I'll send my findings to the court."

"And if all doesn't go well?"

He shrugged. "Same thing, really, except it may take longer for her to get to the fully managing point, if she ever does at all. The only significant difference to me is if she is found to be sane, because then I'll be having to meet with her at a correctional facility instead of here. If I could get Zee to take the medication I prescribed, her anger issues would be much easier for her to manage."

"Why not just tell her she has to take them?"

"Because Zee is the sort of person who delights in doing the opposite of whatever I tell her she has to do." Friesen yawned. "She needs to find her own way to giving medications a try."

"I'll just tell her she has to take them, and won't give her a choice in the matter."

"Well, I can see that going over like a lead balloon."

"A lead balloon would go over quite well, and would go over quickly and efficiently." Abby thought for a moment. "It wouldn't float, however, which is likely its intended purpose."

"That's a different kind of *going over,* but again, it's just an expression."

"Then the expression should be *as stupid as someone who makes balloons out of lead.*"

"Yes, I suppose you're not wrong there. Right, then. Give it a go, and let's see what happens."

Abby nodded. "I'll go and talk to her right now."

Saturday: 12:02 p.m.

Abby marched into Zee's room. Zee was lying on the bed, stretched out, and Abby strode toward her. Zee nodded. "Hey, Abby."

Abby folded her arms. "Why won't you take the medication Dr. Friesen offered you?"

Zee scoffed. "Because I don't trust pharmaceutical companies."

Abby rolled her eyes. "Nobody in their right mind does, but that doesn't mean their stuff doesn't work."

Zee sat up and locked eyes with her. "I'm not comfortable with the idea of brain medicines."

"It's not about what makes you comfortable, it's about what will help you and those who care about you," Abby snapped. "If you want out of here, then you're going to have to try some things you might not be comfortable with. You need to actually try to help yourself instead of focusing on what doesn't work for you. It's like that thing they say about an apple a day keeping the doctor away."

"Anything will keep someone away if you throw it at them hard enough. And once you do that, they'll file a restraining order to keep *you* away instead."

"You know what I think?" Abby shook her head. "I think the real issue is you're scared they'll work."

"Why would that scare me?"

"Because then you'd have nothing to blame your actions and behaviour on, and you'd have to accept that you sometimes make some pretty bad life choices." Abby rolled her eyes. "And don't look at me like that. I know I've made a lot of bad life choices too, but I accept responsibility for everything I've done. I've never blamed any of the lousy things I've done on my brain problems. I made those decisions and I know whatever happens, I brought upon myself."

"Are you done?"

"That depends." Abby glared at her. "Are you going to take your medication?"

"No."

"Then yeah, we're done." Abby stormed out of Zee's room.

Saturday: 12:29 p.m.

Abby found Alyssa in the employee break room. The term *break room* may conjure up images of tables, chairs, and perhaps a sofa of some kind. Perhaps one might think of a pristine, white countertop, with coffee machines, hot water dispensers, a sink, fridge, a dishwasher, and perhaps even an assortment of teas. If, indeed, one had such images in their mind, one would need to utterly disregard any such nonsense, as this room was not originally designed as a place to take breaks. Back when the building was used as a police station, this particular room was a small office supply bay. There used to be a large copy machine, two shelves of office supplies, and a small countertop in the room, and that was it. The space was barely ten feet square. When it was converted into a break room, and this term is used loosely, a small table and two chairs were placed in it. The counter was left intact, but there was no sink or dishwasher. A small bar fridge was provided, and an old electric kettle was available on the counter, though where one obtained water for said kettle was anyone's guess.

Alyssa was sitting at the table with her laptop open. She glanced up when Abby entered.

"You look upset. What's wrong?"

"Zee's wrong," Abby fumed.

"What happened?"

"I'm not upset about something that happened, I'm upset about what *hasn't* happened and *isn't* happening." Abby began to pace in the room, but after taking two steps, she was already at the opposite wall, which made pacing a somewhat unsatisfying course of action. "I just found out the doctor wants Zee to take medications for her mood disorders, but she's refusing to take them."

"Did you ask her why?"

"Yes, and all she offered were excuses." Abby folded her arms and stewed. "By not taking her medications, she's hurting herself, and that hurts me."

"I know, but you can't force people to take good advice, even when they're clearly sabotaging themselves. She's going to have to arrive at that conclusion herself."

"I'd be okay with her arriving at the conclusion herself if she was actually making an effort to travel there. You can't arrive at a conclusion if you don't start the journey. She's not even waiting at the bus stop or trying to hail a cab, she's still at home on the couch eating tortilla chips."

"What are you talking about?"

"Look, I'm not good with metaphors, okay? But at least I'm trying to use them."

"Sorry, Abby, but I don't know what to say, as usual, but I'm sorry you're upset." Alyssa leaned back in the chair. "It must be difficult seeing someone you care about not willing to help themselves."

"It really is." Abby stamped her foot on the ground, then looked at Alyssa. "What are you reading?"

"The investigative report on the fire, which you sent me earlier." Alyssa pointed toward her laptop screen with her chin. "There's a lot of information for me to digest."

"Anything I should know?"

"I'm not sure yet. I'm going to spend the afternoon reading through it and making notes, so I'll have some thoughts for you by this evening."

Saturday: 4:12 p.m.

Alyssa normally enjoyed that time of year, when the summer heat was replaced with mild autumnal days and cool breezes. A time when her narrow street was lined with trees, featuring an explosion of brilliant colours. Many sections of Vancouver's 29th Avenue are busy, but the further west you travel, the narrower the street gets. Where Alyssa currently lived, there was barely enough room for a single vehicle to make it between all the parked cars, whose owners, by and large, realized the value of folding in their side mirrors.

During that particular walk home, however, Alyssa noticed none of those things, as she was too preoccupied with Abby's case. It was far preferable to focus on the case rather than reflecting on how she'd been impersonating a government official.

Abby had always been a creature of habit, so when she met an obstacle in her path, she would take the quickest path around, over, or through that obstacle, and minor things such as laws, felonies, and the threat of incarceration were never factored into her next move. Alyssa had influenced Abby to take laws, felonies, and the threat of incarceration into consideration, which Abby did, immediately before completely disregarding them. Still, it was progress, in a way. Baby steps.

And the temporary facility… so many strange and bizarre people there, from the foul-mouthed security guard to Abby's doom-and-gloom client who hated the world. She had so many questions.

The investigative report and summary of recommendations she'd spent the afternoon reading had been intriguing. There were a lot of health and safety violations, some arguable negligence, and some tragic failure of systems, but she'd seen nothing – neither in the government report, nor anywhere else – to make her believe there was anything resembling a homicide on that fateful day.

What confused Alyssa the most was how Abby had seen the same evidence she had, but ended up convinced there was a legitimate detective case. So far, Alyssa hadn't seen anything even remotely like a mystery needing to be solved, so she could only assume Abby was simply seeing what she wanted to see.

She sighed as she came up the path and unlocked the front door of her home. She walked through the front door and did a double-take upon seeing someone sitting in the living room. She smiled. "Dad!"

Her father, Malcolm Mercer, walked to Alyssa and wrapped his arms around her. "Good to see you, kiddo. I missed you."

The embrace ended, and Alyssa smiled again. "How was your trip overseas?"

"Good," Malcolm exhaled. "Do you want the real answer or the cover story?"

"The real answer."

Malcolm thought for a moment. "Actually, never mind, I can't tell you that, but I *can* tell you it ended great. The cover story's pretty good, too."

"What's the cover story?"

Malcolm walked into the living room and sat on the sofa. "I haven't thought of it yet, but it's going to be amazing."

Alyssa followed her father and stood in front of him. "Are you okay?"

"Couldn't be better. Why?"

"I don't think I've ever seen you in such a good mood." Alyssa gestured with her hand in front of him. "You're almost… *giddy.*"

"Well, I am in a good mood, I have to admit," Malcolm beamed. "Your mother and I have some terrific news to share with you. We're officially retiring, so no more chasing down international criminals, no more facilitating defections, and, best of all, no more boring paperwork and meetings. We're done, and that's why we're late coming home. We had a lot of dull debriefings to attend and a ton of boring paperwork to sign. Your mother will be flying to Washington to wrap up the rest."

"That's wonderful." Alyssa sat beside him. "What will you do now?"

"I don't know, and right now, I don't care." He gave her a weary smile. "For now, I'm just going to relax, and hang out with you. In a few days, I'll be needing something to occupy my time, and then I'll think about stuff."

"That makes sense."

"How's Abby's case going?"

"There's no easy answer to that question." Alyssa chuckled. "Where would I even begin?"

"Anywhere you like." Malcolm leaned forward. "Just be sure to tell me everything. I want to know what you two have been working on."

Saturday: 5:49 p.m.

Alyssa had made herself some tea and sat at the dining room table as her father peppered her with questions as he paced the room. She had a wide array of papers spread across the table, ranging from sticky notes and documents to floor plans and patient summaries.

"Okay." Malcolm stopped pacing and looked at Alyssa. "So, why are you ruling out the owner of the facility as a suspect? There's an obvious financial motive, as it shows he received a sizeable insurance payout."

"Yes, he did, but he didn't profit from the fire." Alyssa found the appropriate sheet of paper and held it up. "If anything, he was underinsured."

Malcolm shook his head. "No, you said he received somewhere around a million dollars, so what am I missing?"

"He did get a huge insurance payout for sure, but between the safety violation fines, renovating the temporary facility, and then the construction cost overruns on the clinic repairs, it's only around eighty percent of what he needs." Alyssa looked at Malcolm. "The owner lost a lot of money because of the fire, plus Celia's family is in the process of filing a wrongful death lawsuit against him."

"I guess that makes sense. Does the owner live locally?"

"No, he lives in Winnipeg."

"Oh, okay." Malcolm nodded. "Then he's being punished enough."

Alyssa set her tea cup down. "What's wrong with Winnipeg?"

"Are you kidding? They get eight months of winter, their official provincial birds are all mosquitos, and every Halloween costume has to be designed to fit over a snowsuit. Let's just say Winnipeg is a great place to be *from.*"

Malcolm's attention was diverted when the front door opened and Abby walked in. She looked up, saw Malcolm, and nodded a greeting to him. He nodded back. Abby closed the door and made her way to the dining room table. "What are you guys doing?"

Malcolm gestured toward the papers on the table. "Alyssa's bringing me up to speed on your case."

"Cool," Abby set down her backpack and sat down. "Continue."

Alyssa looked at Abby. "I was just about to tell him more about Mr. Vollack."

Malcolm chuckled. "Yeah, the guy who thinks he's a demon."

Abby stretched her arms and sighed. "Despite his claim about being more than five centuries old, Mr. Vollack has only been saying he's a demon for the past three years. Prior to that, he was being treated for paranoia and schizophrenia."

Malcolm raised his eyebrows. "How do you know that?"

Abby opened her backpack and pulled out a folder. "I read it in his file."

Alyssa's eyes widened. "You have access to patient files as an aide?"

"Not as an aide, no, but I have access to patient files as Abby Lunay, the former criminal, thanks to my password-cracking software and my handy set of lock picks."

Alyssa shook her head. "This is a huge breach of patient confidentiality."

Abby groaned. "And this is a huge waste of our time when we should be talking about Mr. Vollack. Do you want to read his file or not?"

"Yes," Alyssa exhaled. "I really do, and more than anything right now, because I'm so curious. You said he's only been a demon for three years, correct?"

"Right, so one day he was responding well to his meds and treatments, and the next he was insisting his name was *Armoniel,* some sort of being from the netherworld."

Malcolm guffawed. "I'd call that a step backwards in his progress, for sure."

Abby looked at him. "I think it was a step *forward,* because ever since his demonic possession, he has shown no symptoms of paranoia or schizophrenia, and he hasn't needed any medication in those three years."

Malcolm snickered. "Right, so he's completely cured, except for the small matter of believing he's a demon from the depths of Hell who took up residence inside a mental health clinic."

Alyssa thought for a moment. "Does he ever break character?"

"Quite often, actually." Abby sighed. "Some days he's totally demon, and then for a few days, he seems to become more like his old self, but then snaps back into full demon mode again."

Alyssa tapped a pen against the table, absent-mindedly. "Is there a pattern?"

"Yes, some days demon, some days not."

"No, I mean is there something happening on his *very-demon* days that aren't happening on his *not-quite-as-demon* days?"

"I don't know." Abby shrugged, and then her eyes grew wide. "Wait a minute. He's been claiming to be a demon for three years."

"Yeah," Malcolm prompted. "And?"

Abby looked at him. "He's been with Dr. Friesen for three years."

Alyssa made a note on a piece of paper. "Then maybe we need to find out if his demon days coincide with his doctor visits. We'll need to go back tomorrow and ask some more questions."

"I guess we could do that." Abby drummed her fingers on the table. "Is that really our best way to find out what really happened?"

"Yes, Abby." Alyssa nodded. "It's not as if we can go back in time and watch everything unfold and then gather the facts for ourselves."

"True." Abby pondered this. "And time travel could cause problems, like if you started reminiscing with someone you hadn't met yet."

"We'll head back to the clinic first thing in the morning."

Malcolm leaned on the table. "And I'll go with you."

Alyssa looked at him. "Seriously? You've been retired for ten minutes, and it was too much down time for you?"

"No, I'm glad to be retired from the job, but this is a mystery, and the last mystery I worked on was a year ago, when I was sent to Somalia. Do you know what that country's capital city is?"

"Yes," Alyssa nodded, "Mogadishu."

"Gesundheit."

Alyssa gave her dad an exasperated look. "This is hardly the time to be making country jokes."

"I know." Malcolm winked. "Kenya believe I did that?"

Alyssa closed her eyes. "I get a feeling tomorrow's going to be a long day."

Saturday: 7:18 p.m.

Malcolm was sitting up in bed in the dark, his legs stretched out, as he flipped channels, looking for something interesting to watch. His wife, Mary, liked a bedroom to have pastel colours and lots of natural light, whereas Malcolm liked a bedroom which could be made completely dark, illuminated only by the TV screen. Their compromise was to have a huge window in the room, which had thick, opaque curtains, so they could each have the room the way they wanted it when they were home. For Malcolm, it was more than a difference in aesthetic tastes, the dark bedroom was the one place he didn't get headaches. Night terrors, on the other hand…

His phone rang, and he saw it was his wife. He smiled as he picked up his phone. "Hey, Mary."

"Hi, Malcolm. I'm now at Heathrow, waiting to board my flight to Washington, so I thought I'd just check in with you. I forgot to ask you earlier how your flight was."

"It was long." Malcolm turned off the TV and stood up. "That was nine hours of my life I won't get back."

"Is Alyssa at home with you?"

"Yeah, she's in her room right now."

"Good. Have you been helping her with her end-of-term assignments?"

"No," Malcolm admitted.

Mary hesitated before responding. "No?"

"That's what I said. No, nyet, nein. I'd add the Italian and Spanish words for *no,* but I don't know the no in those."

"It's *no* for both, but I know you don't know those no's."

"No, but I know your nose, and your fingers and toes."

"Enough of the rhyming." Mary's tone of voice was an interesting blend of wildly curious and mildly annoyed. "So, you really haven't been helping her with her school work at all?"

"No."

"I'm going to need a bit more than a simple no."

"Fine." Malcolm smirked. "As Shakespeare wrote in Hamlet, act three, scene three, line eighty-seven, *'no'.* Didn't think I knew that, did you?"

"No, but I'm willing to bet it's the only Shakespeare quote you can reference, though that's beside the point. Why haven't you been helping her with her studies?"

"Because she's got a case."

"A case? A case of what?"

"Not a case of what, she has a *case* case." Malcolm leaned against the wall. "You know, a detective case. A mystery, an enigma, a conundrum."

"Has your brain been replaced with a Thesaurus? I know what a case is, but what are you talking about?"

"Abby has her first detective case, and Alyssa's helping her with it."

"Alyssa can't be on a case with Abby, because she has assignments, projects, and exams." Mary groaned. "You've infected me with your neural thesaurus."

"Who knew it was contagious?"

"This is serious."

"I know it's serious, but Alyssa already turned in all of her assignments, so she's done until her classes resume next Wednesday." Malcolm began to pace. "So as long as she's ready to get back to school by then, there's no harm in her helping Abby for a few days."

"She's a hundred percent up to date?"

"She's a hundred percent up to date, down to prune, and ready to fig. She's totally caught up with all her assignments and whatever other Mediterranean fruits you want to mention."

There was a pause before she answered. "I guess that's okay, then."

"Exactly." Malcolm grinned. "And don't worry. If she needs help with anything, I'm here."

"That isn't as reassuring as you think it is. What are you up to?"

"That depends. Are you referring to my height, or my intentions?"

"Your intentions, of course."

"If I mention my intentions, it may cause some contention."

"Great." Mary sighed. "It's as if I'm trying to get answers from Dr. Seuss."

"I cannot yet leave, I cannot depart. I have a job to do here, so show me some heart." Malcolm chuckled. "That was fun. I should answer in Seuss-rhyme more often."

"Not unless you want to sleep in the garage for the rest of your life." Mary groaned. "Be serious. Is there really a case – like an actual, tangible case – or is this just a reaction to our retirement?"

"No, Mary, I'm seriously committed to our retirement. I promise you."

"Then explain this."

"Well, *this* is a pronoun used to indicate a person, time, or thing. Now that I think about it, it can also be an adverb, such as when you're about to say *I can't believe he's this weird.*"

Mary sighed. "It's true, I can't believe you're this weird, but it's not what I want to discuss. Explain *this* the situation, not *this* the word."

"Hang on a second." Malcolm went to his bedroom door and peeked into the hallway, to ensure Abby wasn't nearby. "Listen, when Abby told me she had a case, I didn't take her too seriously. After decades of chasing international criminals and jumping head-first into high-stakes gambits, a low-level PI case didn't interest me in the slightest. But when I spoke to Alyssa and Abby, I realized Abby's stumbled onto something potentially interesting and important."

"Why do I find that hard to believe?"

"Because I said it?"

"That's usually a good indicator, but not this time." Mary paused. "Look, my flight to D.C. is starting to board, so I have to leave it at that. I'll call you when I get settled in the hotel, because I'll want more details about everything."

"Have a safe flight. I miss you already."

Saturday: 10:06 p.m.

Malcolm went down the stairs and walked into the kitchen. He opened the fridge, reached past Mary's array of healthy foods, grabbed a can of Coke, and then opened it. He closed the fridge door, took a gulp of the soda, and then headed into the dining room. He saw Abby sitting motionless at the table, her eyes staring straight ahead.

"You look distracted, Abby." Malcolm pulled out a chair and sat down opposite her. "A penny for your thoughts."

She glanced at him. "We don't use pennies anymore, and offering me a nickel for my thoughts somehow feels demeaning."

Malcolm set the Coke can on the table. "Are you still annoyed that I referred to your clothes hamper as the Lunay bin?"

"No, I'm still thinking about my case."

"Yeah, I've been thinking about it, too, and I have a few questions about the fire. Alyssa told me a lot, but I'd like to hear it from your perspective. Is this a good time to dive into it a bit deeper?"

"Yeah, go ahead. Shoot." Abby winced. "No, wait, I know you're armed a lot of the time, so pretend I said *go ahead* and not *shoot*."

Malcolm took a drink and swallowed. "So, who was on duty in that section when the fire broke out?"

Abby squinted as she thought. "Robert was on security, Celia was the care aide, and Gina was there as a trainee."

Malcolm nodded. "So, just to be clear, Dr. Friesen wasn't there at any point?"

Abby shook her head. "No, he was there the day before, and was scheduled to be in again the day after."

"And the other guard, Luis Garcia, wasn't on duty that day, and you didn't yet work there, correct?"

"Correct."

Malcolm pulled out a sheet of paper from his pocket, which was covered in his notes. "And the patients in that section were the deceased coma guy…"

"Wing Zhen."

"Yeah, and Suzanne…"

"Zee."

"Right, plus that unresponsive guy…"

"Jeff."

"Right, and the demon dude."

"Mr. Vollack. Yes."

"Okay," Malcolm said as he put the paper back inside his pocket, "so walk me through it all. Just before the fire broke out, where was everyone?"

"Gina was coming back from her break, and she was looking for Celia, Celia was doing the daily care of Wing, and Robert was at the security desk."

Malcolm reached to the nearby kitchen counter and retrieved a full-sized notepad and a pen and got ready to write. "And where were the patients?"

"Mr. Vollack was taking his walk, so you can see him on the security footage for sections at a time. Zee and Jeff were probably in their rooms."

"I'd have preferred hearing *definitely* instead of *probably,* but I guess nothing's perfect, especially with such lousy lighting and crappy cameras in that place."

"I know," Abby rubbed her eyes, "but the security cameras don't cover everywhere, and where they do cover is hard to see. There were a lot of sections where there's no camera coverage at all, which makes this even more difficult."

When you're in a public hospital, one of the things you can't help but notice is how brightly lit everything is. In a private facility, where one of the main priorities is profit, things like the electric bill are looked upon less as the necessary cost of providing an important service, and more as an annoying hindrance adversely affecting the owner's bottom line.

The private hospital's owner had, one day, decided to remove twenty-five percent of the overhead lights, as a cost-saving measure. When he saw the reduced cost on his next utility bill, he went up to fifty percent removal, and then, another utility bill later, took it to seventy-five percent. He kept more lights on in certain key areas, but fewer in less important areas, such as hallways, and, in his mind, this was an idea every bit as bright as the hallways were not.

Once the facility had been at that seventy-five percent point of reduced light, the owner had to decide between the cost of the remaining twenty-five percent of lights, and the cost of possible disability claims caused by people tripping over things they couldn't see, and he opted to keep a minimum number of lights on.

What began as a cost-savings exercise ended with a number of poorly-illuminated areas throughout the facility. The interesting thing about such areas is when they get filmed by the cheapest security cameras available, it results in some particularly useless video footage being entered into evidence later on.

Alyssa came down the stairs and wandered toward the voices. "What's going on?"

"Abby's walking me through what happened during that fire a year ago." Malcolm turned back to Abby. "Okay, and then the fire broke out. Where was everyone once that happened?"

"Gina seemed to be in a panicked state. At first, she froze, but then began running around all over the section. Robert sounded the alarm, called 911, and then went to the patient area."

Malcolm made some notes. "And where were the patients at this moment?"

"At first, as far as we know, Zee and Jeff were still in their rooms, but we can't verify that, and Mr. Vollack had just made it back to his door after his daily walk. The security cameras didn't work well even under ideal conditions, so once there was smoke, there's no useful footage from most of them at all. We can really only go by what everyone said in their statements, which is what the courts had to do. Zee left on her own, Mr.

Vollack, laughing maniacally the entire way, was escorted out by Robert. Jeffrey didn't want to evacuate at first."

"Tell me more about how Jeffrey got out."

"There's nothing to tell, really." Abby shrugged. "Robert just went back inside and got him to leave."

"Any ideas as to why Jeff didn't want to leave in the first place?"

"I can maybe guess." Abby looked off into the middle distance as she thought. "His brain was probably overloaded with everything going on, plus evacuating wasn't part of his daily routine. Maybe he was upset about the disruption to his schedule."

Malcolm looked at his notes and frowned. "You said Robert went back to get Jeffrey. Did he go back to get Wing Zhen, too?"

"He tried to, but he wasn't able to access the room. He said his security card went missing."

"Suspicious timing. And you said Suzanne – I mean, *Zee* – got out on her own?"

"Yes, the rooms unlock automatically as soon as the fire alarm goes off."

"But the door to Wing's room didn't unlock?"

"No, it didn't." Abby frowned. "The investigators later found out that the wire leading to the locking mechanism wasn't plugged in properly, which is why it failed."

"You mean it wasn't plugged in properly, or it had been pulled out by someone?"

"Not sure." Abby shrugged. "What I do know is the owner faced a huge fine as a result. It turned out the fire systems hadn't been checked in nearly two years, which is a violation of health and safety laws."

"The people who weren't there that day," Malcolm referred to his notes. "Dr. Gordon Friesen and Luis Garcia... can anyone vouch for where they were at the time of the fire?"

"No, they both said they were home. The doctor has no witnesses, but Luis says he was with his mom that day."

"That's it?" Malcolm raised his eyebrows. "Luis' alibi is flimsy, at best, and the doctor has none at all. If this was a detective show on TV, ominous music would start playing in the background. Okay, now let's look at things *after* the fire. Those who were able to evacuate did so, right?"

"Right."

"Okay, so then what?"

"Zee tried to escape, but was restrained by a guard from another wing, who was helping to look after the evacuees. Mr. Vollack was heard yelling *burn, burn* and clapping. Gina wasn't in any of the footage for a while, but later, people saw her curled up on the grass crying. Robert was with Jeffrey, trying to calm him down, as Jeff was having what looked like a panic attack of some sort."

"Okay, that all helps." Malcolm flipped the page in his notepad. "In order to fully get the whole picture, I have a few more questions."

"Okay."

"First, why were those four patients in a separate section from the rest of the patients?"

"There were three areas in the hospital where patients were kept." Abby squinted as she recalled the layout. "The main part could hold forty-eight patients, and there were two smaller sections which were added later in phase two. The section on the south side was added a few years after the main section opened, and it could hold another twelve patients. There used to be a huge storage room on the north side beside the laundry room, but they shrunk the storage room and used the extra space to make four more rooms for patients. That's the section where the fire broke out."

"And this section was the only one where fire control systems failed, correct?"

"Yup, but they only partially failed." Abby tapped the table with her finger. "The alarms worked, but the ventilation system didn't. All the doors unlocked, too, except for Wing Zhen's."

Malcolm whistled. "Jesus, it sounds to me like that whole section was just an accident waiting to happen."

"If accidents waited to happen, they wouldn't be accidents, they'd be deliberate and premeditated."

"It's just an expression, Abby."

"Then the expression should be *an accident waiting for the negligence lawsuit to be filed.*"

"That's arguable, but let's just move on. Was a floor plan entered into evidence?"

"Yup. It's still here on the table, folded up, if you want to see it."

"I really do."

"Is it because you have an idea?"

"I don't know yet, but I might, depending on what I see."

Abby opened the floor plan on the table and smoothed it out. Malcolm leaned on the table and pored over the schematic.

Abby looked from the floor plan to Malcolm. "What are you thinking?"

"I'm thinking about how many conclusions were drawn in the investigation, as well as in Zee's trial, which were based on hearsay and poor-quality video evidence."

"I think I know where you're going now." Abby pointed at several points on the floorplan. "There are these dead zones where the cameras don't cover, and there's so many other areas where the lighting and video quality are so poor, assumptions are the only thing anyone can make."

"Exactly. So, on this map, I can see there are cameras at the corners of the halls, but not in the halls themselves. There were also no cameras in the washrooms, patient rooms, or the laundry room."

"Right."

"On the morning of the fire, which people were in one of those dead zones at any point? Or, for that matter, were in one of those areas where the video quality was useless?"

"It would be easier for me to list who *wasn't*. We can't really know who was in those areas, because we're not able to see those areas."

"Yeah, but we can see who passed by one camera and then see how long it took them to show up on the next camera." Malcolm squinted at the floor plan, then pointed. "What's the room there, in the middle of the north corridor?"

Abby leaned in to see what was being pointed at. "Oh, that's the maintenance room."

"Hmm," Malcolm thought for a moment. "Are we talking about a brooms-and-mops maintenance room, or a wires-and-electronics maintenance room?"

"There were both of those together in the same room."

Malcolm swore under his breath. "Just what you want. Sensitive electronics set up beside a water faucet. Somehow, it just gets worse the more I hear. Was the door locked at least?"

"No." Abby made an erasing motion with her hands. "Well, wait, they weren't locked before the fire happened, anyway, but it was one of many safety violations listed in the report, so they started locking it after that."

"You mentioned a report, which means there was an investigation."

"Big time. A team of investigators from the Ministry of Health came by and spent five weeks collecting statements and doing assessments. By the end of it, they submitted a ninety-seven-page report with an additional fourteen pages of recommendations, mostly concerning improvements to safety procedures."

"Can you get me a copy of the report?"

"Yeah, sure. I already sent a copy to Alyssa." Abby glanced at Alyssa then looked back to Malcolm. "I'll forward one to you as well."

"And now for the big question." Malcolm folded his arms. "Why was Zee blamed for the fire?"

"Several reasons. They found her lighter where the fire started, plus she was on record as stating if she was sent to this facility, she'd burn it down, plus she was always fighting with Celia."

"Why was she fighting with her?"

"I don't know for sure. I just know Zee hated her, and the feeling was mutual."

Malcolm nodded. "Yeah, and now Celia's dead. Still, all of that's circumstantial evidence. And they convicted her on that?"

"Zee had a prior arrest for arson, a history of assaults, and dozens of misdemeanors. When she was questioned about the facility fire, she expressed delight in the tragedy and seemed indifferent about the deaths of Wing and Celia. She was their prime suspect, and they had a lot more evidence pointing to her than anyone else, and just enough for the charges to stick. Zee couldn't afford a big-time lawyer, so she used the court-appointed one, who apparently wasn't terribly interested in getting her off charges. The best he managed was getting Zee sent here instead of straight to prison."

"So much about that bothers me, it isn't even funny." Malcolm narrowed his eyes and frowned. "And then there's the security guard, Robert... something about his situation doesn't add up in my head either."

Abby raised her hand. "I usually add things up on the calculator in my phone."

"No, I mean Robert played a big role in the evacuation of the facility. Jesus, he *literally* saved the life of a patient, that Jeff guy. From what you've told me, he also did his damnedest to get to Wing Zhen and Celia Ocampo, so I don't understand why he was demoted."

"The owner said as the on-duty guard and security supervisor, Robert was responsible to know where his access card was at all times. He claimed it was stolen, but he had been using it just earlier that morning. The report said if he'd had his access card, he could have used it to activate the emergency door override, and two lives might not have been lost. His access card was later found melted in the laundry room where the fire broke out."

"So, Robert got demoted, and this Luis Garcia guy was named supervisor."

"Yes."

"Garcia had only been on the job for six or seven months at that time, yet they promoted him anyway?"

"Apparently, yes."

Malcolm thought for a moment, then shook his head. "Nothing about this case makes any sense."

Alyssa cleared her throat, and both Abby and Malcolm looked at her. "It makes complete sense to me." Alyssa shrugged. "After meeting people at the facility and reading the results of the investigation, it looks to me like there was a breakdown of procedures, some negligence on the part of the owner, and a series of screw-ups and tragedies. And Dad, you're so used to seeing crimes and criminal behaviour, it seems to me as though you're looking for something that isn't there. Sorry, Abby, but as much as you want there to be a mystery to solve, I'm pretty sure there's no case here; just a comedy of errors."

"No." Malcolm shook his head. "I completely disagree with you, Alyssa. From what I've heard, there is a case here. A huge case. In fact, there could be an entire luggage carousel of cases here."

"I don't see it."

"Of course not. We aren't at the airport. But there is a case here."

"It looks to me more like a wild goose chase."

"You shouldn't chase wild geese." Abby noted. "They're temperamental, and will try to kill you the first chance they get. And you also forgot to mention we're dealing with a demon."

"For the record," Alyssa raised her index finger, "regardless of what Abby may have told you before I came downstairs, there's no demon involved in this whatsoever. She's way off base if she truly believes that poor, troubled old man is a literal demon, or is currently being possessed by one."

"Whether he's a demon, a leprechaun, or a mentally unstable mess, it's irrelevant." Malcolm unfolded his arms. "We're not here to diagnose anyone, or to debate about who does and does not have a shred of sanity left. Right now, we're only looking at Abby's murder case."

Alyssa held out her hands, palms-up, and looked at her father. "Do you *seriously* think this was an elaborate murder, painstakingly manipulated to look like an accident?"

"It's too soon to rule it out, but so far, yes, it looks likely to me." Malcolm nodded. "And maybe this isn't *a* murder, but perhaps like any good two-for-one special, our killer might have taken advantage of the savings and killed in bulk. One action, two deaths. It's efficient, you'd have to give them that much."

"Okay," Alyssa exhaled. "Based on what you've heard, do you have any suspects?"

"Yes," Malcolm nodded. "Everyone."

"Gee, that really narrows it down."

He looked at his notepad. "I'll need a lot more information about everything before I can start eliminating anyone from the suspect list."

"I guess that makes sense."

Malcolm locked eyes with Alyssa. "Did you really read the entire report Abby sent you?"

"Yes."

"At the end of the report, Zee was the only suspect, I expect."

Alyssa nodded. "You expect correct."

"I can accept her being a suspect, except they didn't closely inspect where the laundry was kept."

"That's circumspect."

"What makes you say that?"

"No reason, actually." Alyssa's face reddened. "Sorry, I thought we were doing a rhyming thing there."

"I find a lot of what happened suspicious." Malcolm looked at Abby. "Then again, I find a lot of things suspicious, so take what I say with a large grain of salt."

Abby nodded. "Fatal advice for slugs."

"Alyssa, you read the report. What did it say about the failure of the ventilation system?"

"The ventilation system runs through the laundry, and the fan was blocked by bags of soiled linens waiting to be washed. The report stated the area in front of the main fan is supposed to be kept clear at all times."

"And yet it wasn't." Malcolm thought in silence for a moment. "I'd love to know if it was routinely blocked out of laziness or carelessness, or if it was only blocked that one convenient time, when the killer needed it to be blocked. I still have so many questions, and we'll only get them answered tomorrow, when we go back."

Sunday: 11:42 a.m.

Abby set down a plastic tray of food on the small bedside table in Vollack's room. He sat up in his bed and looked at it, then wrinkled his nose. "It would appear the dietician failed to implement my suggestion of beef wellington and shepherd's pie for my Sunday lunch."

"Looks like it," Abby replied in a monotone. "You've got ham and Swiss, red jelly, apple juice, and mixed veggies instead."

"Hardly a suitable substitution. I'd have settled for Lobster Thermidore, but not this travesty. Look at this bread, or rather the *alleged* bread, they used. Bread shouldn't be this white, it's unnatural." Vollack studied Abby's face and frowned. "It all makes me wonder why I continue to stay here."

Abby looked at him out of the corner of her eyes. "Why do you think you're here, exactly?"

"Because I wish to be here, that's why." Vollack coughed. "I got tired of working, tired of mortgages, and tired other people, for that matter. It's so much easier to be in a place like this. I get fed, clothed, and taken care of, and all I have to do to stay here is tell you all the truth."

"The truth... that you're a demon and over five hundred years old?"

He leaned slightly closer to Abby. "Can you keep a secret?"

"I forget most things people tell me, so that's a big yes."

Vollack's eyes twinkled. "Okay, in truth, I rounded up here and there, and may have embellished a bit."

"How much did you embellish?"

"Quite a lot, really."

"So, you're not over five-hundred years old?"

"Definitely not." He waved his hand. "I was summoned to this world in 1701, so I've been here considerably less than half a millennium."

"Yeah, that's somehow both better and not better at the same time."

Vollack watched Abby toss his bag of laundry toward the door. He narrowed his eyes. "What is bothering you, Abby Lunay? Do you look lost because something is on your mind, or do you look lost because most of your mind is unfamiliar territory to thoughts in general?"

"No, I'm not lost at all. I'm just frustrated, that's all."

Vollack picked up the ham sandwich, grimaced at it, and placed it back on the tray. "I have *this* for lunch, and *you're* the one who's frustrated? Very well, then I must know why you are frustrated. Tell me now."

Abby scowled and she began to sway back and forth. "I'm trying to prove Zee didn't murder Wing and Celia, but it's taking too long, I'm not having much luck, and I've made no real progress."

Vollack picked up the small bowl of red jelly and then the spoon beside it. "I don't know if this will reassure you or make you feel worse, but I happen to agree with you. Suzanne didn't kill anyone."

Abby blinked. "So, you think the deaths were accidental?"

"Oh, most certainly not." He ate some jelly. "There was most definitely foul play."

Abby wrinkled her brow. "You think chickens did it?"

"No," Vollack set the jelly and spoon back on the tray. "Not *fowl* with a *w,* I mean *foul* with a *u.*"

"Oh, good. That makes a lot more sense, because there'd have been feathers and stuff at the crime scene." Abby sat on the edge of his bed. "Do you know who did it?"

"Yes. Yes, I most certainly do."

"Then tell me."

"I shall do no such thing." Vollack thought for a moment. "Well, I shan't do it *yet,* anyway."

"If you know who did it, then what've you been waiting for in order to come forward?"

"Well, I've been waiting for you, actually."

"It's been a year. Are you serious?" Abby pointed to herself. "You didn't tell anyone such important information because you were waiting for me?"

"Well, I wasn't waiting for you, *specifically,* but I was waiting for whomever came to me with the right questions." Vollack poked his finger into the mixed vegetables as though checking for signs of life, and shook his head. "Honestly, I didn't think you'd be the one, but I do so enjoy a pleasant surprise; almost as much as I *don't* enjoy the look of those diced veggies."

"I don't know if I understand exactly what you're saying, but the main thing is you believe Zee is innocent."

"No," Vollack shook his head. "It's not a case of *believing* she's innocent, it's *knowing* she's innocent."

Abby rubbed her hands together. "Then help me to prove it."

"That's not how this is going to work, but perhaps there is a way I can help to speed things along for you, if you're willing to do something for me."

"What do you want me to do?"

Vollack pointed toward the barred, secure window beside him. "Across the street is a wonderful little delicatessen. Go there now and get me a proper roast beef sandwich with all the toppings on whole-grain sourdough bread, and I'd like a large piece of their cornbread as well. There are so few places here that know how to make a proper cornbread."

"Okay," Abby wrote down his request on a napkin and put it into her pocket. "If you help me with my case, I promise to bring you what you asked for."

"I know you are true to your word, Abby Lunay, as I am true to mine, so we have an accord."

"Great. So, if you want me to defy the dietician's orders for you, you have to tell me what you know."

"Of course. I'll give you a few things to investigate, and if you find the correct answers yourself, then we'll negotiate further for the next pieces, but if you fail to find the answers, then you can't say I didn't try to help you."

"That's fair, and I'm good with that arrangement. Okay, so what should I look into?"

"Read the complete files on both of the victims, including their treatments, their families, and all incident reports. Take a close look at your colleagues, and find out everything you can about them. Review the other patients the same way."

"Including you?"

He waved a dismissive hand. "Only if you wish to waste time, but that's up to you. Do as you wish."

"What am I looking for?"

"That's for you to discover. Next, you go to Suzanne and ask her where she hid it."

"Ask where she hid what?"

"That's also for you to discover." Vollack laced his fingers behind his head and stretched. "She stole something from someone here and hid it. Many of your most important answers are connected to the stolen object."

"Okay, I'll talk to Zee. Anything else?"

"Yes." Vollack's eyes flashed. "A fun little research project for you. Look up Francis Bianchi Russo, a 17th Century Cardinal who died or disappeared in the early 18th Century."

"What am I looking… wait, you're just going to tell me it's for me to discover, aren't you?"

Vollack grinned. "Correct, but I believe you'll find his life story most illuminating."

"Okay, and what else?"

"There's so much more, but that's all you get for now. Once you get me my lunch *and* put those pieces together correctly, only then will I give you what's next."

"That's fair." Abby nodded. "I have one more question for you. Why are you helping me if you're a demon?"

Vollack's grin widened. "It's because you don't yet understand what a demon truly is."

Sunday: 12:38 p.m.

Alyssa didn't know what to make of everything Abby had just told her. The two women sat in the break room, silently for a minute, until Alyssa broke the silence. "I'm not sure whether to spring into action and start doing research, or to talk to the doctor about recommending Mr. Vollack receive high doses of anti-psychotic medication."

Abby shrugged "I'm hoping what he said makes sense to you, because buying his lunch cost me thirty bucks, and I still have no idea what those clues are supposed to mean."

"Sorry Abby, but I don't know, either. At least, I don't know yet." Alyssa squinted in thought. "I suppose I'll need to hit the books."

"But unless you really understand what you're looking for, the books won't hit you back with anything useful."

"Do you have any better ideas?" Alyssa threw her hands into the air. "Because I don't, and when I'm stuck, I do research. What do you do when you're stuck?"

"The same. I wait for someone else to do research."

"And then what?" Alyssa retrieved her phone and began tapping on the screen.

"And then I go and kick some ass, once I know which asses I need to kick. Just make sure your research results in finding the right ass, because I can't un-kick the ass if you're wrong."

Alyssa was unlike many people her age, in that she didn't keep her eyes glued to her phone's screen. She didn't have friends to text with, she rarely used social media, and preferred paper books to electronic ones. Her phone was primarily used as an actual telephone. From time to time, however, she greatly valued the ability to look things up on it when needed.

"Here's something." Alyssa read from her phone. "Cardinal Francis Russo led a team of religious scholars who were translating old books into Latin."

"Religious scholar." Abby snort-laughed. "Now *there's* an oxymoron."

"Focus, Abby."

"Sorry."

"This bit here is interesting." Alyssa scrolled down. "It says the last thing they translated was a text which supposedly was some kind of guide to summoning angels."

"What happened to it?"

"It doesn't say, but it notes at the bottom that the Cardinal disappeared in 1701, when they were done."

Abby's brow furrowed. "Disappeared?"

"Yes, he allegedly vanished into thin air."

Abby blinked. "Would the Cardinal vanishing into fat air have made things any less confusing? And what happened to the other people doing the translating?"

"It doesn't say anything about the rest of his team after that."

"Huh. Weird." Abby shook a finger. "And yet also kind of curious."

"Why?"

"Because Mr. Vollack claims to be a demon who was summoned in 1701."

"I wouldn't read too much into that."

"Why not?"

"Well," Alyssa shrugged, "if I may play Devil's advocate for a moment…"

"It wouldn't hurt to do that, because I haven't ruled out the Devil's involvement at this stage."

"Mr. Vollack is the one who told you to look up this Cardinal in the first place, so he already knew we'd see the Cardinal died or disappeared in 1701, so he pointed you to that information so you'd believe his crazy story. He chose 1701 as his date of summoning, so you'd think he was the Cardinal in a new body, and you'd believe every strange thing he said to you after that."

Abby thought for a moment. "But why else would he put together such a weird reference like that if it wasn't true?"

"I don't know for certain, but just off the top of my head, the answer might lie in the fact that he's lived for nearly twenty years in mental health clinics, where he's been treated for a deep-rooted neurological disorder. Sorry, Abby, but he's not a demonically-possessed Cardinal from the early 18th Century. He's a troubled man with mental health issues, who wants to share his delusions with a willing listener."

"Maybe." Abby shrugged. "Look, there's something I need to go and do."

"What?"

"I have to talk to Zee. Alone."

Sunday: 12:50 p.m.

Abby strode into Zee's room. "I need to talk to you."

"Oh, great," Zee scoffed. "Are you here to start another fight over my pills?"

"No, there's something else that's come up. I need to know where the thing is that you stole."

Zee sat up; her face wrinkled in confusion. "What thing?"

"The thing you stole from someone here which you then hid." Abby held up a finger. "And just to be clear, I'm saying you hid the *something,* not the *someone.*"

Zee sat, mouth agape. "How do you know about that?"

"What's important is that I do know." Abby's voice softened and she sat down in the nearby plastic chair. "I don't care about you stealing something, because I've been stealing things since I was six years old, so I can't and won't judge you."

Zee frowned. "Seriously? You stole things as a child?"

"Yeah, and then more as a teen, and then an astonishing amount as an adult."

"I didn't know that."

Abby shrugged. "There's a lot about me I'm not proud of that you don't know. You said you wanted to know my story, well, here's the short version. I was raised by criminals, so while other children were learning history, math, and science, I was learning lock picking, computer hacking, and bypassing alarm systems. Until a little over a year ago, I worked for a guy who used me to steal whatever he wanted. I need you to know that as of a year ago, I'm not in that life anymore. I've left my criminal past behind me, or at least most of it, and I'm trying to start my life over as a detective."

Zee sat on the edge of her bed. "I didn't know you had a past like that. Why didn't you tell me any of this?"

"Because I don't want anyone's judgment and didn't want to risk being rejected by you. Plus, I was afraid of what you'd think of me as a person if you knew about that."

Zee had just the slightest of smiles on her face. "I like you regardless, Abby." Zee shrugged. "So what if you stole some shit and did some computer crime. I've hurt people and I've wrecked stuff. When I was a kid, I set fire to the house of the kid who was bullying me in school. So, stealing? Are you kidding me? I *wish* I'd only been stealing."

"I'm relieved you understand." Abby let out a long exhale. "But listen, I need to know right now what it was you stole."

"Okay, I'll tell you." Zee rubbed her face. "I stole someone's phone."

"That's it? You just stole a phone?"

"Yes."

"Whose phone was it?"

"Celia's."

Abby looked confused. "Why did you steal her phone?"

"Because there was something on it that I couldn't let her keep."

"What?"

Zee hung her head. "She hated me, and one day she filmed me when I was having a meltdown. She said she was going to use it to get me transferred out of the facility and into a maximum-security psych ward."

Abby took Zee's hands in her own. "This is going to be hard for you, but it's really important. What was on the video?"

"I was so angry at her, and… and I told her I was going to kill her. She recorded the whole thing and said it would be what she needed to get me sent away."

"So that's why you have it hidden." Abby nodded. "It would show you threatened to kill someone who ended up dead. How come you didn't delete it from her phone once you stole it?"

"I couldn't get past her password screen."

Abby stood up. "I could have helped you with that."

Zee shrugged. "You weren't working here at that time, so it wasn't one of my pre-trial options."

"When did she film the video?"

"The day of the fire. She filmed it maybe an hour or two before she died."

"Where's the phone hidden?"

"I can't let anyone know where it is, not even you."

Abby pinched the bridge of her nose. "I can't help you unless I get my hands on it."

Zee irritably wiped a tear from her eyes. "But that video would get me thrown in prison for twenty to thirty years."

"Did you kill Celia?"

"No," Zee wailed. "Of course not."

"Then you have nothing to worry about with me on the case." Abby handed Zee the nearby tissue box. "I think it's time for a little cloak and dagger."

Zee took a tissue and blew her nose. "I have a wide variety of both, but not here."

"I meant it's time to sneak around, and you can work with me so we can prove your innocence. I think that's what it means when people say two heads are better than one."

"That would depend on how well the heads are preserved, as well as the size and composition of the container they're being stored in. But, yeah, working together to solve this sounds great and all, but there's not much I can do to help you from in here. I'm a convicted killer according to them, remember? I can't go anywhere unless I'm handcuffed or restrained, and I hate it. Kind of ironic, really, because that used to be my favourite way to start an evening."

"When do you get released from here?"

Zee shrugged. "There was no set release date, but the range given was between twenty and forty years. What the final year count will be is determined by the results of my psych evaluation, which I happen to think is going poorly. Anyway, when my evaluation is presented to the court, my first hearing will be ten years from that date, so that'll be my first shot at a conditional release."

Abby frowned. "I can't wait ten years, though mostly because I'm not likely to live that long."

"The hearing could be made sooner, depending on what the doctor decides in his evaluation of me, but I don't see that as possible."

"Why do you think things are going so badly?" Abby shrugged. "I mean, what if he says you're perfectly okay?"

"It doesn't matter what he says, because I'm screwed either way." Zee locked eyes with Abby. "If he says I'm mentally fit, then I'll be taken to prison to serve out two murder sentences. If he says I'm crazy, then I'll be here for at least the same amount of time. No matter which way his report goes, the next two to four decades of my life will be spent in one locked cage or another."

"But I need you out now."

Zee scoffed. "Then it sucks to be you, though still nowhere near as much as it sucks to be me."

"Wait a minute. You just said no matter what the doctor says, you're looking at decades locked away, but that's only if you're the one who committed the murders, right? What if I was somehow able to prove you didn't kill anyone?"

"You really think you can find proof my moronic, court-appointed lawyer missed?"

"Maybe, I don't know, but I'm going to need your help if I'm even going to have a chance. Where's the phone you stole?"

Zee looked down at the floor. "It's… not here."

"Yeah, but where is it?"

"I put it into a post office box I own under a fake name."

"How did you manage that?"

"Easy." Zee sighed. "I mailed it to myself from here."

"Hmm. If I could somehow sneak you out, would you be willing to take me to your secret postal box to get that phone you stole?"

Zee looked up. "Are you being serious right now?"

"Yes."

Zee shrugged. "Then sure."

Sunday: 1:11 p.m.

Malcolm had spent the last twenty minutes listening to Mr. Vollack regale him with the summarized version of his life story. He'd heard some pretty wild tales in his time, but Vollack was next-level. Malcolm wasn't sure if he hated this long, rambling journey, or if it was a fascinating rant by an unhinged lunatic.

Vollack continued. "The last time I had hope was in the 1960's, but they proved no better than anyone else."

Malcolm pinched the bridge of his nose. "Meaning…?"

"They sold out, the selfish bastards."

"Yeah." Malcolm cleared his throat. "I simply asked you about the fire at the facility, not for your views on Woodrow Wilson, the New Deal, or what constitutes good art."

"It was probably all a waste of breath anyway." Vollack huffed. "What would someone like you really know about art?"

Malcolm shrugged. "I know it's short for Arthur."

"Bah."

"Well, thank you for this enlightening discussion." Malcolm stood up. "But I can see you have nothing to offer me with respect to the fire, so I'm just going to retreat from here now."

"Retreat," Vollack nearly spat the word. "Go ahead and leave. From now on, I'll call you Dunkirk."

"That was an *evacuation,* you moron."

"An evacuation is a type of retreat." Vollack made a disgusted noise. "Be gone, Dunkirk. You are like a cloud. When you disappear, it's a beautiful day."

Malcolm left and closed the door behind him. He went into the hall, leaned against the wall, and exhaled.

Alyssa saw him and went over to see him. She smiled. "So, how did it go?"

"That man is exhausting, irritating, and completely obnoxious."

"Oh," Alyssa was taken aback. "I thought you two would get along. You have a shared disdain of humanity."

"He and I are nothing alike." Malcolm began walking down the hall with Alyssa. "Yeah, sure, we both dislike most people, but he just sits there and complains, whereas I go out and try to change society. I worked to make the world a little better, but he just sits and heaps scorn on everything he lays eyes on."

"That's a fair point." Alyssa quickened her pace.

"Where are you going in such a hurry?"

"I have to meet Abby. She says she has a plan, so I want to hear it before she decides to go ahead and do it anyway."

Sunday: 1:13 p.m.

Alyssa sat quietly in the break room while she listened to Abby's plan. When Abby was done, Alyssa groaned. "I can't believe you're actually going to help Zee escape."

"I didn't say anything about helping her to escape." Abby stomped her foot on the floor. "I said I want her to take me to the location of her secret hiding place."

"Yes," Alyssa nodded in an exaggerated fashion, which was a rare example of non-verbal sarcasm. "You'll take her out of here, where she will then escape, run far away, and you'll never hear from her again. You will be held a hundred percent responsible for her escape, so why would you take such an extreme risk?"

"Zee told me she has something that can help us with our investigation, but it's in a post office box."

"What is it?"

"It's a small, locked box where people can send you mail."

Alyssa squeezed her eyes shut. "I should have known better, and been more specific with my question." She opened her eyes and exhaled. "What I mean is, what does she have in her postal box that can help us?"

"The phone of one of the victims." Abby looked at Alyssa. "I think it's going to be a huge breakthrough in my case, so I think I should take her there to retrieve it."

"Abby, please listen to me," Alyssa stared deep into her eyes. "There's an extremely high probability she's going to try to escape, and you'll be the one who's held responsible if she succeeds. It's a horrendous idea, and it's also not going to be possible."

"Why not?"

"For starters, how do you propose getting her out of the hospital?" Alyssa shrugged. "She has court-ordered security measures in place, due to being a convicted killer, who has, and this is worth repeating from earlier, a history of spontaneous violence. They're not going to allow you to just take her out for a stroll."

"I know all of that, which is why I have a second part to my plan."

"Okay, I've braced myself. Let's hear the second part."

Abby grinned. "She'll wear some scrubs and a blonde wig and pretend to be me, and I'm going to put on a black wig and dark clothes, and then take her place in solitary confinement."

"Then who's going to look after her if we take her out?"

"The two of us."

Alyssa wore a confused expression, which she had become all-too-familiar with since she met Abby. "But you just said you're going to be in her room, locked away."

"Right," Abby nodded. "I'll look after her presence in solitary, and you'll look after her presence on the outside."

Alyssa's wide eyes gave hint to her sudden onset of alarm. "Let me see if I have this straight. You want me to sneak someone out of this facility who was found guilty of a double-homicide, who has a reputation for violent outbursts, and who recently stabbed someone with a piece of pointed cutlery, and I'd be the only thing standing between her and an escape to freedom?"

"Yes, it sounds to me as if you understand everything perfectly."

"Then it's an insane plan with too many risks to take seriously." Alyssa massaged her temples. "How about I cover for her in solitary instead? It sounds a whole lot less potentially stabby."

"That won't work, because Gina will know you aren't Zee."

Alyssa blinked. "Who's Gina?"

"She's the other attendant who looks after the patients here with me."

"And Gina won't know *you* aren't the patient?"

"She'll figure it out eventually, but Gina knows me, so she'll be cool about it. If she finds out I'm in

Zee's cell, she won't care, but she'll freak out if she sees you."

Alyssa realized her mouth was agape, so she closed it, and then organized her thoughts before she responded. "How can seeing me be the thing she'd freak out about? How would she not be freaking out about a violent patient with two murder convictions being missing from the clinic?"

Abby held up two fingers. "There's a couple of reasons. The first is Gina is my workplace bestie, so she knows and trusts me. She'll believe me if I tell her everything is okay."

"I guess that sort of makes sense," Alyssa conceded. "And the second reason?"

"Gina's either hung over or high most of the time, so she won't stress unnecessarily."

"Just a moment." Alyssa rubbed her face, then let her hands fall slack at her sides. "You're telling me she looks after patients while she's in an altered state of mind?"

"Yeah, but she's surprisingly capable, half of the time."

"And the other half of the time?"

Abby made a face. "If I'm being honest, in those times, the line between caregiver and patient gets a little hard to define."

"And she still has a job?"

"We're short-staffed and largely unsupervised, to tell you the truth, so nobody really knows or cares much about what goes on here. As long as we're capable when the doctor or the owner shows up, it's all good."

Alyssa closed her eyes and shook her head. "People often ask me why I always assume the worst in any given situation, and yet it keeps ending up being even worse than I thought possible."

"See?" Abby beamed. "Only a team like us could go further than you ever imagined."

Alyssa folded her arms. "What are you not telling me?"

"What do you mean?"

"There's too many inexplicable things happening, and I need this to somehow add up in my head."

"It all makes perfect sense to me."

"Yes, I know it does, which makes me need to ask this next question." Alyssa took in a deep breath. "This case means more to you than simply getting some hours logged, doesn't it?"

"Well, yeah, of course." Abby shrugged. "I believe in my client's innocence."

Alyssa shook her head. "No, this is something deeper than wanting to do *pro bono* work for your client."

Abby screwed up her face. "Probing what?"

"Huh?"

"You said I was doing probing work?"

"No, I said *pro bono* work."

Abby shook her head. "What's that?"

"It means you're working for free."

"Working for free?" Abby made a retching sound. "That sounds awful. No wonder I wasn't familiar with the term."

"I can't help but suspect you're doing this because the case is somehow personal."

"Yeah, sure, it is personal, and so what?"

"So what?" Alyssa's surprise caused an increase in her voice's volume. "How can you *so what* me when it's an important and legitimate question? The more personal this is, the less objective you're going to be, that's what's *so what,* so don't ask *so what* when this is what the *what* is in the *so what*."

"I'm not sure if I want to respond to your doubt first, or the fact that I was able to understand that sentence." Abby tilted her head. "Never mind. It doesn't matter if it's personal, as long as I'm still able to be objective."

Alyssa folded her arms. "How personal is it?"

"Somewhere between a little and a lot, but it's hard to measure such things."

"How about you tell me the personal connection, and then I'll help you measure it."

"Okay, fine." Abby rocked back and forth. "You know how some nights I don't come home from work?"

"Yes."

"It's because I'm with Zee."

"Wait, you're with Zee as in you're *with* Zee?"

"Yes," Abby nodded, "me and Zee, and Zee and me. I'm with, accompanying, beside, and sometimes under Zee, okay?"

Alyssa put her hands on top of her head. "Oh my God."

"There are other positions as well, but we'd best not go there."

"No, we'd best not, as I'm already starting to feel all twisted up."

Abby simpered. "That's one of the other positions."

Alyssa covered her ears. "No, I don't want to hear about it. I don't need those images in my head."

"What's the problem?"

"The problem?" If Alyssa's jaw hadn't been secured to her head, it would have landed on her shoes. "Where would I even begin to list the problems? It's just so wrong."

"Wrong?" Abby snapped. "Why? Because I'm a woman dating another woman?"

"No, that part is fine. I don't care about same-sex relationships."

"Actually, so far, we've never had the same sex."

Alyssa pressed her hands tighter around her ears. "No, no, no!"

Abby whistled. "She's got quite the surprising imagination."

"Just stop, will you? I don't want to hear about it."

Abby's eyes met Alyssa's. "But I still don't understand the problem."

Alyssa let her hands fall to her side. "It's completely unethical, for starters, because she's your patient, and you're her caregiver. That kind of relationship is strictly forbidden in professional circles, and it's utterly inappropriate."

"I wonder if that's why she keeps telling me she wants to be punished."

"For the love of God, please stop sharing your intimate details."

Abby scoffed. "Don't blame me, you're the one who brought it up."

"Listen, Abby. This goes against the code of conduct of every hospital and clinic. If your workplace finds out, you'll be fired."

"So what?"

"Are you seriously going to *so what* me again?"

"Yes, actually, I am. I don't care if I get fired. I'd rather be a full-time detective anyway."

"But you've only just started out as a detective, so you don't yet have enough clients to support your business. You don't want to jeopardize your steady job until you're earning enough money as a detective to support yourself. Is this really worth the risk?"

"Yes, it is. It's worth every bit of risk, because I might be in love with her."

"Listen to me, Abby. I swear upon everything I hold dear and from the depths of my heart and soul, I want you to be happy. I truly do want you to find someone who will give you the love you deserve and who will treat you well. If Zee is that person, then of course I'll give you a hundred percent of my support."

"I appreciate that."

"At the same time, though, I also don't want you to get used and hurt. There's a part of me – a really big part of me – that's worried about you."

"What are you so worried about?"

"What if Zee is just using you to get you to help her? I know that sounds like a terrible thing for me to say, but you're my best friend and I love you dearly. If Zee was using you and I didn't say anything, I'd never forgive myself."

"Alyssa, it means a lot to me that you care. It was also brave of you to tell me what you're worried about, so I know you meant well when you said that. When Zee and I first started getting close, the thought did cross my mind, but here's the thing. I told her I wanted to help her way before we got involved. She's an artist at heart. She talks tough and acts all scary on the outside, but beneath the surface, she's a frightened, sensitive, and creative woman who is feeling lost and alone. I'm convinced in her case, instead of the art getting framed, the painter was."

"And that may be the case."

"Right. So, you've said what's on your mind, and voiced your concerns, and I've heard them."

Alyssa managed a weary smile. "That's all I wanted to do, so thank you."

"So now that you've said what you wanted to say, don't ever say it again. It makes me feel hurt and it also makes me mad, and I'm feeling sadder the more I think about it."

"I'm sorry, Abby." Alyssa looked wretched. "I'm just being protective. I care about you."

"I know, and that's the only reason I'm not screaming at you right now. But if you want to remain my friend, don't ever bring that subject up again."

"I won't." Alyssa groaned.

"What was that eye roll for?"

Alyssa avoided eye contact. "It's better if I don't say anything right now."

"Why not?"

"Because it drives me crazy sometimes when you're so…."

"What?" Abby prompted. "When I'm so what? Stupid?"

"No, you're definitely not stupid. You're a very bright person, Abby, but sometimes you're a little clueless when it comes to trusting people."

"You're one to talk." Abby's laugh was derisive. "You're never able to figure out what people think of you, so you make a lot of completely wrong assumptions instead. So, fine, maybe I am a bit clueless when it comes to trusting people, but you wrote the book on the topic."

Alyssa was about to say she wasn't aware Abby felt that way, but stopped herself when she realized it would only serve to prove her point. Instead, she said, "You know what? We should probably work separately for a little while, until we're both in a better head-space."

"Suits me. I'm going to go and talk to Zee about the plan." Abby's eyes narrowed. "So, yeah, it's probably best if you don't come with me until I'm calmer, because I don't like you very much right now."

"Fine, then I'm going to… I'm going to… *I'm going.*" Alyssa stormed out of the tiny break room and continued to storm down the hallway. As the initial anger ebbed, she felt less stormy and more like general precipitation with a persistent breeze. By the time she got to the end of the hall, she felt like a light drizzle.

She sighed. As she stood there, trying to collect her thoughts, Alyssa saw a disheveled young woman in light blue scrubs stagger past the security desk. Her hair was in disarray, she was wearing dark sunglasses, and she was massaging her own temples. Alyssa approached her.

"Are you Gina?"

"Yes." The woman moaned. "But right now, I really wish I wasn't."

"Why?" Alyssa guessed the women to be close to her own age. "Are you feeling under the weather?"

The woman removed her sunglasses and squinted through her bleary, red eyes. "Everyone's under the weather, except maybe astronauts, because I'm guessing they're probably feeling *above* the weather when they're in space."

"Wow." Alyssa bit her lip. "You look as though you're in really rough shape."

"Yeah, but don't mind me, I just woke up with the world's biggest headache this morning, that's all. I took some extra-strength ibuprofen, but there's only so much it can help with, so if you wouldn't mind speaking, like, *way* softer right now, I'd really appreciate it."

Alyssa made a face. "Do I smell alcohol on your breath?"

"Hair of the dog." Gina began walking somewhat awkwardly. "It doesn't count as drinking if it's medicinal."

"So, you're hung over."

"Oh my god, yes, I am so hung over, and I was puking all morning." Gina managed a weak smile as she attempted to steer herself toward the coat cupboard. "But the main thing is, as of today, I'm two weeks sober."

Alyssa wrinkled her face. "Two weeks sober, yet you were drinking just now to cure a hangover, which itself implies you were drinking yesterday."

Gina grabbed hold of the cupboard doorknob on the second try. "Well, I mean, I do allow myself a couple of lapses here and there, but otherwise I don't drink."

Alyssa folded her arms. "What exactly do you mean by a couple of lapses?"

She took a coat hanger off the pole, dropped her jacket, and then dropped the hanger on top of it. "I lapse every Friday and Saturday."

Alyssa couldn't help the eye roll. "That sounds less like a lapse, and more like a schedule."

"Look," Gina tried to make eye contact but gave up after a couple of failed attempts. "If I'm doing one thing *most* of the time, and I do a different thing *some* of the time, then doing the second thing is still kind of under the general heading of a lapse."

Alyssa raised an eyebrow. "So, you're drunk on Fridays and Saturdays, but sober during the week."

"That's right." Gina flashed a smile and needed to grab the cupboard door to steady herself. "Five out of seven days, I don't touch a drop of alcohol. I just do mushrooms and weed, but that's it. Well, okay, and sometimes the occasional hit of acid, but I never do meth or heroin. I mean, you've got to have strict standards when it comes to what you put into your body, am I right?"

"So, you're alcohol-free five days a week, and drug-free the other two days a week."

"Yeah, and that makes seven sober days a week, so I'm golden." Gina held out a bag. "Want a weed gummy?"

"No, thank you. You know, most hangovers occur as a direct result of the dehydration caused by the alcohol consumed. What you need right now is a large glass of water."

Gina made a horrified face. "Hell no, girl. I never drink water."

"Why not?"

"Are you kidding me?" Gina ate a cannabis gummy. "Do you know how many different types of sea creatures poop in the water? And you want me to drink that?"

Alyssa nodded slowly. "Interesting thought process there, and I can now see why you and Abby are close colleagues."

"She's my sister from another mister." Gina stared at Alyssa for a moment. "Wait, who are you, anyway?"

"I'm Alyssa Bristol, Abby's friend."

Gina smiled. "Oh, cool. Nice to finally meet you, girl. Abby talks about you sometimes, and it's all good stuff." Gina closed the cupboard door. "I got to get to work. I was supposed to start at one o'clock, so I'm like, ten minutes late."

"You're almost twenty minutes late. And it was nice meeting you, too."

Gina stood still for a moment, then shook her head. "Whoa, that was so bizarre. I totally forgot where I was for a second."

"Are you okay to be working?" Alyssa wrung her hands. "Like, if a person was impaired, should they be working at a place where they're looking after other people? You know, hypothetically?"

"Hypothetically? Well, people can decide for themselves about the *pathetically* part, but I'm definitely *high*. It's way too early in the day for riddles. Later, girl."

Sunday: 1:40 p.m.

Abby was taken aback by Zee's reaction to her plan.

"No," Zee folded her arms. "It has to be you who takes me. And *only* you. That's the only way this is going to work."

"But I was thinking of getting Alyssa to take you instead, so I can take your place here."

"No, that won't work at all, and I don't know how you think it will work." Zee took one of Abby's hands. "I don't trust anyone but you, so I won't go with her. If you really stop and think about it, this only works if it's just the two of us going to the post office."

"Okay, fine, but if we do go there together, you have to promise me you won't decide to run away from me and go into hiding."

Zee's eyes flashed with anger and released Abby's hand. "I'd never do that to you, so what kind of thing is that for you to say to me?"

"I trust you, but you're only human." Abby sat down. "Once I take you out of here, you might be tempted to run away at some point. It's only natural for it to cross your mind."

Zee scoffed. "If I escaped your custody and ran off, you'd be in so much trouble."

"Exactly. And I know you wouldn't do that to me."

"Of course not." Zee locked eyes with Abby. "I would never risk that happening to you, which is why we're going to run away together."

"We're what now?"

"Come on, Abby." Zee put her hand on Abby's shoulder. "We both hate the clinic, even if it's for different reasons. We're both misunderstood by everyone around us, and we love and support one another, so it's a perfect plan."

"But if we retrieve that cell phone you took…"

"Wait, taking me out of the facility was your idea." Zee stood up and stared at Abby. "I thought you taking me to the post office box was just a pretext so we could be fugitives together."

"No." Abby took a step back. "I was taking you to get the cell phone so I could use it to help clear your name. Once you're cleared of the charges and released, *then* we can run off together if we want to. That's how this is going to work. So, are you going to take me to the post office box, or not?"

"No," Zee looked wretched, "because the cell phone isn't in a post office box."

"It isn't?"

"No, I have the cell phone hidden here in my room. I made the post office box story up."

"You lied to me?"

"It was necessary so you'd have plausible deniability if things went wrong." Zee returned to the bed and sat back down. She reached between the section where the mattress and headboard met and the pulled out a phone, then handed it to Abby. "I don't want you to go to prison for helping me if the escape doesn't work, so I provided you with a reasonable excuse for you to take me out of here. I thought that's what you wanted."

"You could have told me that." Abby put the phone in her pocket. "I hate being lied to."

"I hate lies, too, but I'm not risking you being put in jail for me."

"I can protect myself; I don't need you to do that." Abby's eyes welled up. "What I can't take is being lied to like that."

Zee made a disgusted sound. "Yeah, well, I can't believe you aren't willing to get me out of here."

"I am willing to help you, and that's what I've been doing these past few days, but if I'm going to help you, then I have to do it my way."

Zee folded her arms and stared at the floor. "Your way will take too long, because I need to get out of here now."

"Why right now?"

"Because the justice system doesn't work," Zee pouted. "Once the judge looked at my dumb threat, my past convictions, and the fact they found my lighter at the crime scene, it was decided ahead of time I was guilty, and the writing was on the wall."

"That's called graffiti, and it's hardly a reliable source of evidence."

"It doesn't matter," Zee snapped. "They weren't looking for clues to find out who did it, they were only looking for evidence that pointed to their top suspect; me."

"Maybe, but that's why we have to work together on this, so we can find the stuff that got missed. We have to take the time to make sure we do this right, so it will clear your name."

"You were supposed to understand, but it turns out you're just like everyone else."

"And so are you." Abby turned toward the door. "I'm going to leave right now before I start screaming."

Sunday: 2:03 p.m.

Alyssa leaned against the wall of the doctor's small office, as she listened to Dr. Friesen. She had asked him for a summary of the patients he looked after in the facility, and was trying not to dwell on the fact she had no legal right to be asking such questions.

"There's only three patients in this temporary facility, yet they run the gamut." He leaned back in his chair. "Jeffrey spends his time saying very little or nothing at all, Zee spends all her time denying the murders she was convicted of, and Mr. Vollack spends his time confessing to every crime committed over the past five hundred years."

"At least he aims high."

Friesen chuckled. "Yes, quite unlike Gina, who only aims to *get* high."

"So, you... you know about Gina's... *state of being?*"

"Oh yes, I know all about her state of being." He laced his fingers behind his head. "Or, more specifically, her state of being under the influence of one substance or another, but I can't discuss the specifics."

"Don't worry, Abby told me that Gina's working through some personal problems."

Friesen sighed. "Yes, well, I'm doing what I can to help her through it all."

"Help her how?"

"A few months ago, when I first met Abby, she and I talked about how everyone has their own inner battles against the darkness within them. Well, Gina is no different, and she's struggling with some darkness of her own. If she weren't a staff member here, she'd most likely be a patient."

"I'm a bit worried about her."

"Yes, well, I'm helping to guide her through the darkness until she can see some daylight, for lack of a better metaphor. But I have hope." He grinned. "After all, it's always darkest just before the dawn."

"Technically, it's always darkest at the exact midpoint between sunset and sunrise."

Friesen moaned. "Not you, as well. Doesn't *anyone* appreciate these old sayings anymore?"

Sunday: 2:09 p.m.

Malcolm was in the facility's central quad, the main intersection for the four short hallways in the building. He was going through his notes, when he observed a security guard who was much younger than the gruff fellow he'd met prior. He guessed the man to be in his very early twenties, and observed he had a slender build, with short, wavy, black hair, and an olive complexion. Malcolm made a face at the skin colour reference he'd just made in his mind. *Olive complexion?* Olives were either green or black, and this fellow had a creamy, light-brown skin tone, which you would never see on an olive, except maybe the one you needed to throw away. Malcolm shook the distracting thought out of his head, and then approached him. When the guard turned to look at him, Malcolm showed him the government-access pass Abby had provided for him.

"Hey, pal." Malcolm squinted at the name badge on the man's chest. *"Luis.* You got a second?"

"Sure." Luis looked at the man dressed in black. "How can I help you, sir?"

"We're doing some follow-up on the fire at the facility last year, and I have a few questions for you."

"A year after the fact?" Luis wrinkled his forehead. "Sure, I guess. What kind of questions?"

"The particular question you can help me with is a big one." Malcolm leaned against the wall. "You see, I'm trying to figure out who had a motive to ensure Robert got demoted, aside from you."

"Me?" The guard put his hands on his hips. "What motive do you think I have?"

"It should be obvious." Malcolm shrugged. "With him demoted, you were clear to take over his position."

"The supervisor job?" Luis scoffed. "That was no big prize to win, I'll tell you that. It's only an extra two dollars per hour, and it comes with a lot more responsibility than that two dollars in pay makes up for. I wasn't qualified to take over his job, and I told the owner that exact thing when he first offered the position to me. If you ask him, he'll tell you I flat-out refused to take it. A day later, the owner came back and said he'd arrange for me to get all the training I needed, which is the only reason I finally agreed to take the role, but I'm still waiting for the training he promised me."

Malcolm stroked his chin, one finger tapping his jaw. "If you weren't qualified, then why do you think they demoted the other guy and promoted you?"

Luis threw his hands in the air while shaking his head. "I have no idea. Seriously, none at all. It makes no sense to me."

"You weren't working the day of the fire, correct?"

"Right." Luis gave a slight nod. "I wasn't on duty that day, but if I had been, there would have been three deaths instead of only two."

"Why is that?"

"Have you met Jeffrey?"

"The catatonic patient?" Malcolm sighed. "No, but I'm familiar with his case."

"Well, Jeffrey wouldn't evacuate when the place was filling up with smoke, and I don't think I could've gotten him out, because he didn't know me well enough at the time. Jeff trusted Robert, so he was willing to follow him out of the building."

Malcolm pretended he wasn't familiar with the investigative report. "Oh, Rob got Jeffrey out?"

"He really did." Luis whistled. "It was so unfair he ended up getting demoted and reprimanded, when he's the true hero of that day."

"Do you get along with Robert?"

"Before the fire, yes, we got along pretty well." Luis frowned. "But once they demoted him and put me in charge, things between him and I went south. Look, Robert didn't deserve to get demoted. He knows hospital systems, security, and operations better than anyone. He's a way better guard than I am, that's for sure. It's in his blood."

"What do you mean by that?"

"Robert's father and uncle were both cops, so he's a chip off the old block."

Malcolm shook his head. "Only if *the old block* is on his shoulder, because that's the only place on him there's a chip."

"I need to get back to my rounds, if that's okay with you."

"Yeah, sure," Malcolm nodded. "We can chat some more later."

Sunday: 2:10 p.m.

Gina staggered into the women's washroom and attempted to see her reflection. After a few seconds, she realized she was staring at the hand dryer, so moved to her left until she was facing the mirror. She stared at her reflection until there was only one of her looking back.

"You need to get it together, girl," she scolded the image staring back at her.

Gina was startled by the sudden, loud noise behind her. Someone in the bathroom stall had just blown her nose, and it sounded as though an elephant had a digeridoo stuck in its trunk.

"Abby?"

The stall door opened, and Abby exited. Her face was red, her eyes bleary and moist, and her hands were full of crumpled tissues.

Gina blinked. "Wow, girl, you look like me just before I pass out at night."

Abby dumped the tissues into the trash, then went back into the stall for more paper to wipe her eyes and blow her nose with, and took some satisfaction in doing those two things in the correct order.

"What's wrong, Abs? Seriously, you're freaking me out right now."

"I'm just upset," Abby croaked. "There's no reason for you to be freaked out."

Gina leaned against the bathroom counter. "Yeah, there is. Listen, Abs, you're the most together person I know."

Abby scoffed.

"I'm serious. I mean, sure, you've got more loose wingnuts in your head than anyone I've ever met or hallucinated, but you're also the most kick-ass, capable, and clever person I've ever met, though I think I once hallucinated seeing Sherlock Holmes in a ballerina skirt, so you may have to take second in that category."

"Thanks for that, Gina, but if I'm the most capable person you know, then you need to upgrade who you hang around with."

"Okay, look, I don't know what's upsetting you, but I do know you'll find a solution to it. You always do."

"I hope you're right."

"Of course I'm right." Gina winked at her. "Don't sweat it, girl. Whatever it is, I'm sure it'll all work out."

"No," Abby snapped. "I don't know how you can say that. *Nothing* is working out. Things are the opposite of *working out,* they're... *idle in.*"

Gina stood silently and Abby looked wretched. "Sorry, I didn't mean to shout at you."

"No biggie, for real. I just... you know, you always help me when I need you, but I don't know what to do to help you."

Abby shrugged. "You're listening to me, and I think that's all I needed. So, thanks."

Gina saw something out of the corner of her eye and looked to her right. There, on the counter, was a phone, plugged into the wall.

"Is that your phone charging there?"

"No," Abby answered eventually. "But I'm looking after it for now. There's stuff on there I need to see."

"Like what?"

"I don't know yet, but I'm charging the battery right now in order to can find out." Abby locked eyes with Gina, which took some effort, as Gina's eyes weren't often still. "Maybe you can help me. You worked at the facility when the fire broke out."

"I've put in a lot of effort to forget about that day, and I'd like for that effort to not go to waste. I don't know if it's my state of mind, or trauma, or what, but I no longer have any memory of that day. Yet I can still remember commercials I watched as a kid, word for word, so memories are weird."

"It is weird, for sure." Abby leaned against the bathroom stall. "I can remember exactly what I was wearing twenty years ago, when I was smuggled out of the hospital. Like, I remember it all, right down to the tiny pink and white striped socks I had on, yet there's so many day-to-day things I can't remember from this week, because I blank out."

Gina nodded. "I totally hear you. I blank out *and* black out a lot. Some things, I remember vividly, even if it was, like, years ago, yet I also can't remember what clothes I had on yesterday."

"I do, and you're still wearing them."

"Oh, hey, you're right." Gina smiled. "Hey, that completely explains why I didn't remember putting these scrubs on this morning."

Abby's gaze fell to the floor.

"What's wrong?"

Abby sniffed then looked back up at Gina. "Did you ever look at your life and feel both lucky and cursed at the same time?"

"Every day. Hey, did you ever wake up in a weird place you didn't remember going to? It's happened to me a lot over the past year."

Abby sighed. "Were you drunk or high the night before?"

"Yeah, I was."

"Then mystery solved." Abby scoffed. "That's about the extent of my detective skills, apparently. I thought I could solve hopeless cases, but it turns out the only hopeless case is me."

"Are you kidding?" Gina approached Abby, stood beside her, and then wrapped her arm around Abby's shoulder. "You're seriously the coolest person I've ever known."

"I've never been cool in my life." Abby thought for a moment. "Maybe that's what Alyssa meant. One time I asked her if she was ever cool, and she said no, but she'd had moments when she was arguably a few degrees below room temperature."

"I have no idea what you mean, there."

"I think it means she wasn't actually cool, but she could be considered cool if she's being compared to something less cool than her."

Gina blinked a few times. "Nope. That is way too much for my brain right now."

"I don't know what to do in this case." Abby groaned. "I had a fight with Zee, I had a fight with Alyssa, and I feel so lousy and completely alone right now."

"Listen, girl, the weed gummies kicked in a while ago, so I don't know how good this advice is, but I think you need to go and talk to your bestie and work all this stuff out."

Abby mulled the words over for a few seconds. "Yeah, that's probably the best advice for the situation."

"I'm glad you think so, because I don't remember what I just said."

"I probably should go talk to her, but we didn't leave on the best terms."

"Look," Gina squeezed Abby's shoulder, "you've told me a lot of stuff about her. Was it all true? The stuff you said?"

"Yeah, she's been great to me."

"Well, then, like, if you two have such a great thing together, then it's probably stronger than whatever other things and stuff come up between you, right? So go talk to her."

"Thanks, Gina. You're pretty great, too."

"Sorry, I totally blacked out there for a second. What did I miss?"

"Nothing. I was just going to give you a hug."

"Awesome. Then bring it in, girl."

They hugged for a few seconds, and gently rocked one another. Eventually, Abby tried to pull away. "Hey, Gina, the hug's over."

"Hug? Oh sorry, I thought you were helping to hold me up."

"I'll get you to the chair outside the door. One sec."

Sunday: 2:55 p.m.

Abby was in the small laundry room at the end of the hallway. She was loading the washer with patient clothing, soiled linens, and, for reasons unclear, a rubber spatula. Alyssa appeared behind her.

"Oh, there you are."

Abby glanced back at her, then resumed loading. "Yes. No matter where I go, I always seem to be there."

"I know you're busy," Alyssa walked over and stood beside the washer, "but I really need to talk to you."

"There's no need." Abby shut the glass door of the washer and switched the machine on. "I know you were only trying to help me, but what you said still hurt."

"I know, and I'm so very sorry." Alyssa's head drooped. "I'm a bit hopeless when I have strong feelings, or am nervous, and then everything comes out the wrong way, and it always causes me problems."

Abby exhaled, then leaned on the machine. "I know what you're like, and I also know I'm even worse. We both said some stupid things, and I hate these bad feelings we have."

"I was just trying to look out for you, but so much of it came out wrong. I say dumb things when I'm frustrated, but that's no excuse. I don't want silly misunderstandings and minor spats to cause bad feelings and come between us like this."

"Yeah, me neither." Abby leaned against the washer; in silence for a few moments. "I know I'm not a good talker, so it's hard for me to put feelings into words. Like, I'm really good at letting someone know essential information, but when it comes to stuff about what's going on in my heart, it's so much harder for me. I can't get my inner thoughts out, so I tend to under-explain rather than over-explain."

"You do a great job in your own way, Abby, and I need to be more patient with you. You're my best friend."

Abby scoffed. "That would be more of a compliment if I wasn't also your *only* friend. I can't be your best friend if there's nobody else to be best against. The thing about being your only friend is that I'm both the best *and* worst, because there's only one person in the competition."

"Then let me put it a different way. You're the most important person in my life who isn't family."

"Again, I'm the only person outside of your family you spend time with. And, by the way, I've met several members of your family, so that's not saying a whole lot. Your parents are nice to me, and your Aunt Isabella is a sweetheart, but the only thing separating the rest of your family from piranhas is they don't live in the Amazon. If there's ever a family gathering down at the river, I won't be going into the water."

Alyssa chuckled. "We're quite the pair, aren't we?"

"We're quite the what?"

"The pair."

"No, pick another fruit. I don't like pears. I prefer berries."

"Which one is your favourite?"

Abby blinked. "Which is my favourite what?"

"Your favourite berry."

"Oh, that would be Barry Gundersson."

Alyssa sighed. "I should have seen that coming a mile away. And who's Barry Gundersson?"

"He's the guy who taught me how to pick locks when I was a kid."

"Where is he now?"

"He's locked up." Abby snickered. "That's kind of ironic, now that I think about it."

"What were we originally talking about?"

"I don't know." Abby shrugged. "You started talking about fruit, and then things got weird from there."

"So, how about you tell me about what happened."

"You were right about Zee, that's what happened." Abby sniffed. "She didn't want to go to the post office, she only wanted to escape."

"Oh lord, and did she get away?"

Abby was unable to bring herself to talk about what she viewed as Zee's betrayal, at least at that moment, while that particular wound was still raw. The only thing that lessened the pain was the realization that Zee admitted to the subterfuge when confronted. Abby instead decided to summarize her discussion with Zee. "No, I didn't let her out, and we ended up in a big argument instead."

"I'm so sorry. I swear to you I didn't want to be right."

"Now I can't trust her, so I don't want to be with her anymore."

"You're upset, and it's okay to be upset, but it's not the state of mind you want to be in when making relationship decisions. I don't want you to burn your bridges behind you."

"Why not? It would be really stupid to burn the bridges in front of me."

"I'm sorry you and Zee had a fight. I don't know what to say to help you, and I really wish I did."

"I'm just happy we're good now."

"Me too." Alyssa smiled. "Come here, you."

The two hugged one another, and they gently rocked back and forth. When the embrace ended, the two left the laundry room and saw Malcolm walking toward them.

"Oh, hey," he said. "I was looking for you two." He saw Abby's damp eyes. "What happened? Are you okay?"

"Yeah, I'm fine." Abby sniffed. "I had a fight with Zee."

Abby summarized what had happened in Zee's room, as well as the subsequent argument.

"I'm sorry that happened." He patted her shoulder. "Are you sure you're fine?"

Abby nodded. "I will be, yeah."

"Glad to hear it." Malcolm sighed. "Abby, one of the things I love about you is your determination to see the best in people. It goes against everything I believe, personally, but I admire that you cling to it anyway. If there's one thing I'd like for you to take away from this is the knowledge that desperate people will do terrible things to alleviate that desperation. What Zee did to you was inexcusable, but at the same time, you didn't help yourself with that scheme to sneak her out of here. It's your ass on the line, so can you promise me you'll be a bit more cynical when people ask you for help?"

"I'll try."

"I guess that's good enough for now." He faced Alyssa. "What's next on your list?"

"I need to talk to the second security guard." Alyssa looked at her notes. "I think his name is Luis Garcia."

Malcolm nodded. "Yeah, I just spoke to him a few minutes ago myself."

"Yeah, Luis is cool." Abby dabbed the corners of her eyes with her sleeve. "Come on, Alyssa. I'll take you to him."

Malcolm narrowed his eyes. "And while you do that, I'm going to go and have a word or two with Zee."

Sunday: 3:00 p.m.

Malcolm stepped into Zee's room. "You and I need to have a little chat."

Zee recoiled in surprise, quickly gathered her composure, and then fumed. "Who the hell are you?"

"I'm a friend of Abby's."

Zee scoffed and nodded. "Then I'm guessing you're her friend's dad."

"Yeah, I am." Malcolm slammed the door shut behind him. "So, what's the deal with you, huh? Are you mentally ill, being set up, or a goddamned selfish sociopath looking to blame others for the things you actually did?"

"You're a straight-shooter like me." Zee nodded. "I respect that." She then shrugged. "Yeah, I guess I can't blame you for asking all of that. The answer is it's definitely the second one, it could possibly also be the first one, but it's definitely *not* the third."

"Okay, then let's keep the straight-talk going." Malcolm picked up the plastic chair, plunked it down near where Zee was, and then sat in it. "According to the court transcripts, you had a motive to do the very thing you were convicted of. You apparently told the prosecutor in your trial that if he sent you to a facility to get a psychological evaluation, you'd burn the place down, and sure enough, the section you were in went from hospital to inferno in record time. That's pretty damning, if you ask me."

"I did say I'd torch the place, but there's a huge difference between uttering an idiotic threat in the heat of the moment, and actually doing it. I was just lashing out at my accusers. I sometimes say stupid things because I have anger management issues, and I know and admit that, but I don't have a homicidal bone in my body, and that's the truth."

"Don't make me laugh." Malcolm glared at her. "You have a rap sheet four pages long, all showing an extensive history of assaults and violence."

"Okay, sure, I might have some ill-tempered cartilage, some resentful ligaments, and some unpredictable tendons that can lash out from time to time, but no homicidal bones." Zee's bluster deflated and she began to stare at the floor. "Look, I act out because of anger, desperation, and, I don't know, *maybe* even some psychological issues, but I have never crossed the line and killed anyone. *Ever.* As a kid, yeah, I lashed out a lot, and my anger issues were out of control, but I'm a lot better now. I mean, I still have problems and occasionally slip, but I would never take a life."

"You're seriously wanting me to believe you wouldn't hurt a fly?"

Zee shrugged. "Yes, unless you mean zippers, in which case I've put my knee into quite a few flies in my life."

"I guess that's a fair response." Malcolm's voice softened.

"Look," Zee wiped the corner of her eyes. "I don't want to be in this cell. It's not as if one day I woke up and thought how wonderful it would be if I did stupid shit and got locked up. I didn't plan for this to be my life."

"Yeah, well, there's a support group for that. It's called *Everyone on Planet Earth*." Malcolm shook his head. "If everyone wrote an autobiography and gave it an honest title, then ninety-nine percent of all books would either be titled *Well That Didn't Work Out How I Planned*, or *How the Hell Did I End Up Here,* so you're not in a unique position." He took a breath and exhaled slowly. "According to your arrest report, they found several preserved internal organs in your possession."

"Yes, and just so we're clear, they were internal organs of *animals,* not people." Zee peeked through her bangs at Malcolm. "I don't want there to be any misunderstandings about that."

"Why did you have internal organs of animals in your home in the first place?"

"I'd been learning about animal anatomy." Zee gave a slight shrug. "I was saving money so I could get into veterinary school. I would never harm an animal; I just took dead ones and worked on them so I could learn. I learned about their anatomies, organs, and bone structures, so that when I finally did go to veterinary school, I'd already be up to speed."

"Jesus," Malcolm chuckled. "That sure as hell wouldn't be my cup of tea."

"Give tea another try. Perhaps with the subtle almond flavouring cyanide would add to it."

He smirked. "You know, when people say they have skeletons in their closet, it's usually just a metaphor. I hope those animal parts weren't being kept in your sock drawer or anything."

"No, I have a special storage unit which preserves them." Zee rolled her eyes. "Well, *had,* past tense, because the cops took the machine when they searched my place, and it's in an evidence locker now."

Malcolm leaned back in the chair. "Then there's the trifling matter of you planning an escape from here with Abby."

"She told you that?"

"Abby's like family to us, so you're damned right she told me. Abby doesn't have a lot of people in her life who she can rely on to keep her out of trouble, and she was crushed to find out you weren't one of them."

"That really sucks. I didn't want that." Zee rubbed her face. "Whether you believe me or not, I was only looking to protect Abby. I hate that I hurt her feelings, but, whether you believe me or not, I was seriously only trying to protect her."

"You can't lie to someone like Abby, even if it's to help her. She needs the truth at all times, no matter how unpleasant it may be."

"I don't always know what to say." Zee shrugged again. "I'm not what you'd call a people person. There's *maybe* a dozen people I've ever met whose company I didn't find grating, and Abby's one of those precious few."

"I can relate to that." Malcolm leaned forward. "You know, I may not like you, but in some ways, you're a person after my own heart."

"I have no interest in your heart. At least not until my storage unit gets returned to me."

Malcolm stood up. "So, no more lies, no more escape plans. If you hurt Abby, I'll make you my mission, and you'll end up with a fate worse than death."

"I'm already suffering a fate worse than death." Zee scoffed. "I'm living. Tell Abby I'm sorry, will you?"

"No, you need to tell her that yourself."

"Fine." Zee scoffed. "Whatever. Can you at least tell me if she found anything on the phone?"

"What phone?"

Zee put her hand over her mouth.

He put his hands on his hips. "What phone?"

Zee dropped her hand. "Nothing. Forget it."

Malcolm left the room, not saying another word.

Sunday: 3:02 p.m.

Abby pointed. "That's him, right there."

Alyssa and Abby strode along the dim corridor toward the guard. As they drew close, Abby turned to

Alyssa. "Alyssa, this is Luis de la Rosa Garcia, the security supervisor here."

Alyssa smiled and waved at him. "Hi, it's really nice to meet you."

He looked at Alyssa and gasped. "Oh, sorry, I… it's… yeah, same here."

Alyssa continued. "Will you have some time to answer some questions for me?"

"Yes, of course, but later." Luis fidgeted. "I'll answer anything you want. I mean, whatever you need. I mean… I need to go now."

Luis hurried down the hallway and then rounded a corner. Alyssa exhaled and shook her head. "Gee, that wasn't suspicious or anything."

"Yeah," Abby sighed. "And things just got weird."

Alyssa faced Abby and blinked. "What do you mean by weird?"

"Luis has the hots for you."

"No, he doesn't." Alyssa fidgeted. "He was just nervous, that's all."

"Oh, come on, Alyssa."

"What?"

"You're serious, aren't you?" Abby glared at her. "I will never understand how someone so bright and so smart can be so oblivious."

"Sorry, but I'm really not following you, because I don't understand why you think he likes me."

"Just because you believe you're unattractive, doesn't mean everyone shares your opinion. Maybe you don't like your appearance, but other people do. I've known Luis since I started here, and believe me when I tell you he's totally smitten with you."

"I've never heard you use the word *smitten* before."

"Yeah, well, it's the first time I've had to, so don't let it happen again." Abby stewed. "But you are right about one thing, and that's about Luis being nervous. He was so flustered, it makes me wonder if it's because he likes you a lot, or because he's got something to hide and he's worried we'll find out what it is. It might even be both of those things. What's next on your list?"

"I wanted to speak with Mr. Vollack again, please."

"Follow me."

Sunday: 3:18 p.m.

Alyssa tilted her head back, until it touched the wall of Cenk Vollack's room. She shut her eyes and groaned. "Don't get me wrong, I enjoy hearing your views on Nineteenth Century society, but my question was about the facility fire last year."

"You have all of that information already," he paused to cough, "and it's as boring a subject as it is tedious."

"But I still need some additional information."

"Bah. You get nothing until Abby gets back to me."

"Back to you?" Alyssa blinked. "Back to you about what?"

"Has she found the stolen phone yet?"

"What stolen phone? What are you talking about?"

"You know, I moved around a lot, but I settled in Belgium and lived there until the Napoleonic Wars."

"Can we go back to the phone for a second?"

"Belgium didn't exist back then, of course, as it wasn't established until after the 1830 Belgian Revolution. I use the term so you're aware of the geographical location I'm referring to."

"Where or who was the phone stolen from?"

"You know, prior to the Revolution, that area was part of the United Kingdom of the Netherlands. I was living in Brussels at that time, as they had the best fabrics in all of Europe. Nowadays, it's not a big deal to find excellent clothing, but in the 19th Century, it was all the higher classes could talk about. It was all fabrics, wigs, and perfumes. The perfumes were the most important, in my opinion, as this was back in the days before regular bathing was common. Anyway, I digress. I had to leave Brussels behind once Bonaparte started his conquests."

Alyssa gave up for the moment, and decided to just go with it. "Did you ever meet Napoleon?"

"No, have you met the Canadian Prime Minister?"

"No."

"So, you see, just because I was around at the time doesn't mean I knew everyone."

"Fair point."

"However, as I said, I was living in Europe during the time Napoleon was running France. That was a chaotic time, I'll tell you that. I got out of Belgium and moved to Prussia, and then to Denmark. Denmark was delightful and it had the best pastries, but I wasn't there long enough to regularly enjoy them. I mistakenly thought I was a safe distance away from that crazy Frenchman, but he had greater ambitions than any of us realized at the time. When the war got too close for comfort, I got on the next ship to England, and it cost me everything I had, and I landed there with just the clothes on my back. I had to start my life over from scratch, and that wasn't easy, let me tell you. Anyway, that's how I ended up living in Britain for the next hundred and ninety-two years."

"Did you ever meet anyone famous?"

"Quite a few who were famous in their time, but they're mostly forgotten now. I doubt you'd have heard of them. I can tell you, though, that I have met some very powerful people in my life who were likely famous enough that you'd have heard of them."

"Oh really? Who was the most powerful person you've ever met that you think I'd know?"

"The most powerful? That would be Britain's King George the Fifth."

"When did you meet him?"

"That was back in 1914, about three years after his coronation."

"1914. That was more than a hundred years ago. How did you meet him?"

"At the time, I was the senior advisor to another very powerful person."

"Who?"

"None other than Britain's Navy Secretary, and I worked out of his London office." Vollack winked, knowingly. "The Secretary was summoned to the palace, and I went along with him. The King wanted to ask about fleet readiness in the event it came to war."

"And that would be World War One, right?"

"Yes, but I'm a little surprised that was your first question."

Alyssa blinked. "What should my first question have been?"

"Young people always forget their history. I thought you'd have asked me if I really knew Winston Churchill."

"Why would I ask you that?"

"Because he was the Navy Secretary in 1914."

"I thought he was the British Prime Minister in the second war."

"He was, but that was around two decades later. I didn't work with him by then."

"What was he like?"

"I completely admired him." Vollack leaned back. "He's one of the few people I look back upon with any genuine fondness. He was an arrogant, bold, bigoted, clever, and drunken statesman, with the heart of a lion. He was a gifted orator with an unequalled wit as well."

"Wait, which of those qualities did you admire?"

"All of them. Churchill was a package deal. You had to take the terrible because it also came with the great."

"I don't think I could accept a package that included drunken bigotry."

"Which is why there are so few great leaders any more. If you were around in the early Forties, you'd understand so much better what it was like at that time.

There was the Great Depression, there was despair, there was war on three continents, and there was widespread hopelessness."

"There was also systemic racism, sexism, and xenophobia."

"True, but those were different times."

"It makes me angry when people say that." Alyssa knitted her brows. "Sure, it was a different time, but you weren't a different species. There's no excuse for treating people poorly based on their race, gender, or ethnicity in any era."

"Only a generation like yours could look at the man who stood up to fascism, helped us get through the Blitz, and saved Europe and then say *well, yes, but he could be a racist drunk sometimes, so he was obviously bad*. This is truly the era of idiocy."

"At least we don't make lame excuses for our own rotten behaviour. We're a lot smarter than you give us credit for."

"No, humanity is utterly hopeless." Vollack cleared his throat. "It's not entirely your fault, as some of it is due to your short lifespans. You don't live long enough to see the same cycles repeating or to acquire the wisdom you need to be any better. Instead, you view the world so simply, dividing people into good and evil and then not understanding when evil people do good and good people do evil. Allow me to let you in on a little secret. Good and evil exist inside of everyone."

"In a general way, sure, I already know that. But I'm not talking about the vast majority of people who occupy the moral centre and can do varying amounts of good and bad in their lives, I'm talking about some people who are pure evil. They have no positive qualities."

"Who would you say has no positive qualities?"

"Adolf Hitler, for one."

Vollack scoffed. "Everyone always mentions Hitler when I ask that question. He was a vegetarian, and he loved dogs."

"That's hardly--"

"He was a reasonably-skilled painter, and he loved children."

"He loved *Aryan* children, at any rate."

"He was a mesmerizing speaker, and was devoted to Eva Braun."

"None of this comes anywhere close to making up for the atrocities he committed."

"I never said it did. He was a vile, loathsome, and utterly irredeemable human being, but even a terrible human being can have one or two good qualities along with their thousands of despicable ones. They are in no way redeeming qualities, and the person is still vastly more evil than good. Now that I mention it, I could argue the most wretched person was the dimwitted lunkhead who rejected Hitler's application to art school. Could have dodged a lot of bullets if Adolf was a struggling painter instead of a bitter madman."

"We can only speculate." Alyssa waved her finger. "And none of this has anything to do with the question I asked you about the stolen phone or the fire."

"Because there's nothing to tell you. Abby should have the phone by now, so that's all I need to say on that subject. And yes, there was a fire last year, which was the most entertainment I've had since I'd arrived at that other facility. The fire was inconvenient to some, but it was a chilly morning, so I approved of the unconventional heating strategy."

"People heard you yelling *burn, burn* when the fire was at its worst."

"It's as I told you." Vollack shrugged. "It was the most exciting event of the past few years. Why shouldn't I enjoy the spectacle?"

"Because, and this is just off the top of my head, two people died."

Vollack made a sour face. "Who cares? Two people down, eight billion more to go. What should I care if some people get killed, maimed, or wounded? It matters not to me."

"My, aren't you a real Mother Theresa."

"I should hope not." Vollack looked disgusted. "Horrible woman. Despicable."

"Despicable?" Alyssa's mouth was agape. "She helped feed thousands of starving people in Calcutta."

"Bah! She was horrid because most of the charity money she raised to help the poor, she instead funneled to the Church."

"I still believe she did more good than bad."

Vollack scoffed. "Now who's making lame excuses for rotten behaviour? I disagree with your feeble argument. Sure, she set up clinics for the poor, but rather than treating their illnesses all she did was provide an unsanitary bed for them to die upon in utter agony. Of course, when she was on her own death bed, no expense was spared for her own treatment."

"Is that true?"

"Absolutely. Look it up. Mother Teresa was a big believer that suffering was a gift from God, and it was a gift she enjoyed giving out, but not receiving, being the hypocrite she was. Good and evil are nothing more than points of view based on your own experiences, opinions, and ambitions."

"I suppose."

"It's as I said: humans are all too simple. You can't hold two differing ideas inside your heads. A beloved politician, activist, or entertainer is discovered to have an unpleasant side to them, and then suddenly everyone decries how bad they are, and subsequently refuse to acknowledge any of their good qualities, even though those same people have their own unpleasantness they try to hide. Like I told you earlier, every person is a flawed mix of positive and negative qualities."

"Like Winston Churchill?"

"Among many, yes. As I said, Churchill was a great leader, inspiring orator, and a bulwark against fascism, while at the same time a racist drunkard, to use your term, and an ill-tempered human being."

"I've heard it said you are the sum of the company you keep, so if I met a racist drunkard, I would avoid them."

"A ridiculous outlook."

"It's like they say: if you lie down with dogs, you will get up with fleas."

"But if you lie down with people, you won't get up at all, due to the knife in your back. I'll take the fleas if it means I avoid the knife and get the dogs. Every generation, I see people shaming the previous generation for smoking, racism, their treatment of women, and so on, yet they're all hypocrites who can't see their own folly. Future generations are going to look back at your generation and laugh at how high and mighty you're acting when you're just as bad."

"In what way?"

"They'll see all the vapid and insipid videos people take of themselves doing idiotic things, or they'll watch TV shows from today and ask you why there are single-use plastic containers in every scene. Voters allow elected officials to plunge their countries further into debt, because that's for a future generation to worry about. Everyone is so short-sighted, refusing to look beyond their own short lifespans. Oh, and lawns!"

"Lawns?"

"Yeah, lawns. Stupidest idea you've ever had."

"Lawns? As in grass?"

"Yes, can you imagine having all this rich, fertile soil and not planting crops in it? Unless you have hungry cows or goats roaming around, growing grass is a waste of arable land."

"We don't need that soil for food."

"Then what about the water? So many idiots watering their lawns, wasting a precious resource to grow a useless weed. Humans must be the dumbest apex species in the entire universe."

"Wait, you're doing it again."

"Eh?"

"Every time we start to discuss the fire, you change the subject and start a debate or argument about something unrelated."

"Because the fire is a boring subject. I'd rather have a rigorous debate any day."

"Maybe, but I'm here to learn about the fire, not debate ancient history."

"Ancient? It isn't ancient. The same behaviors which fueled the Salem witch trials are still fueling atrocious actions today. You see progress over the years, but I just see the same actions and same fates recurring again and again."

"Maybe that's why some people say time is cruel and spares no-one."

"I don't think time is cruel at all. It's about as fair as anything can get." Vollack scratched his head. "Time is just something we've invented to measure age. It's just a *thing* - it has no feelings and it doesn't care, pass judgement, or discriminate. If a piece of lumber isn't long enough, do you blame the tape measure? No. If we are a little overweight, do we blame the bathroom scale?"

"I generally do."

Vollack thought for a moment. "Okay, perhaps that last one was a flawed example, but you get the idea. Regardless, I believe we are done. I now wish for some solitude."

"Thank you for the talk."

He waved a general acknowledgement as she opened the door to leave.

Sunday: 3:25 p.m.

Abby noticed Alyssa leaving Mr. Vollack's room, and shutting the door. She also observed Alyssa begin bumping her head against the nearby wall.

Abby approached her. "Um, I'm pretty sure what you're doing is a hint, but how did it go with Mr. Vollack?"

Alyssa began massaging her temples. "I have a bit of a headache, and not from banging my head against the wall. I was trying to get Mr. Vollack to answer questions about the fire, and the next thing I knew, I was arguing with him about Mother Theresa."

The two began a slow walk down the hall, side-by-side.

Abby snickered. "I think he's pretty cool to talk to, for a demon."

"Are you seriously telling me you still believe his demon possession story?"

"I'm not going to rule it out just because it's not considered possible." Abby glanced at Alyssa. "Are you seriously telling me you're going to dismiss a potential answer just because you don't happen to believe it's likely?"

"Okay, fine." Alyssa folded her arms. "Then tell me what you think is going on with Mr. Vollack."

"What I think isn't relevant, so I don't care."

"I think it's very relevant, and I'm surprised to hear you say it's not. Why don't you care?"

"Because it really doesn't matter if he's possessed or not."

"I certainly think it *does* matter, and I'd have to say it matters an *enormous* amount. How can you possibly say it doesn't?"

"He truly thinks he's a demon, right?" Abby waited for Alyssa to nod before continuing. "So, to him, that's as real as it gets, and someone telling him, *no, you're not a demon* isn't going to change his mind. Whether he's crazy, possessed, or an actual demon, it doesn't change who or what he thinks he is one bit, which is why it doesn't matter."

"But it is relevant and it does matter, because it would change any potential treatment he receives, right? I mean, depending on what he really is, he needs medication, therapy, or an exorcism. I think you'll agree that's quite the wide range of possible treatments, so what he really is matters a great deal."

"He's never harmed anyone, as far as we know, and he's peaceful in his room. He's become a model patient since the whole demon thing started, so if he's harmless and able to function without his meds, then why worry about whether or not the demon thing is real?"

"I'm sure there are plenty of excellent reasons which will come to my mind later, but right now I can't think of any."

"Exactly." Abby nodded. "I think the reason you're having problems with the whole demon thing is because of the backwards way you've been looking at the patients here."

"I may regret asking, but what do you mean by backwards?"

"You're looking at this through a black-and-white filter. To you, everyone is either well or unwell, crazy or sane, instead of looking at this the right way."

"And what would you suggest is the right way?"

"Instead of looking at this in terms of the two extremes, try looking at the patients as though they're on a grid."

Alyssa made a face. "A grid? How would that work?"

"Imagine a big grid. On the left edge, you have completely crazy, and on the right edge, you have completely sane. Then at the top of the grid you have completely functioning, and at the bottom you have completely *non*-functioning."

"Okay, I can visualize that."

"Okay, so absolutely no person is ever going to be right at the edge in any of those categories. Nobody is *completely* sane, as everyone has some stuff in their heads that they need to work on."

"If I understand where you're going, then everybody would end up at a unique spot on the spectrum, depending on where they're at."

"Yeah, that's right. So, Jeff is non-functioning, but he's sane. Zee is functioning and sane, but more in the middle of the grid. And Vollack is functioning, but not particularly sane. All three patients are at different points on the grid, but the only one who has harmed another person is the sane and functioning one."

"Zee."

"Yeah."

"Maybe you're right. I don't have a lot of experience with mental health patients, so I have to be open to the possibility that my views are rooted in my own lack of knowledge and experience."

Abby pointed to herself. "You've known me for two years."

"Sure, but your brain is physically damaged, and it affects how you think. What you have isn't an illness, but an injury."

"True, but both of your parents have PTSD, so you've seen them struggle with that."

"You're right." Alyssa mulled over the information. "I hadn't really looked at their struggles as an illness. To me, that's just how they are and have always been."

"And maybe this is how Cenk Vollack has always been."

"That's a fair point. I'll tell you what. I will be open to whatever the evidence points to."

"And so will I."

"And speaking of evidence," Alyssa cleared her throat.

"What?"

"I understand you've come into possession of a phone?"

"Yeah, but it's still charging. It's been idle for a year, so it will take a while."

Alyssa's eyes grew wide. "A year? Whose phone is it?"

"Celia Ocampo's."

"Why didn't you tell me about it?"

Abby shrugged. "Right now, there's nothing to tell you. Once it's charged and I've cracked the password, then I may have something to share."

"Abby, that's potential evidence in a police investigation."

"A *closed* police investigation. A *concluded* police investigation. But it's fresh evidence in *my* investigation, so it's all good."

Alyssa decided any further argument about the legal status of her keeping the phone would accomplish nothing except make her headache worse, so she dropped the subject.

Sunday: 3:33 p.m.

Malcolm approached the security desk and nodded a greeting to the guard. The guard, Robert, glanced up at him, scoffed, and shook his head. "What?"

"Hey." Malcolm leaned against the counter. "I need to ask you some questions about last year's fire."

"Yeah, well, too bad. I'm busy."

"I'm sure you are. Those screens won't stare at themselves."

"Another damned comedian." Robert grunted. "Then again, idiocy isn't a crime, so you're free to go. Hopefully, sooner, rather than later."

"Wow, whatever is eating you must be suffering terribly. Who ate your bowl of sunshine this morning, thundercloud?"

"Most people don't like the way I talk to them, but I don't give a shit about their opinions. I always speak the truth, so if they can't take it, screw 'em."

Malcolm chuckled. "You're just a regular, honest guy, huh?"

"Hey, pal, I'm as honest as the day is long."

"Then I'll need to ask my questions while there's still daylight."

"Well, good luck with that. It doesn't matter if it's daylight or midnight, because I'm not telling you shit."

"That's perfect, because I don't want any of that from you, so we're already on the same page." Malcolm narrowed his eyes. "Listen, I don't care how you answer my questions, as long as you do."

"Why would I answer your questions, when you're the human equivalent of a participation trophy? And maybe I don't feel like talking right now."

"Fine, you don't have to talk." Malcolm shrugged. "Hell, you can sing it to me, for all I care. What's your favourite song?"

"Piss off, you moron."

"I don't know that one. Sing a few lines, and maybe I'll recognize it."

Robert stared at Malcolm, studying his face, and frowning all the while. "If you want to ask me questions, then let me ask you something first."

"Sure."

"Why do you give a shit about the fire anyway?"

"Easy." Malcolm leaned on the counter. "It's because I think the wrong person was charged and convicted for the fire and both deaths."

Robert scoffed. "And I think all of that's damned obvious."

"You do?"

"Hell yeah. Suzy – or Zee, or whatever name she's going by – didn't set that fire."

"Did you voice your views to the police?"

"Yeah, and it didn't do nothing to help. My statement was entered into evidence by the public defender, but it was obviously shit-canned, because Zee got charged and sent here anyway."

"Who do you think was responsible for the fire?"

"Easy. Garcia did it."

"Luis? Why would he do such a thing?"

"I used to be the supervisor of security here, and I'm sure Garcia wanted my job." Robert shook his head. "That useless moron wanted the extra pay that came with the supervisor title, so he orchestrated the whole thing."

"I spoke with him earlier, and I'm not sure he could organize a urination at a bar, let alone a murderous conspiracy." Malcolm tapped his finger on the counter. "You saying he arranged this elaborate murder plot sounds less like a reasoned conclusion based on proof, and more like a bitter allegation with no evidence to back it up. A house of cards would be more stable than your accusation."

"Yeah? Then here's something that'll blow your mind." Robert leaned in. "He sabotaged the security door, stole my access card, and then set the fire."

"But, again, can you prove any of that?"

"Who needs proof when you have a motive?"

"What was his motive?"

"I already told you his motive. I was standing in the way of his career advancement."

Malcolm sighed. "Help me connect the dots here. How does killing two people benefit his career?"

"Listen, it's all very simple." Robert leaned back in his chair and folded his arms. "When a crime has taken place, whether major or minor, there's a process to figuring out who did it, and it starts with two big questions. The first question is *who benefits from the crime?* You make a list of those people. And then you ask the second question, which is *who profits?* You then make a list of *those* people. Then, it's all about seeing who is on both of those lists, as the person who benefits *and* profits automatically becomes my top suspect."

"That's a reasonable yet overly-simplistic way to start."

"Yeah, it is, and that, by the way, is why Garcia is at the top of my list of suspects. With me demoted, he directly benefitted through the promotion, and he profited due to a pay raise, so it's a slam-dunk, as far as I'm concerned."

"Look, what you're saying is within the realm of *possibility,* but it's nowhere near *probability.*" Malcolm looked heavenward, fighting the strong impulse he was feeling to use the word *stupid* to describe the man's theories, and then looked back at Robert. "It seems like a hell of a stretch to assume this kid – and let's face it, he's still just a kid – planned and carried out this elaborate plot which killed two people in order to get a raise of just a couple of bucks. The payoff doesn't match the effort."

"I've seen people do worse things for even less payoff." Robert scowled. "Hell, I also have first-hand experience of being demoted for less."

"And I know first-hand that people don't need any incentive at all to do terrible things, because most people are so stupid, you can understand why there's instructions on toothpaste."

"Yeah, when I look at most people, they're like an envelope with no address on it."

Malcolm grinned and nodded. "It appears that we both believe humanity is the pizza burn on the roof of the world's mouth."

"I'd insult more people, but then I'd have to explain it to them later, so it's not worth the effort."

"I look at some people, and assume their birth certificate is just an apology letter from the condom manufacturer."

"Huh." Robert looked Malcolm in the eyes and the slightest of grins appeared on his face. "When you first walked in here, I figured your brain cells weren't exactly holding hands, but it does seem we share the same views on humanity. You're a little brighter than I thought."

"Yeah, my wife says I'm like a lighthouse in the desert, in that I'm bright but not very useful." Malcolm chuckled. "But at least I'm bright. Jesus, I look at most people, and figure their lives are more about regret management than goal achievement."

"People suck." Robert cracked a small grin. "So, what gets you out of bed each morning?"

"Usually my wife's cold feet, but until I recently retired, it was the knowledge that every day I went to work, I was keeping the worst of the two-legged locusts under control and holding them accountable."

Robert grunted with disgust. "There is no real accountability for most of the shitheads out there."

"It's kind of funny." Malcolm smirked. "When people are twenty, they want to change the world. When people are forty, they want to change their jobs and/or their lives. When people are sixty, they are fed up with change and they insist on talking about how things were so much better back in their day... you know, back when they were unhappy with the world and wanted to change it."

Robert nodded. "Irony is alive and well. I believe when life gives you lemons, you add tequila and salt and hope you get drunk enough to tune out all the idiots."

"I look at things a little differently. When life gives you lemons, forget the lemonade. You hand those lemons back with explicit instructions on where to shove them, how deep to shove them, and what size hammer to use to pound them in even further."

Robert chuckled. "You know, you're the first sensible person I've talked to in this place in a long time. I wouldn't trust most people I meet to sit the right way on a toilet seat. Honestly, the amount of shit I have to deal with each day keeps piling up."

"Yeah, once the pile starts, it continues to grow *excrementally.*"

"You know what, jackass?" Robert grinned. "You're okay, so I'll answer your bullshit questions. What do you want to know?"

Sunday: 3:39 p.m.

Abby nodded in the direction of the security desk, where Malcolm and Robert were chatting. "Looks like Rob's making a friend."

"Yeah," Luis nodded. "I miss being on good terms with him. Robert is a real salt-of-the-earth type."

"And we all know how salted earth can prevent anything from growing for generations." Abby was silent for a moment. "I noticed you got really nervous when my friend Alyssa asked you about the fire."

"Yeah, sorry. That wasn't my proudest moment."

"So, what's the deal with you and her?"

Luis' brow furrowed. "Um, we didn't make any deals, so there's no deal to talk about. Why would you ask about a deal?"

"Because you obviously have the hots for her."

"Ugh." Luis squeezed his eyes closed. "Is it that obvious?"

"Let me put it to you this way. I have lousy social skills and can't read emotions from peoples' faces, and even I noticed it, so yeah; it's going to be blatantly obvious to anyone on earth with functioning eyesight."

Luis lowered his voice. "So, did Alyssa say anything?"

"About what?"

"About me liking her."

"No, because she's as clueless as you are when it comes to that kind of thing."

"Look, Abby, I know I just met her today, but she seems totally amazing. How well do you know her?"

"She's my best friend, so I think I know her pretty well."

"Great!" Luis rubbed his hands together. "So, is she seeing someone?"

Abby reflected on his question. "Do you mean like dating or like hallucinating?"

"I mean like a date. Is she dating anyone?"

"No, she's kind of hopeless when it comes to love and other indoor sports. I've dated more than she has, and I've hardly dated at all."

Luis leaned closer. "Do you think she'd mind if I asked her out?"

"Are you kidding? She'd love that."

"Do you think I'm her type?"

Abby shrugged. "I guess. You're young, male, and alive, so you're pretty much everything she... hang on a second. You're perfect."

"Perfect?" Luis rolled his eyes. "No, you must have me confused with somebody else."

"No, I wasn't meaning you're perfect as in flawless. Let's face it, you're so imperfect, you'd have to upgrade in order to qualify as a factory second. You make me seem well-adjusted, and I have permanent brain damage."

"And that's what you think of as perfect? Okay, then. Thanks a lot."

"No, what I'm saying is you're not a perfect person, but you just might be perfect for her. She told me recently she wanted someone reliable, intelligent, supportive, and secure. You're definitely reliable and supportive, so full marks there. I think she'd be okay with someone who was bright instead of specifically intelligent. And you have some self-esteem issues, but are otherwise secure. Yeah, you'd fit the bill. Just go up to her and ask her out."

"Okay," he smiled. "I'll do it tomorrow. Any idea what I should say?"

"I'm not the right person to ask because I'm told I don't always understand social situations." Abby looked at him. "The person I'm seeing now? I just told her she was hot, and then asked if she'd like to get naked and see if we could break her bed on the first try."

Luis blushed. "I could never say that."

"I should hope not, because she's my girlfriend."

"No, I mean I couldn't say such a thing to Alyssa."

"You got that right." Abby snort-laughed. "If you even tried to say that, her dad would kill you before you finished getting the first few words out."

"Her dad?"

"Yeah," Abby nodded. "Have you seen that scary-looking guy walking around the hospital, dressed in black, and asking a lot of questions?"

"The guy with the permanent frown, who always looks like someone just cut him off in traffic when he was in a hurry?"

"Yup."

Luis' eyes grew unusually wide. *"That's her dad?"*

"Yup again."

"Wow." Luis whistled. "I think I'm getting a clearer picture as to why she hasn't dated much."

Sunday: 3:58 p.m.

Dr. Friesen made a tut-tutting noise as he walked toward his office with Malcolm. "No offense, Mr. Mercer, but I already answered that same question when the young lady asked me. The two of you should exchange notes if you're going to be investigating together."

Malcolm chuckled. "Yeah, that's a fair comment. I apologize. Mind if I ask you something I know she didn't ask you?"

"Go right ahead."

"Aren't you a little overqualified to be working in a nothing little facility like this?"

Friesen laughed. "Not when you consider how lucrative these private clinics can be. This is only one of three facilities I go to for work, so my billings keep me quite comfortable, even in this over-priced city."

"Yeah? Where else do you work?"

"There's a clinic downtown, which treats drug addicts."

"And what do you do there?"

"I suppose you could say my job there is trading. I counsel people, and help them to quit one drug, so I can help them get dependent upon a completely different one instead. For every opioid, there's a methadone."

"Maybe, but at least the new one won't kill them."

"Well, more accurately, the new one is *less likely* to kill them."

"Either way, I'm sorry I asked."

"Yes, I thought you might be." Friesen grinned. "I also visit a correctional facility in the valley. It's a truly massive place. I spend at least half of my time there each week. There's a lot of mental health challenges in a place like that."

"I'd have guessed as much."

"This is the smallest facility I visit, but it's also by far the most interesting."

"Yeah?" Malcolm raised an eyebrow. "How so?"

"Mr. Vollack is one reason. I'm generally fascinated by anyone who claims to have supernatural or paranormal abilities, so you can imagine how interesting I find someone who insists they're a five-hundred-year-old demon. I'm always delighted to come here to see him so I can hear his latest reasons why everything in the world is terrible and why we're all doomed."

"But what about Zee? She doesn't claim to have any abilities at all."

Friesen rubbed his chin. "No, her demons are purely metaphorical, but her case is still interesting for other reasons."

"What reasons?"

"For starters, and against all probability, she somehow dislikes people even more than I do. I can't help but find that fascinating on a personal level. I can't condone her violent tendencies toward people, but I can certainly understand the feelings behind them. I figured I could help her, so I informed the judge that I'd be happy to do her evaluation if he was willing to assign her to me. He approved my request immediately, as I have many years of experience with patients like her. It's my hope I can bring her some sort of inner peace, or, at the very least, less inner torment."

"That was nice of you to take her on."

"Not really, no." Friesen frowned. "Don't get me wrong, I don't mind at all if you think I'm a nice person because I set Zee up here in this facility instead of her being locked up in God-knows-where, but if I'm being completely honest with you, it was more out of pure selfishness than any desire to be nice. It's to my advantage to have her here with some of my other patients, because it's one extra billing I can do with no extra time or travel required on my part. The reimbursement allowance I get for mileage doesn't completely cover the cost of the petrol, let alone any of my time, so the fewer places I need to drive to the better."

"Makes sense. Hey, thanks for taking the time to answer my questions."

"Delighted I could assist you. Cheers."

The doctor approached his office door and saw Alyssa approaching from the other direction.

"Oh dear."

Alyssa waved to him. "Hello again. What's wrong?"

"I literally just left Mr. Mercer and his questions, and here you are again. More interrogating, I assume?"

"I only have one question, and it's an easy one."

Friesen smiled. "Well, that's finally some good news. Fire away."

"I forgot to ask you what you thought about the security guard."

"Which one?"

"Luis Garcia."

"Well, he's a nice enough young man, but I often wonder if his elevator is spending quite enough time on the top floor."

"When you say that, do you mean his upstairs is vast and self-sustaining, or that there's no actual upstairs, just a small, unused attic?"

"Somewhere in between, I'd say." He winked. "He's a lot brighter than he appears, so I wouldn't dream of underestimating him, but at the same time, I can safely predict we won't be seeing him winning any Nobel Prizes, unless they create a new category for general adequacy. He's not the blandest person on earth, but he'd better hope that person doesn't die. Why do you ask?"

"I was just curious."

"Yes, he is a rather nice-looking fellow, isn't he?" Friesen grinned as he saw Alyssa's face redden. "I abhor social media, but I have no doubt you'll be posting all sorts of nonsense about your feelings toward him on such sites."

"You'd be wrong, then. I have a couple of social media accounts, but I use it more as a public photo album than a way of over-sharing."

"Delighted to hear it. So many of these online social sites are little more than a way for shallow people to present a superficial persona to the world. A mask, of sorts, to cover their own inner insecurities and wretchedness."

"For many people, maybe, but I only use social media to keep in touch with friends and family. I don't post any filtered vanity photos, or exotic locales, or anything fake. I just have a simple profile page, where I can tell the people I'm overdue to visit that we should catch up soon, and then completely fail to do so."

"Then perhaps a better term for it would be *antisocial* media."

Alyssa chuckled. "After what I just told you, I'm obviously in no position to argue with that term."

"You know, there's a splendid invention for keeping in touch with people, and I believe they named it the telephone."

"I can keep up to date with a greater number of people easier online than I ever could manage by calling them. I have some social anxieties, and talking on the phone with people makes me nervous, so I end up saying stupid things."

"But it's only through saying stupid things today that we can learn to say wiser things tomorrow. How can you improve your social skills if you don't practice? Don't be too hard on yourself for learning and growing."

"I appreciate that. I mean, my intentions are good."

"Without actions, I'm afraid good intentions are useless." Doctor Friesen groaned as he stood up and stretched. "I believe that's where that old saying came from, about the road to Hell being paved with good intentions."

"But Hell itself is paved with *bad* intentions. Did you ever stop to think that the road to Hell is also the road leading *away* from Hell? And it's paved with those same good intentions."

"If I ever did stop to think about it, I'd probably conclude you were overthinking the saying. You know, I do so miss the days of hand-written letters and cards. It was so much easier in my day, and it sounds as though you would have loved it as well. Back then, nobody knew your business unless you shared it. You could be an anonymous face in the crowd, and there weren't those dreadful cameras all over the place. It's appalling how little privacy we get these days."

"Listen, there's another reason I was asking you about Luis." Alyssa took in a deep breath, and held it, while she tried to find a way to word it.

"And what reason is that?"

"Do you believe there is any chance that Luis was involved in the tragic events of last year? Whether willful or not?"

"Heavens no." Friesen made a sour face. "He has a good heart, and is far too insipid to concoct a murderous scheme. A year ago, and against all probability, he was even more banal than he is today, so I can safely say there isn't a trace of villainy in that young man."

Alyssa gave an appreciative nod.

"Now," he opened the door to his office, "I've enjoyed our little chat, but I have my daily reports to write."

Alyssa nodded. "I understand. Thank you."

He nodded and closed the door between them.

Sunday: 4:20 p.m.

Malcolm saw a bedraggled young woman in scrubs coming out of the staff room. She stopped, lowered herself to the floor, and then sat there, leaning against the wall. He walked over to her and saw a small bag of cannabis gunnies in her hand. "Are you Gina?"

"Yeah." She looked in his direction until there was only one of him and in reasonable focus. "Uh, which patient are you trying to find?"

"None."

Gina giggled. "Dude, nobody in this place is a nun, trust me." She looked at him again and she wore an expression of realization. "Oh, wait a minute. Are you the delivery guy from the cannabis store?"

"No, I'm here to look into the fire from last year."

"No way." Gina gasped. "There was a fire at the weed store too? Wow, can you imagine being downwind of that? You'd get a buzz for free."

Malcolm pinched the bridge of his nose. "No, I'm investigating the fire at the hospital where you worked a year ago."

"Oh, you're looking into *that* fire."

"Yes. Finally. I've struck brain."

Gina held up a finger and began to wave it, slowly. "But if you're looking into the fire that happened over there, then why are you over here?" Her eyes widened. "Wait, are you from the future, and you're here to warn me about a fire that's going to happen here?"

"No, I'm not from the future, because if I knew we were going to have this conversation, I'd have avoided it with every ounce of my being."

"Hey, speaking of ounces, if you're not my delivery guy, then I should text the store and find out when my order will get here." She squinted at Malcolm. "Wait, so, if you're not from the future, then how can you know there's going to be a fire here?"

"I can't and don't." Malcolm's sigh was long and weary. "The fire was *your* assumption. *My* assumption is that you've had more of those edibles than is recommended in a single day."

Gina lifted the small bag up to her face and looked at the packaging. "There's a recommended daily amount?"

"Yes, though it now occurs to me a person has to be lucid enough to read the dosage, which is unlikely considering the target market and subject matter. I'd like to ask you about the fire last year at the facility."

Gina returned the bag to her pocket, then spent the next twenty seconds getting up on her feet. "Can't. I've got vitals to take and patients to chart, and I'm already way behind in my daily tasks."

"Then how about later?"

Gina shook her head. "I'll still be working later."

Malcolm folded his arms. "I mean how about *after* work?"

Gina snort-laughed. "Are you kidding? I'll be way too stoned by then to answer you."

Malcolm's eyes grew wide. "You mean you think you're lucid *now?*"

Gina backed away. "Look, I have to go."

Malcom watched her stagger hurriedly down the hallway.

Sunday: 4:42 p.m.

Gina and Abby were unloading the dryer in the laundry room and folding the contents together. Or, more specifically, Gina unloaded the dryer, and Abby got what was missed. Then Gina would fold things, and Abby refolded them, so they didn't look as though they performed this task during a hurricane. In order to keep Gina focused, Abby made an effort to have a conversation with her, even though social interactions weren't her strong suit.

"So, I didn't know Celia or Wing. What were they like?"

Gina stopped her chaotic folding and flashed a grin. "Celia was nice. Like, she was super uptight and totally vain, but still nice, you know? She was, like thirty-five, but wanted to look, like, twenty-one, so she was obsessed with her appearance. I met her younger sister once, and, like, I can tell you that vanity totally runs in that family."

"Did you get to know Celia outside of work?"

"No. Well, one time, she wanted me to check out her church, but I wasn't interested. Then she started talking about sex, drugs, gambling, and sin, and I was like, hell yeah, girl, what night does your church group meet? But then she said they were all bad things, and then I was like, way to get my hopes up, lady. Sheesh. Talk about a total buzzkill."

"And Wing?"

"Wing Zhen was an awesome guy, seriously. He was the best patient I ever looked after."

"Did you know him before he slipped into a coma?"

"No, but that's why he was so great to look after. No complaining, no resisting, zero attitude, and, like, totally chill. He was just an all-around great dude. Why are you asking about them?"

"I want to find out who killed them."

"You know, I'm pretty high right now, and even I know they already solved that one." Gina attempted to fold something that she had already folded. "Our resident girl Suzy went all pyro on us, and that's why she's, like, here."

"I'm working on a theory that Suzy – *Zee* – didn't set the fire."

"Cool, but… you know, she was already convicted and stuff, right?"

"I'm aware of that, yeah. Hey, I have a question for you about Wing Zhen."

Gina made finger guns. "Sure, shoot."

"I've been told that even before the fire, Wing already had one foot in the grave. Is that true?"

"That would be consistent with the kind of person he was."

"I'm not sure what you mean by that."

Gina suppressed a chuckle. "He didn't like making commitments in his life, so having only one foot in the grave totally makes sense."

Abby patted a towel she'd just folded, which was the final piece to be done. "Thanks for helping me finish up the laundry."

"Whoa, you're right, it is finished." Gina's eyes widened. "I don't even remember folding these."

Sunday: 5:02 p.m.

Abby opened the door, flicked on the lights, and then gestured for Malcolm to enter. She walked into the room behind him.

"And this is the secondary storage room."

The twelve-by-twelve room contained metal racks, which covered every wall from floor to ceiling. There were dozens of boxes, which filled every shelf in the room, each labelled with a black marker. Some of the boxes were labelled as office supplies, while others were marked as copy paper, or surgical masks, and everything else from paper clips and staplers, to rubber gloves and gauze.

"So, the big room we saw was for food and perishables, and this one is for everything else. Look around as much as you like, but there's mostly just boring medical supplies, skin creams, and other junk in here."

"What kind of junk?"

"Like that box," Abby pointed. At the end of the shelf beside Malcolm was a large box labeled *decorations.*

He turned toward it and pulled it off the shelf so he could peer inside.

The decorations were mostly for Halloween and Christmas, from what he could see. Aside from a few pastel-coloured plastic Easter eggs at the bottom and a few red cardboard hearts, it was otherwise all witches, garland, ghosts, stockings, skeletons, and plastic Santas.

Malcolm held up one of the Santas in his hand.

"See?" Abby pointed again. "Just useless junk."

"You're not a fan of Santa Claus?"

Abby shrugged. "He wasn't part of my childhood, so, to me, he's just another stupid fairy tale."

"You know," Malcolm set the box down and waved the Santa at Abby, "this version of Santa Claus may be a myth, but he's based on a real person."

"A fat bearded man who lives with elves and makes toys at the North Pole?" Abby glared at him. "I'm not stupid, you know."

"I know you're not, but I'm serious." Malcolm tossed the Santa back into the box. "The real guy was from the 4th Century. Saint Nicholas, the Bishop of something or other in what today is the country of Turkey, or as it's now known, Türkiye. He was a real guy, I swear, and he was skinny, to boot."

"Then how did that Saint Nicholas dude morph into the chubby red representation of shopping sprees?"

"He evolved." Malcolm shrugged. "The stories changed over the years, and with it, people's understanding of him changed, too."

Abby opened her mouth to answer and then froze. She waved her finger. "So, you're saying he was just some nice guy hundreds of years ago, and he kind of changed over time into that."

"Well, yeah, the stories changed. The legend of the actual man was exaggerated, changed, and then made into something else." Malcolm leaned against one of the racks. "Religions did similar things as a way to teach people about morals and crap. There weren't schools as we know them today, so people were taught with stories, fables, and legends. As the stories were retold over the years, they evolved into something no longer resembling what it started out as."

"So, the Santa Claus we know today is the result of people retelling a story so many times, it became something completely different."

"Yeah, that's what I've been saying. Why are you asking like that?"

Abby stood silently for a moment, still waving her finger. "That means a lot of things we know today may also be the result of stories being retold and no longer resembling what they really are."

Malcolm's brow wrinkled. "It's just Santa Claus, so I'm not sure what the big deal is."

Abby looked at him. "If Santa changed, then maybe what we know about demons is the same."

"Okay." Malcolm narrowed his eyes. "Help me understand where you're going with that thought."

"What if Mr. Vollack is really a demon, but we're so used to demons being these creatures from Hell with horns and stuff, but what if we've got it wrong? What if demons were originally something else? If this magic snow-bound toymaker was originally some old bishop from the Middle East, then maybe a demon was originally something else entirely, too."

Malcolm smiled. "I love how you think, Abby. Mary's the theological one. Let me see what she thinks and I'll get back to you."

"Okay." Abby headed toward the door. "I'll be down the hall in the kitchen when you're done."

She closed the door behind her.

Malcolm looked at his watch and then pulled out his phone. He called Mary. She answered immediately.

"Hi Malcolm, how are things going?"

"I was thinking about Santa Claus."

His wife paused before responding. "It's a bit early for you to be hanging your stocking, isn't it? Plus, I don't know how to break this to you, but it may be wishful thinking for you to believe you made it off the naughty list. Did you seriously call me to talk about symbols of Christmas?"

"No, I'm calling because I asked myself an interesting question and got a truly bizarre answer."

"Oh, so now you know how I feel every time we speak."

"So let me tell you what I asked."

"I don't remember encouraging you to continue, but here we are."

"I asked myself to consider the possibility that the ridiculous could be real."

"You mean like the two of us being married?"

"No, like what if there was a grain of truth to vampires, demons, and other mythical beings, much like there is to Santa Claus."

"Santa Claus?"

"Yeah, Saint Nick, the fat guy, the milk and cookie addict; him. The jolly old elf himself, who's probably jolly because he has a list of where all the naughty people live. The guy who built a toy factory on a melting sheet of ice up north."

"What about him?"

"You're Catholic, so you must know the rotund symbol of December shopping is based on the Fourth Century Bishop of something in Turkey, right?"

"He was the Bishop of Myra."

"Right, but the point is that he was a real guy. He helped the poor, helped kids, and that sort of thing, correct?"

"Yes, which is why Saint Nicholas is the patron saint of children. Over the years, the setting somehow changed from Turkey to the North Pole, and the Bishop of Myra morphed into a toy-making symbol of rampant consumerism."

"Exactly, plus flying reindeer, elves, and an ability to stop time so he could deliver everything in one night. Can you imagine having the ability to stop time and wasting it on expedited delivery? But yeah, all of that stuff. The myths and legends about Santa Claus grew out of a real event, and a real person. So, along the same lines, Abby was wondering if the same evolutions also happened with demons, werewolves, and the like? What if these mythical creatures are also based on real events and real people, but no longer bear no resemblance to what they used to be?"

"I have to admit, much to my surprise, that you and Abby have constructed an interesting and thought-provoking hypothesis of the theoretical."

"Right?"

"But is it at all relevant to the case you're helping with?"

"It is, because it may tie into something Abby thought of." Malcolm leaned against one of the metal racks. "She's the one who asked about the Santa legend, and that got me to thinking..."

"After all these years, *that's* what did the trick? I wish I'd known it was that easy, and you'd have started thinking long ago."

Malcolm pressed on, undeterred. "What if angels and demons are real, but they aren't what we think they are?"

"The answer to that is obvious."

"It is? Then tell me."

"You're clearly still jet-lagged and sleep-deprived."

"This was Abby's theory, and I'm being serious."

"I know," Mary sighed, "but even if she's right, you're not going to change six thousand years of theology just because she came up with an interesting but completely unprovable hypothesis. That's the whole point of religion. It's about faith, not facts."

"Hence my atheism."

"And hence why we don't usually discuss theology. I need to head into another debriefing with the ambassador, so we'll chat some more later."

"Okay. Take care." Malcolm hung up his phone and went to find Abby.

Sunday: 7:41 p.m.

Alyssa sat at the desk in her bedroom, focused on the research her laptop computer. Abby was leaning on the back of Alyssa's chair and peering over her shoulder.

"There." Alyssa pointed to her screen. "I found a reference to the name *Armoniel.* In the Book of Enoch, he's mentioned as an angel. Armoniel was a *Watcher,* whatever that means, and the name can mean *cursed one* or *accursed one.*"

Abby made a face. "Either way, not a good title to have."

"It said in Cenk Vollack's file that when he first claimed to be a demon, he referred to himself as a *Baku.*"

"What's that?"

"Not sure, but I'm looking it up right now." Alyssa typed and clicked. "Okay. I've found two references to that word. Baku is a city on the coast of the Caspian Sea, and it's the capital of Azerbaijan, so I suppose he could be from there. Ah, and the other reference is from Japanese mythology, and it's a mythical creature which is believed to eat nightmares."

Abby whistled. "If that's true, then he should hang out with me, and he'd never go hungry."

"It says in Japanese folklore, a person who wakes up from a bad dream can call out to the Baku, asking that they devour their nightmare so they can go back to sleep."

"That sounds useful."

"It does, for sure, but be careful what you wish for, because there's a serious down side." Alyssa pointed to a section of text on her screen. "Along with eating your nightmares, this paragraph says he can also eat your hopes, dreams, and desires, leaving you feeling as though your life is empty."

"Maybe the Baku already visited me and I didn't notice. It would explain so much about my life. Oh, and maybe this Baku's name is Armoniel."

Alyssa turned to Abby. "But that can't be right, because a Baku is depicted as an animal-like demon creature from Chinese and Japanese legend, whereas Armoniel is a Judeo-Christian angel. Oh wait, now that I read further, it says Armoniel was a *fallen* angel."

"Like the Devil, right?"

Alyssa shrugged. "If you believe in such things, yes, but keep in mind these are just stories and legends, to say nothing of the fact that these are obviously two different entities."

"Are they? I'm not so sure about that."

"Explain."

Abby smiled. "Maybe it's like Santa Claus."

"Okay, you've completely lost me now."

"The woman who taught me to break into computer systems was raised in Germany, and she told me about their version of Santa Claus, except he isn't Santa Claus."

"I believe they use the name *Weihnachtsmann.*"

"Yeah, but their Santa doesn't do the flying sleigh and breaking into houses. Instead, he travels with his evil version."

"He travels with an evil version of himself?"

Abby frowned. "No, I explained it wrong. It's not a version of himself, it's more like… an evil companion who goes by the name of Krampus."

"And the good kids get the nice Santa, and the bad kids get the evil Krampus?"

"Pretty much." Abby leaned on the back of Alyssa's chair. "Father Christmas would ride in on his white horse and reward the good children, while Krampus would torture and frighten the bad ones."

"Okay, I think I understand all of that." Alyssa gestured toward her screen. "So, are you suggesting Armoniel and this Baku are, what, a team?"

"I was thinking they're more like two sides of the same coin."

"But they're so vastly different."

Abby paced around Alyssa's room. "I'm just thinking how possible it is that two very different cultures viewed the same demon and interpreted it their own way based on their existing beliefs. Over the years, the stories changed and evolved, and they ended up being two very different things. One culture named him a watcher and it evolved from there, and the other culture named him a dream-eater and it evolved from there, so Mr. Vollack could easily be both of those things."

Alyssa gave a conciliatory nod. "That was surprisingly insightful and thought-provoking, Abby, but the simpler and much more likely explanation is that Mr. Vollack is a man with mental health problems, who needs someone to help him reconnect with reality. It also explains why he's been in one hospital or another for so many years."

"Maybe," Abby shrugged, "but I think my theory is far more interesting. Your dad also thought it was an interesting idea."

"I'm not surprised." Alyssa leaned back in her chair. "Most of his ideas are interesting, but they're more the *I wonder if he needs medication* sort of interesting."

"I need to think about this some more." Abby stopped pacing. "I'll sleep on it and will hopefully have some more ideas when we go back to the facility tomorrow. But first, I need to go and see your dad."

Sunday: 7:59 p.m.

Abby found Malcolm in the kitchen, making a sandwich. He looked up and gestured toward the bread on the counter. "Want one?"

"No, a piece of plain bread doesn't do it for me."

"I meant… never mind." Malcolm added some slices of ham upon his creation. "You need anything?"

"Yeah, I wanted to ask you a couple of things about the case."

"Sure." He added a piece of lettuce, so if asked by his wife later, he could say he had a salad.

"Have you eliminated any suspects, yet?"

"No." He put the remaining bread slice on top, then sliced the sandwich. "I suspect some people more than others, but nobody's off the hook just yet."

"You want it to be Luis, don't you? You hate that he likes Alyssa."

Malcolm sat the knife down and put the sandwich on a small plate. "At this point, he's a perfectly legitimate suspect, but yeah, sure; I can't deny my unhappy feelings about him. Especially now that you've confirmed what I've been suspecting about his interest in Alyssa. I want him to stay away from her, you're right about that, but that doesn't mean I'll pin blame on him just because of that. And before you say anything, I know I'm being bit over-protective of my daughter, but it is what it is."

"No, what you're doing isn't over-protectiveness, what you're doing is adding a ton of fuel onto all the anxieties she's already dealing with."

"How do you figure?" He took a bite.

"You lived on the streets of New York for six years, starting when you were fourteen, right? I mean, you went through a lot of bad stuff. And then your decades in national security made you see even worse stuff. So, because of the dangerous life you've led, you've made her aware of all the bad things in the world, but you've left her unequipped to deal with any of it."

Malcolm held up his finger until he was able to swallow the mouthful. "I hope to hell you're wrong."

"Just talk to Luis. He's a good guy."

"Fine. I'll… see if I can… talk to him without, you know, vomiting." He got ready to take another bite, but stopped. "You have something else on your mind, don't you?"

"Yeah. You're friends with a police detective. I think his name was Browne or something."

"Yeah, Neil Browne."

"Are you still in touch with him?"

"Do tics tick? Yeah, Neil and I have become pretty good buds. Why?"

"I need some information, so do you think he would be up to making a deal with us?"

"What do you have in mind?"

Abby smirked. "He's a cop, so it's fair to say he's going to hate everything about it."

Monday: 7:42 a.m.

Neil Browne saw Malcolm waving him over, so he strode to the entry door of the take-out doughnut shop. Neil was in his early thirties, dressed in slacks, a golf shirt, and a blazer. He had close-cropped black hair and a skin tone that reminded Malcolm of milky coffee. When Neil got to Malcolm, they opened the door and stepped inside the shop. As they scanned the menu, Malcolm nudged Neil. "Hey, thanks for meeting me on short notice."

"No problem." Neil cast a sidelong glance in Malcolm's direction. "You know, whenever I see your name pop up on my phone, I tense up, because I never know if you're calling me so we can sneak off and eat doughnuts without our wives knowing, or if it's because you need something that's going to make me regret ever becoming a cop."

"Hypothetically, how bad would it be if it was the latter option today?"

"That depends. Are we talking about you buying me a doughnut, or about you buying me a dozen?"

"Have you ever had one of those boxes of twenty-four? I haven't."

"Please tell me you're kidding."

"No, I truly haven't had the twenty-four-doughnut box, but I also truly know that wasn't what you were asking me."

"On a scale of one to ten, how much am I going to regret ever meeting you?"

"On a scale of one to ten, I'd guess your regret will clock in somewhere around the number of doughnuts in the box we were just talking about."

"So, a score of twenty-four on a one-to-ten scale." Browne exhaled, sharply. "That's a lot of regret there. Why don't you tell me about it, so I know how many antacids to buy at the pharmacy next door?"

"You think knowing me today is stressful? You should be glad you didn't know me thirty years, thirty pounds, and thirty percent of my hair ago."

"Be glad it's only thirty percent of your hair. Alright. I start my shift in twenty minutes, so let's go with the summarized version of what you need."

"You remember the fire at the hospital last year? Two people died, and a young woman ended up being charged with arson and two counts of murder?"

"Yeah, I definitely remember that case. And, if I recall, the owner of *Saint Raphael's Hospital* was found negligent and fined. Some troubled youth was sent for a psych evaluation or something."

"Yeah, that's the one. Listen, I'm helping a private detective who is looking into the case, so I'm wondering if you could accidentally leave a copy of the police report behind when you meet me for all those doughnuts I'll be buying you."

"The file's digital, but there's a lot of information there. What specifically are you looking for?"

"One of the patients who died was Wing Zhen. I'm looking to review his wife's testimony as some new information has come to light."

Browne made a note.

"And the other victim was Celia Ocampo, a care aide. Her sister was interviewed, so I'll want that information as well. Plus, the witness interviews, and whatever else was discovered which wasn't made part of the trial."

"I think twenty-four doughnuts doesn't come close to reflecting the risk I'd be taking."

"No, but there is a payoff for you. If our investigation works out, you'll be the one who will get to make the arrest and take all the credit. Our evidence will be inadmissible in court because of how we obtained it, so you can be the one to collar the bad guys."

"I see."

"It worked out last time, didn't it?"

"Barely. You nearly ruined the career of my former partner."

"And you nearly charged my daughter with a murder she didn't commit."

"Touché, Malcolm. I guess we both learned something important in that last case."

"So, what do you say? Are you with me?"

Browne grinned. "Yeah, I'm in. I'll give you what you need either later today or early tomorrow."

Monday: 7:49 a.m.

Alyssa and Abby walked together in the rain toward the temporary facility. Alyssa had her umbrella up and was trying to keep them covered. Abby wasn't one to use rain gear, and would often show up at work or home completely drenched. When prompted, Abby would shrug and offer her opinion that rain was harmless. She'd say, *there's no danger in getting wet, as long as you don't stay wet* and that would be that. Abby kept a towel or two at work and home, as well as a change of clothes, to be able to dry off at either location.

Nevertheless, it bothered Alyssa to see someone getting wet, so she did her best with the umbrella.

"I was just thinking about something." Abby shook the rain off her uncovered jacket sleeve. "If the detective thing doesn't work out, maybe I can be a comedian."

Alyssa made a face. "You can't be serious."

"I'm aware of that. It's part of the requirement of being a comedian."

"I mean, why do you think you'd make a good comedian?"

"I don't really, but when I told Robert I was going to become a detective, he said I was hilarious, and added that he didn't know I had such a knack for comedy."

"I'm going to go out on a limb here and say he was being sarcastic."

Abby shrugged. "We're close to solving this, aren't we?"

Alyssa returned Abby's shrug with one of her own. "I don't know."

She didn't share Abby's view about resolution closeness. There were still too many pieces that didn't fit together, and even more unanswered questions.

When talking about detective cases and mysteries, people often use the analogy of a jigsaw puzzle. All the pieces are there, you just need to assemble them until everything fits together to form the final picture, but Alysa had formed the opinion that the puzzle metaphor was enormously inaccurate.

In her mind, solving a crime was nothing at all like a single jigsaw puzzle, which is neat, a single theme, and no leftover pieces. She now believed no real detective case could realistically ever work out so neatly like that.

A real-life mystery was more like taking a large grocery bag, emptying at least a dozen different jigsaw puzzles into it, shaking the bag up, removing two random handfuls of pieces and throwing them away, and *only then* dump out the pieces and try to put them together.

Real detective work wasn't just finding clues, it was about poring over all the information, and then figuring out which pieces were relevant and which ones were unrelated. The main objective may be to finish one particular puzzle, but before one can find which pieces one needs, one also must sort through all of the pieces first. Some pieces may be the right shape, but not have the right picture. Some pieces appeared to have the right image, but it was unclear which puzzle it was part of and where it might fit.

Each suspect was his or her own unique puzzle. No detective, no matter how clever, would ever get all of the pieces, but he or she might get enough of them to understand where they fit. Each suspect – whether they were on-site that fateful day or not – could be the guilty party, but the possibility also existed that there was no crime committed at all.

The two made their way up the stairs and entered the facility.

Monday: 8:00 a.m.

Doctor Friesen entered Zee's room and flashed his usual smile. "Good morning."

Zee scoffed. "Can you prove it is?"

"Of course not." He closed the door. "It's a greeting, not an observation. It's little more than polite noise."

"It's rare, but sometimes you say something that I actually agree with."

The doctor beamed. "Then we're already making progress." He sat down and glanced at Zee. "This morning, I'd like to talk a little bit about the people who passed away in last year's fire."

"I'd rather not."

"I know, but it's important to do so as part of your healing journey."

"I don't like traveling."

"One of the reasons you were sent here was due to your complete lack of empathy over the loss of life. In fact, I may go so far as to state you seemed joyous at their deaths."

"No." Zee shook her head in an emphatic way. "There was no joy. None. I was sorry to hear about Wing, but I hated Celia because she was the equivalent of a sentient menstrual cramp. I actually envied everyone who had never met her, so her death was no big loss to me."

"She was a human being with a life and loved ones. Shouldn't that matter?"

"To her loved ones, maybe, but not to me." Zee tilted her head back and stared at the ceiling. "She treated me badly, so isn't it natural that I feel some contentment that she's no longer able to make my life miserable?" She looked at the doctor. "Well, *more* miserable?"

"To a certain extent, sure. It's one thing to feel some satisfaction she's gone, but a healthy mind will also feel guilty about feeling that way. It's very simple: empathy is part of the human condition; it's hardly rocket science."

"Of course it isn't. It's not science at all. It's art. And like all art, it's entirely subjective. And to me, subjectively, Celia was a total pig who would fail a personality test."

"Celia was hardly a pig." Friesen frowned. "She believed cleanliness was next to godliness."

"They're only next to one another if your dictionary is missing the pages in between those two words."

"She took great pride in her appearance, perhaps, admittedly, to an unhealthy extreme." Friesen recalled Celia and smiled. "She was always made up, her hair and everything, right down to her manicured fingernails, was always perfect-looking. In my opinion,

Celia didn't need to do so much preening, because she was naturally as cute as a bug's ear."

"You think bug ears are cute?" Zee scoffed. "And here I thought my fetishes were strange."

"I know you didn't like her, Zee, but biases aside, you must admit she had a face that could launch a thousand ships."

"Yeah, and a personality to get a thousand crews to mutiny." Zee stared at him. "I'm surprised Celia didn't get worn out each day, putting makeup on her two faces every morning. Beauty is only skin deep, but being a superficial, mean-spirited manipulator goes all the way to the bone, and Celia was the living proof of that."

Friesen tut-tutted. "I still can't quite wrap my head around why you despise her so much."

"There are a number of objects I could try to wrap your head around if you like."

Friesen made another tut-tutting sound. "You know, there are some doctors who would take your comments seriously, but I prefer to take the road less travelled."

"Because the road less traveled is the preferred hiding place for stalkers and serial killers?"

"I really do need to stop serving these comments to you on a silver platter." Friesen exhaled sharply. "Perhaps Celia could be a difficult person to you sometimes, but she was a very capable employee at the hospital. I believe that somewhere inside of you is the humanity you keep suppressed. I continue to treat you because of that belief. Celia's gone, but it solves nothing that ails you. Your life is no better with her gone; you just have one less person to blame for your perceived life problems."

Zee shrugged. "Maybe you're right, but at least I don't have to see her anymore, so that's still a win as far as I'm concerned."

"So, for you, it's all *out of sight, out of mind.*"

"According to the courts, I might be out of my mind, and yet here I am, within your field of vision."

"You're not out of your mind, Zee, you just need some help." Friesen flashed a quick smile. "So, we'll continue moving along with our session. Like they say, a rolling stone gathers no moss."

"I'm pretty sure I heard Mick Jagger once dated Kate Moss."

"I'm surprised you even know who those two people are."

"Only because my grandfather was a fan of the Stones."

"And now, somehow, I feel even older than I did a moment ago. I don't know if the Mick and Kate rumour is true, but, regardless, it's the wrong kind of rolling stone, wrong kind of gather, and wrong kind of moss for this idiom. I suppose I could have said *a tumbling boulder accumulates no flora,* but it really loses its impact."

"A tumbling boulder would have a big impact on whatever it hits, and it may not accumulate any flora, but it would gather any vehicles, bystanders, and houses in its path."

Friesen scowled. "You really know how to take the charm out of these old expressions, don't you?"

Monday: 8:07 a.m.

Malcolm noticed Luis Garcia up ahead in the hallway, staring at something. He looked in the direction Luis was watching, and he saw Alyssa walking into the break room. Malcom approached him. "Hey, did you just ogle my daughter?"

"No, sir. Um, and I think it's pronounced *oh-gull,* not *aw-gull*."

"Oh-gull, aw-gull, either way, there's a gull involved." Malcolm waved his finger at Luis. "The main point is about a certain bird watcher, who'd better watch what birds he watches."

"But then I'd be watching the bird you don't want me watching."

"Watch it, pal." Malcolm put his hands on his hips. "So, what's the deal with you and my daughter?"

"She seems like an amazing person. She's smart and she's pretty." Luis looked panicked for a moment. "I mean she's smart and pretty *capable*."

"Yeah, she is."

"A nice-looking woman is great, and everything, but there's something about a woman with… I don't know how to say it."

"I'd suggest using words, and preferably English ones. We can start with one-syllable words if you like, and then see how it goes from there."

"I only just met her, but I already feel inspired."

"What do you mean by *inspired?* In what way?"

"I just think a woman like her could inspire someone to be their best. It's like that old saying about how behind every great man there's a woman."

Malcolm scoffed. "Yeah, and behind every great woman is a man staring at her ass."

"It's not like that. Listen…" Luis took in a deep breath. "I really like Alyssa and I want to ask her out."

"Maybe you should wait for a while."

"How long?"

"I don't know, maybe one or two… *thousand* years."

"I don't think this can wait." Luis locked eyes with Malcolm. "I want to let her know how I feel. In cases like this, I think it's better to wear my heart on my sleeve."

"I'll assist you in expediting that organ relocation if you're not careful."

"Wait," Luis blinked a couple of times. "You don't want me to ask her out?"

"No, of course I don't. Jesus, read the room, will you?"

"I haven't been able to do much reading lately."

"You don't say. How the hell were you the fastest sperm?" Malcolm sighed and cast a wary eye on him. "Let me ask you something. Where do you see yourself in five years?"

"Probably in a mirror, much like now."

Malcolm pinched the bridge of his nose. "I'm asking you about your career plans. Do you want to be a security guard for the rest of your life, or do you have some kind of life plan?"

"I'm where I need to be for right now, and that's all that matters to me." Luis shrugged. "So, five years from now? It's kind of hard to look that far ahead."

"Unbelievable. Do you live alone, or with roommates?"

"Right now, I'm living with my parents."

Malcolm's gaze fell to the floor. "Against all probability, it keeps getting worse with each question I ask."

"I don't think –"

"Yeah, I'm seeing that, but I'm sure you have other qualities, though I doubt any of them are meaningful." Malcolm shook his head. "It's as if your parents said you could be anything, and you chose disappointment. I'm going to walk away before my headache worsens."

As Malcolm left, he sighed. *That kid's as useful as an ashtray on a motorcycle. I sure as hell hope he's the guilty party in all this.*

Monday: 8:55 a.m.

Dr. Friesen exited Zee's room and closed the door. He was surprised to see Abby was there waiting for him. "Good morning, Abby."

"Hey Doc. Got a sec?"

He smiled. "I'm sure I can rummage a second up for you. What's on your mind?"

"Can I ask you something about Cenk Vollack?"

"I haven't checked on him yet this morning. Is he alright?"

"Physically, yes, but I think the rest is up to you to decide."

"You can certainly ask me about him, but I can't disclose anything confidential."

"No, I'm already familiar with his file, I just want to ask a hypothetical question."

He raised an eyebrow. "Then do go on."

"What if he's telling the truth about everything?"

"Oh dear." Friesen chuckled. "If he is, then I'd love to know which moisturizing cream he's using, as he looks superb for a man of five-hundred."

"I was reading some stuff about vampires, and they can live for centuries without showing their age."

"This sounds like the sort of conversation I might enjoy more after I've had three drinks too many and the floor has begun tilting." He raised an eyebrow. "You do understand that vampires are simply a myth, yes? They aren't real."

"Just humour me. What if he was a vampire?"

"Very well then, I shall indulge you and consult my invisible Vampire Identification Manual." Friesen pretended to open a book and flip through some pages. "I vaguely recall reading somewhere in here that vampires need to drink blood regularly in order to survive. He's been my patient for the past three years, and has been locked up in the Ministry's care for another fourteen years prior to that. I've seen every incident report filed here since I started, and there are no reports of missing plasma, no mention of puncture wounds in necks or anyplace else, and nobody has reported seeing any bats flying around, so I'm quite confident in stating we're safe from Count Dracula here."

Abby shook her head. "The real-life guy, Vlad Dracula, didn't change into a bat and didn't drink blood."

"True, but the real Dracula also wasn't a real vampire."

"But that's kind of what I'm getting at." Abby made wild motions with her hands. "We know what vampires are thought of today, but what were they originally? And the same with demons. What were they originally?"

"The details may have changed, Abby, but at the end of the day, demons, vampires, werewolves, the Loch Ness Monster, Big Foot, and the Headless Horseman all have but one thing in common: they're nothing more than legends, fables, and stories." Friesen sat on the edge of his desk. "Stories which have been retold and repurposed since mankind's beginning. For example, Noah's Ark was based on the legend of Gilgamesh. It's the same story, but the details were changed for a new audience. No matter what the changes are, it's still just a fable." He flashed a kind smile to her. "Now if you'll excuse me, my dear colleague, I must get back to reviewing the patient charts you and Gina filled out."

"Sure."

He squinted at one of the charts. "Oh dear. Gina spelled that completely wrong."

"Which word did she spell wrong?"

"Her name." He sighed and sauntered down the hallway.

Monday: 9:22 a.m.

Malcolm was on his phone, pacing in the supply room. "That's not the worst of it."

"What else happened?" Mary asked. Where she was, three time zones away, in Washington, DC, her day was already half over, and she had gotten back to her hotel for lunch. She had called him to check in and to hear about how the case was going. She had been surprised at how animated Malcolm was at such an early hour. She made a mental note to later ask him just how much coffee he'd consumed this morning.

"Get this," he fumed. "Then this security guard walks up to me and says he wants to ask Alyssa out."

"That's wonderful."

"Wonderful?" Malcolm all but spat the word. "No, it's not *wonderful*. It's not even *wonder-half-full*. It's more like *wonder-empty*. Wonder's picture is on the side of a milk carton because there's been no sightings of wonder in this situation at all."

Mary sighed. "You're being over-protective again."

"No, I'm not, and I can prove it."

"How?"

"He's still alive and has all of his limbs intact, so I think I've been showing remarkable restraint."

"You're showing remarkable *something,* alright, but it isn't restraint."

Malcolm let out a loud breath. "Are you seriously okay with our daughter being asked out?"

"Yes, of course I am."

"I can't believe you're not on my side." He groaned. "How are you okay with this?"

"Let me try to reason with you this way, if I can." Mary paused for a moment. "Alyssa's never been on a second date with anyone, so what does that tell you?"

"That I clearly need to work harder to prevent the first dates?"

"No, dummy. I need you to get it through your head that she's old enough to date, and you need to figure out a way to be okay with that."

"She can date all she wants, as long as she does it after she graduates from college, after her thirtieth birthday, and after I'm dead."

"My days of not taking you seriously are certainly coming to a middle." Mary sighed. "She doesn't live in a cloister, you know."

"I didn't realize that option was on the table, but it's a concept I could get behind." Malcolm fidgeted. "We should explore that in greater detail."

"No, she's nineteen, and legally an adult."

"Then let's move some place where she needs to be older."

"No." Mary let out an exasperated sigh. "You're going to have to accept that she's no longer a child. She's a young woman who needs to date people in order to get some experience in the dating world and grow as a person."

"There's a particular nine months' worth of growing a person I'm trying to avoid. Look, I know you're probably right, but I can't help but hate the thought of some guy hurting her."

"I know, and I worry about that, too, but there's no need for you to be so protective. We raised and educated her well, and she has a solid foundation of ethics and morality. Do you not trust her?"

"I trust Alyssa completely; it's everyone else I don't trust."

"If you trust Alyssa, then let her handle it on her own."

"I'd rather she not handle it at all. And if her date takes it out, I'll cut it off."

"Stop being a Neanderthal, will you?" Mary snapped. She let her voice soften before continuing. "Alyssa needs to be able to date men without you hitting the panic button every time. She knows we're there for her if she needs us. You don't need to run background checks on everyone she looks at, and then proceed to follow them home."

"Oh, come on," Malcolm fumed. "I only did that once, and I've never heard the end of it."

"The boy was her assigned lab partner in science class."

"I didn't know that at the time."

"In Grade Six."

"You can't be too careful."

"In your case, you can *easily* be too careful." Mary cleared her throat. "And after the subsequent restraining order you were served with, I thought you'd have learned something about being too suspicious."

"Hey, my built-in *bastard detector* has gotten us out of a lot of scrapes, and has helped to solve a lot of our assignments."

"It has, but there's a time and a place for everything. We've also benefitted from me knowing multiple languages and martial arts, yet I didn't help

Alyssa with her homework by speaking Farsi and putting a choke-hold on her biology book."

"That's both true and an interesting mental image at the same time. What's your point?"

"Remember when Alyssa was learning to crawl, and you said not to baby-proof everything? You said she should bang into some things so she could learn from it. Remember that? And you were right."

"Was that painful to admit?"

"Excruciating, but the principle behind your idea was sound." Mary paused to let her statement sink in. "If you make the environment too safe, she won't learn how to deal with the world she has to grow up in."

"So, I should let her get her heart broken in order to find out men are creeps?"

"Yes, to the heartbreak, keeping in mind it heals with time, and no to all men being creeps. The only way she's going to find the right guy is to date a few wrong ones first, so she can find out what kind of guy she *doesn't* want to be with. Do you remember the first girl who broke your heart?"

"Of course. I'm reminded of her every time I see trash on the street."

Mary suppressed a laugh. "Thank goodness you're not bitter or anything. My point is, you got over her. It was only by moving past her that you ended up finding me."

"I found you outside a café when you walked into the crossfire of the gang hit I was caught in the middle of."

"You're missing the point, which shouldn't surprise me, but yes, we did have an unconventional first meeting. And now, Alyssa needs to have her own first meetings in order to grow. And, if you recall, I was eighteen when we met, so she's older than I was at the time." Mary heard silence on the other end, so decided to press forward from another angle. "Look, by preventing her from dating, she'll be angry and resentful toward you, and she'll have every reason to be both."

Malcolm made a sour face, and it came across in his voice. "I really hate it when you make sense."

"Why? Is this young man a terrible person?"

"I don't know, but I suspect his only purpose in life is to become an organ donor."

"Don't be so petty. What was the first thing you noticed about him?"

"His audacity."

"Okay, this isn't working, so listen to me closely." Mary's tone turned serious and emphatic. "I want you to go and find that young man right now, and let him know you'll butt out. Do you understand?"

"The number you have reached is not in service. Please check the number and dial again."

"I'm serious," Mary fumed. "I'd better get a text from you in the next hour letting me know you've done this. Let her work this out with him on her own."

"For the record, he's a suspect in Abby's case."

"Everyone's a suspect in Abby's case, so that's not saying much. Does Alyssa seem to be in any imminent danger?"

"No," Malcolm answered eventually.

"Well, then?"

"So, just to be a hundred percent clear, you're saying I should let her make some potentially terrible choices?"

"You say *potato,* I say *starchy tuber of the Solanum tuberosum plant.* She can't grow if she doesn't learn, so that's a big yes to your question."

Malcolm scowled. "Damn it."

Monday: 9:25 a.m.

"Luis Garcia." Alyssa scurried down the hall toward him. "I have some more questions for you."

Luis' eyes darted from one side to another. "Um, sure."

She arrived at his location and smiled. "Is this a good time?"

"No. I mean, I don't know." He squeezed his eyes shut. "I mean yes. Maybe."

Alyssa made a face. "I didn't think I'd get every possible answer to that question, but you somehow managed to do exactly that."

"I'm sorry," he moaned. "I'm not trying to confuse you. I'm just... I'm really nervous right now."

Alyssa's eyes narrowed. "Because you have information for me, or because you're afraid of what I'll find out?"

He looked away. "It's neither of those."

"Then what?"

"You're just," he stammered, until he finally got the next words out. "You're very pretty."

Alyssa's eyes grew wide. "Sorry, what?"

"You're, like, so amazing, and you're..." He shook his head. "No, you wouldn't believe anything I say like that."

Alyssa blinked. "I wouldn't?"

"No, because if I say something good about you, you'll think I'm just trying to flatter you so you'll be nice to me in your investigation report. Not that people believe compliments anyway."

"They don't?"

"No. I mean, if you tell someone they look great, they'll think, *oh, he's just saying that to be nice, but he doesn't really mean it* and they won't believe you." He glanced at her. "But if you were to tell that same person their hair looks strange today, or that their eyes are disproportionate to their face, they'll run to a mirror and obsess over the comment for days or weeks."

"Just to be clear, those were just random examples, and not anything to do with my hair and eyes, right?"

"No, nothing to do with you at all. No, your hair is great, and your eyes are beautiful." Luis froze, and his face reddened. "I mean, just as an example, right? I don't want you to think I'm trying to…. you know… like, flatter you or something."

"You're probably right about people not accepting compliments, because the first thing that came to my mind was how you didn't mean any of the nice things you just said about me." She shrugged. "I figured you were just being polite."

"But I did mean them. Seriously, you're the most… I'm sorry, I shouldn't be saying these things while you're working."

"Um." Alyssa wrung her hands and bit her lower lip. "I've decided I'm on a break right now, so please continue. I really want to hear what you were going to say."

Garcia looked at her. "Are you absolutely sure you're okay with me saying what I think?"

"Yeah, go ahead. Spill it."

"I think you're very pretty, and I think you have the most amazing eyes I've ever seen."

"That's so sweet." Alyssa blushed. "Seriously, that means a lot to me, because I don't generally hear things like that. And, wow, it suddenly feels as though somebody turned up the furnace in here. I mean, turned up the thermostat. The thermostat for the heating system, which I'm not sure means forced air or a boiler. Or it could be radiant heat in a building this size, which, now that I think of it, would require the boiler I already mentioned, so I suppose I should've quit talking around twenty seconds ago. Regardless, it's become uncomfortably warm in here. My God, why am I *still* talking? Will somebody please stop me from talking?"

"You're funny," he smiled and then looked alarmed. "Wait, I meant funny in a good way, not funny like a clown, or funny like an odd smell. I mean funny like endearing and sweet. Although when I think about it, they're not synonyms, are they?" He covered his face with his hands. "Sorry, I'm not normally this awkward. Well, I am normally awkward, but I'm not usually *this* awkward. It's your eyes." He lowered his hands. "When you look at me, I get completely lost."

"They're just normal, average, every-day eyes." Alyssa stared at the floor. "There's nothing special about them."

"No, there's everything special about them. They're really nice, and they let you see, too, which is great." Luis cleared his throat. "Not that you'd look bad if you were blind, you'd still be great-looking. Not that you'd know you were great-looking if you were blind, you'd have to take my word for it, even though you'd probably just think I was being nice to you, when I wasn't. Not that I wasn't being nice, but instead wasn't meaning it. Which I was. And do. Now I'm completely lost in this conversation, and I don't know what to do."

"Nobody's ever said so many nice things about me before, and it's probably the sweetest thing I've ever heard." She shrugged. "Not that I have any other compliments to compare it to, because guys don't normally notice me, especially handsome guys like you. I don't know why I just said that, and I'm totally embarrassed now. Pretend I didn't say how handsome you are, even though I just did it again there. Yes, I think I need to walk away right now before I say anything else, and then think seriously about taking a permanent vow of silence for everyone's sake."

Abby appeared from around the corner. "Oh my god, I can't believe what I'm hearing. You two are completely, totally, and utterly pathetic. It's no wonder neither of you are dating right now. You both need to go find an empty room somewhere and just throw down."

Alyssa gasped. "Abby, you're somehow managing to embarrass me even more than I already am."

"You should be embarrassed." Abby pointed to herself. "People think I'm dense, but you two are so dense, I bet light would bend around you. I'm socially inept, and even I know that conversation was pathetic." Abby looked into Alyssa's eyes. "Do you like Luis?"

"Well, yeah, he seems nice."

Abby turned to face Luis. "And do you like Alyssa?"

"Very much, yes."

"Well?" Abby made wild gestures with her hands. "Then why do you two still have your clothes on?"

Alyssa covered her face with her hands. "Abby, that's wildly inappropriate."

"Why? Does he repulse you or something?"

"No, of course not."

"Then what?" Abby shook her head. "Did you not shower this morning, or something? You could always do that afterwards, you know."

"No. I mean, yes, I did shower, but no, that's not the reason. I'd just like to take things slowly at first, before stampeding toward anything intimate, you know?"

"No, I don't know." Abby's eyes met Alyssa's. "I have a short life span, so I can't afford to take anything slowly. If I like someone and they like me, then the next step is to get any and all barriers out of the way, such as clothing, and then take care of business. There's no hope for you two." Abby let out a disgusted sound and walked away.

Luis faced Alyssa. "Are you two really best friends?"

"Yes."

"I work with her, but I've never seen her like... *that*." He pointed to the retreating figure of Abby. "Is she always that forceful with her opinions?"

"No, usually she's not that restrained."

"Good to know." He shifted his weight from one foot to the other and then back again. "Are you feeling as uncomfortable as I am right now?"

"Probably even more so." Alysa glanced briefly at him. "I need to leave before my face turns any redder than I'm sure it already is."

"Wait, before you go, I need to say this."

Alyssa looked into his eyes. "What?"

"You're adorable, and I'd like to invite you out to dinner sometime."

"Are you being serious right now?"

"Yes." Luis rubbed his hands together. "Well, I am as long as your dad isn't going to react violently."

"No, he's just over-protective. He'll be fine with it."

"Are both of your parents that protective?"

"No." Alyssa shook her head. "My mom is mostly sunshine and roses, whereas my dad is mostly thunderstorms and crabgrass."

"And you?"

She shrugged. "I'm an equal share of both, which I guess makes me crabgrass in the sunshine."

"I think you're more like a rose in a thunderstorm."

"That was… weirdly poetic and bizarrely romantic, in its own nonsensical way."

"So, maybe dinner some time?"

She nodded. "I'm accepting that invitation before you change your mind or realize your mistake. I need to go right now."

Alyssa hurried down the corridor. As she rounded the corner, she stopped and pumped her fists into the air. "Yes!"

Monday: 9:44 a.m.

Abby had managed to charge Celia's phone once already, but ended up running the battery down while she had it plugged into her password hacking software. Once she obtained the password, she could do nothing with it until the phone had recharged. She tried to access the phone while it was plugged in and charging, but the screen wouldn't stay on. She had little choice, except to wait until it recharged so she could try again.

The phone was plugged in and hidden in the supply room, behind a box of gauze. While she waited for it to charge, she remained haunted by one particular thought: *What if Zee really is guilty?*

Abby ran out of patience and checked the phone. It had charged to thirty-two percent, and she could no longer wait. She unplugged the phone, entered the password, and got to work, knowing the battery charge would only give her thirty minutes or less. She checked emails, texts, and whatever social media she could access, but nothing leapt out at her. She then opened the camera application, and went through the myriad of selfies Celia had taken. She then looked at some older pictures, and did a double-take.

"Oh, now *that's* helpful."

Monday: 10:02 a.m.

Abby bounced toward the security desk. Upon seeing her, Robert nodded a quick greeting.

"Hey, Rob. How's your day?"

"As always, Abby, today is making me wish I had more than two middle fingers." He saw her holding something. "What do you have there?"

Abby held it up. "It's Celia's phone."

"Celia's? Now where the hell did you get that?"

"It doesn't matter. The main thing is I have it."

"Whatever. And?"

"I didn't know you and Celia went out."

"Yeah, it's kind of funny how you don't know about things that aren't any of your goddamned business."

Abby raised an eyebrow. "She ended up dead, which is the only reason I'm asking, because I don't care about any of your relationships."

"Who told you?" He held up his hands. "You know what? Forget I asked that. It's ancient history, anyway." He frowned. "Celia dated anyone who could benefit her. The more she wanted from someone, the more they got from her, if you know what I'm saying. So yeah, she wanted something from me, so I dated her for a while. It wasn't love, romance, or any of that shit. It was just my turn on her list."

"How did you benefit her?"

"She was the unemployed friend of a friend, so I helped Celia to get a job at the hospital."

"I see." Abby drummed her fingers on the counter. "And why did you two break up?"

"That's also none of your business, but it should be obvious." Robert shrugged. "She got the job here, so she had no further use for me. She sunk her claws into the doctor next."

"You mean Dr. Friesen?"

"Yup." Robert tossed his pen onto the desk. "And they were pretty hot and heavy there for a while."

"Did that make you angry or jealous?"

He scoffed. "Nah, I knew from the start our relationship was purely transactional. We each got what we wanted from the other."

"What did you get?"

"What do you think, genius?" He rolled his eyes and looked at her. "What any hot-blooded man wants from an attractive woman."

"Validation, an ego boost, and something to make you feel as though your life has some sort of meaning?"

"Harsh." Robert leaned back in his chair. "You're still a comedian I see."

"No, I'm still a detective."

"You're not a detective, Abby, you're a care aide with delusions of grandeur."

"Yeah, I'm a non-comedic, non-delusional care aide detective." Abby wrinkled her face. "Wait, no, that's going to be too long to put on a business card."

"Look, Abby, I'm busy, so would you mind pissing off?"

Abby nodded. "I'll leave you in peace, Rob. I have something to take care of anyway."

Monday: 10:52 a.m.

Alyssa and Abby each held one of Jeff's arms as they made their way to the spare janitor closet, pushing him along in a wheelchair. Abby had spent the last twenty minutes emptying the room and setting up a microphone and headset.

They walked him into the dark room and sat him on the chair. Abby put the blindfold on him and then the headphones. She positioned the microphone so it was in front of him and then shut the door as she left. Abby and Alyssa leaned in close to Abby's phone, which was on speaker.

"Hello, Jeff." Abby paused. "Can you hear me?"

"Yeah."

Alyssa spoke next. "Do you understand what's happening?"

"Yeah."

"Can you tell me?"

"Yeah," Jeff repeated. "By covering my ears and eyes, you've reduced the number of things that can enter my head."

"That was the idea, yes." Alyssa licked her lips. "We'd like to ask you about the fire last year. Is that okay?"

"My mattress is too hard, I hate peas, and I want a better blanket, because the wool one itches."

"What does that have to do with the fire?"

"I haven't been able to speak for years, so I'm not going to waste it only on what you want. I want things, too, you know."

"I'll take this." Abby took hold of the phone. "You're right Jeff. We're being selfish. I'll start writing stuff down, and we'll make you more comfortable, I promise."

"I want to be in a room like this at least a couple of times each day."

"The best I can promise is I'll bring you in here on the days I work. When Gina is looking after you, I can't promise anything, and I mean that literally."

"Okay."

Alyssa spoke up. "Okay, what?"

"I'll answer stuff about the fire, even though I hate thinking about it."

"I'm sure it's painful to relive that day."

"No."

"No?" Alyssa looked at Abby, who just shrugged. "But you were reportedly quite distressed that day."

"I was."

"But it wasn't due to sensory overload?"

"I mean, that was part of it, yeah, but it was more that I hate how people were acting to what was happening."

"What did you observe?"

"The deaths weren't an accident. You know, I saw Celia doing bad things."

"What did she do?"

Several seconds passed by before he spoke again. "There's a killer in this clinic."

Alyssa again looked at Abby. Abby took over the speaking. "I don't know if you're aware of this, Jeff, but Celia died a year ago in the fire."

"Yeah, I know that, but she didn't do this on her own."

"How do you know?"

"Celia was always on her phone, you know?" He sat quietly for a few seconds. "She spoke freely in front of me, because she thought I was a vegetable, and I hate her. I heard her coordinating with another person."

"Who?"

"I don't know, but I hate them as well. She was planning to kill that Chinese guy."

"Wing Zhen," Abby sighed. "And are you aware she accomplished that?"

"Yeah, I know."

"But she didn't accomplish it the way she had in mind," Abby continued. "I somehow doubt getting herself killed was part of the plan."

"It wasn't. She was getting money for it, you know?"

Alyssa nodded. "But something went wrong. An accident of some sort."

"Not an accident. Sabotage."

"What kind of sabotage?"

"I don't know, but after the fire, I heard someone say how the investigators found a door release wasn't plugged in properly."

"I don't understand," Alyssa scratched her head. "How can you be so sure that was sabotage?"

"The IT guy comes in every night and checks everything, you know? He's very thorough."

"So, you're saying he sabotaged the wire to the door lock?"

"No, I'm saying it was fine when he left the night before the fire. I'm saying somebody unplugged it after that."

Alyssa frowned. "Sorry, Jeff, but I'm still unclear about this. How can you be sure about that? The IT guy could have made that mistake."

"If he did, the door wouldn't have opened for Celia. The wire to the door was tampered with after she went in to see the Chinese guy, Wing."

Abby looked at Alyssa. "That narrows down the when."

Alyssa nodded. "It does, yes."

Abby resumed the conversation with Jeff. "Robert was able to get you evacuated, is that correct?"

There was more silence for a while. "Is he that old guard who complains all the time?"

"Yes."

"Then yeah. I may hate him, but he saved me."

This time, it was Alyssa who paused for a few seconds. "Why do you hate him?"

"I hate everyone who can function. They get to live their lives, but I don't." Jeff took a deep breath and let it out. "I hate the doctor, too. He promised me some help, but nothing happened."

"Um," Alysa began, "I should probably tell you that the doctor did recommend help for you, but the owner of this facility rejected the idea. He wouldn't let it happen."

"Then I hate him as well."

Abby nodded. "That's fair."

"The owner has been trying to break his lease, and the doctor is real messed up, you know?"

"Why is the doctor messed up?"

"When he's checking up on me, he says a lot of things about how much people irritate him."

"And how do you know the owner is trying to break his lease?"

"I already told you. People speak freely around me, especially on their phones, and nobody more than Celia. She loved to gossip and talk trash about people, you know?"

"Listen, Jeff," Alyssa took in a deep breath. "Is there anything you heard Celia talking about that might help us with our investigation?"

"And," Abby added, "if I can get this case wrapped up, I promise I can help get you much better treatment."

"You know, I used to hate you as well, Abby."

Abby made a face. "Used to? When did that change?"

"Just in these last few minutes, when you took me in here and actually spoke to me like I was a person."

"I will continue doing that, Jeff. You deserve it. Now, Celia?"

"Celia's sister, Jenny, runs an adult website. I hear Celia arguing with her on the phone. Celia screams at her to shut it down, but it sounds like Jenny is telling Celia to stay out of her business. They were fighting about this a lot."

Abby pressed the mute button on her phone, and turned to Alyssa. "This is amazing. Why didn't we talk to this guy sooner?"

Alyssa closed her eyes. "You mean aside from his inability to respond, and his neural overload and resulting response paralysis? No reason."

Abby un-muted the phone. "That's great information, Jeff. Did they sort it out?"

"I think so. Celia promised to send Jenny a lot of money to shut down the website, and take a training program for what Celia referred to as a real job."

"Did Jenny accept?"

"It sounded like it."

Alyssa cleared her throat. "Jeff, I need to ask you this. How are you managing in that dark room?"

"I hated it at first, but at least I can think." There was a brief silence. "And in here, I can lift my arms and legs, so that's cool, too."

"My turn." Abby took over the phone. "If I could make your regular room silent and dark, would you prefer that?"

"Yeah. I'd hate it, but it's better than the way it is now. I hate that even more."

"In that case, I'll make that happen."

"Great." Jeff sniffed. "Can we talk some more about how much I hate peas?"

Monday: 11:20 a.m.

Luis Garcia shuffled toward the security desk. When he arrived, he rapped on the counter with his knuckles. Robert turned in his swivel chair, looked at his watch, then scowled at Luis. "You're here early."

"I know." Luis fidgeted. "Um, before you head off on your break, we should probably talk about a few things. Can I have a minute?"

"No, you can't have a minute, pal." Robert poked the air with his finger. "You took my job, so you think I'm going to let you take one of my minutes as well? If you want to take something, how about a hike?"

"I don't understand why you can't let bygones be bygones."

"Because it isn't just the bygones that bug me about you." Robert stood up and glared at him. "The *herenows* are pissing me off every bit as much."

"Listen, Rob, if we work together, we can both succeed here. After all, a rising tide lifts all boats."

"So do tsunamis, but that doesn't make them good."

"You never know what will happen down the road." Luis gave a reassuring nod. "Not getting that promotion could end up being a blessing in disguise."

"If it is, then the blessing isn't just in disguise, it also had facial surgery, took on a new identity, and moved to the Botswana desert."

Luis made a face. "The Kalahari?"

Robert raised his eyebrows. "I don't even like fried squid, so why would you bring that up? You know what, never mind." He began walking away from the desk. "I'll be back in thirty."

Monday: 11:55 a.m.

Abby knocked on the doctor's door, and then opened it. She peered inside and saw Dr. Friesen putting on his coat. "Can I bother you for a moment?"

"If it was just for a moment, then you'd set a record today for who bothered me the least."

"I was wondering if you had a comment about this." Abby turned Celia's phone around and showed Friesen the photo she had on the screen. "You're not the sort of person I'd imagine in leather restraints." She turned the phone back towards herself. "Now that I look closer, they might be hospital-issue restraints." She glanced at him. "Have you been taking your work home with you?"

"Wherever did you get that picture?"

"It was on Celia's phone, along with a few others."

"Her phone was found?"

Abby looked at him closely. "You knew it was missing?"

"Not as such, no, but I was under the impression her phone was burned in the fire."

"The way you said that sounded really suspicious."

"Sorry, I'm just surprised it suddenly turned up, a year after the fact, that's all."

"You two seemed to have an interesting relationship."

"That's one way of describing it, I suppose."

"You seem… I don't know… *uneasy* right now."

"Well, of course I'm feeling uneasy. Celia's death hit me rather hard."

Abby glanced back at the photo. "Based on some of those red marks I see, it looks like she'd hit you rather hard, too." She put the phone into her pocket. "Celia had a reputation for being with people who could help her to get what she wanted. Would you say that description was accurate?"

"Oh, yes. I most certainly would."

"What did she want from you?"

"You know, she never specifically told me. Perhaps it was power, influence, or a simple boost to her ego."

"To what end?"

"Who knows? Maybe it was to fill the empty, superficial void she clearly had inside of her."

"If you don't know, then I need you to make your best guess."

"If I had to guess, and I clearly do, then I'd say she was using me to get free therapy."

"And were you giving her therapy?"

"In a manner of speaking, I suppose. I would sit and listen to whatever she wanted to say, try to help her through whatever she mentioned, and then give her advice. Nothing extraordinary."

"And she, in turn, gave you companionship."

"Yes. I'm old, not dead, so one takes what one can get sometimes."

"She had compromising photos of you on her phone. Some people might look at that as a motive for murder."

"I suppose some people might, indeed, but I might also point out that the word *compromising* is entirely subjective. We were two, single, consenting adults, so whatever we did or wore in the privacy of our bedrooms was our own business. There was nothing scandalous in the photos, in my view, and it certainly wouldn't have hurt my career had the pictures made it to my employer."

"I guess."

"Now, if you're quite done with your attempts to embarrass me, I'd like to head out for lunch."

Monday: 12:18 p.m.

Cenk Vollack frowned. "Lunch was, once again, as big a tragedy as a burning orphanage. Take my lowest meal rating so far, and then place that lunch beneath it."

"Maybe dinner could be better." Abby met his gaze.

"I want to doubt it could be any worse, but I'd rather not tempt fate. Do you have a proposition in mind?"

"I do, actually, yes." Abby sat on the edge of his bed. "Another sandwich from across the street if you help me with my next steps."

"That depends." Vollack spent the next few seconds coughing. "How far have you gotten into what I asked you to investigate?"

"Quite far, actually."

"Do tell."

"For one thing, I'm pretty sure Celia's sister Jenny didn't set the fire, because she was across town the whole day."

"Ah, I see." Vollack wagged his eyebrows. "Then it appears we do need to make that sandwich arrangement."

"Done. Okay, so what do I have wrong?"

"Your turn of phrase, for starters." Vollack sat up higher in the bed. "Perhaps it would be more accurate for you to have said you *believe* she was across town. If you are to be a great detective, Abby, then you need to dig deeper. Peel back more layers, and see what they reveal. Only then, will you find the truth."

"I already saw in Celia's will that her entire estate would go to her sister, Jenny, so that's who I need to speak to for more information and answers."

"Well done, Abby." Vollack beamed. "I once again need to say I underestimated you. Yes, Celia's sister is, indeed, where the money trail leads, so you've successfully solved that part of the puzzle."

"Okay, then. So, what's next?"

"It's time to see if you're worthy of calling yourself a detective. Once you've spoken to Celia's sister, you'll have all of the pieces, assuming you ask her the right questions. All that will be left to do after that is to find out how all the pieces fit together. If you succeed, then the murder charges against your troubled girlfriend will get dropped, and if you fail, then she's here for decades."

"It doesn't feel like I have enough of the pieces, but I'll give it my best shot."

"You have everything you need." Vollack extended his hand. "Now, help me up. I'm going for my walk now."

"I'll walk with you, because I still have some more questions."

Abby helped pull Vollack up, and he maneuvered his feet into a pair of waiting slippers on the floor. He linked elbows with Abby, and the two shuffled their way into the hallway.

They walked for nearly a minute until Vollack broke the silence. "Well?"

"Well what?"

"You said you had some more questions."

"Oh, right. I've seen your file, and I noticed your behaviour changed shortly after Doctor Friesen showed up. You began being more, well, *demonic* after that."

"Indeed." Vollack coughed. "He's a very clever man, so the change was necessary."

"Yeah, he's… wait a second." Abby wagged her finger. "You didn't say he was clever as a compliment, did you? You said it in response to what I said."

"Then it would seem the good doctor is not the only clever person on staff." He grinned at her. "Tell me what you're thinking."

"I'm only guessing here, but after meeting Dr. Friesen the first time, you probably realized he'd eventually figure out you weren't a paranoid schizophrenic, so you'd be at risk of being forced to leave here."

"And…?"

Abby thought for a few seconds. "And so you changed your symptoms to a delusional person who thinks himself a demon in order to remain here."

"You may be far from being a great detective, Abby, but you've already shown you're a good one."

"We were looking at your behavioural patterns over the past few years, and as best as we can tell, the days you are at your most demon-like are when the doctor is visiting you."

"Clever."

"So, I'm right about your symptom changes?"

"Yes. Yes, you are." Vollack coughed. "Doctor Friesen asked me a lot of questions when we first met, and although I presented all the right symptoms to him, his line of questioning progressed and he was constantly adapting to my answers. I could tell what he was doing. He was suspicious of me, and likely saw through my charade. At first, I wasn't certain what to do, but then it dawned on me. The doctor is a man deeply-rooted in facts, logic, and science, so the best way to convince him I was ill was to tell him the truth."

"Because everyone knows demons aren't real."

"Precisely. But in a mind like yours which is… well, *less* rooted in logic and reason, you will be more likely to take what I say at face value."

"You must have wanted me to learn your secret, or you wouldn't have given me the Cardinal's name."

Vollack's brow furrowed. "I wanted to help you solve your first case in order for the guilty to be punished, but unless I established my credibility in a way you'd accept, I didn't think you'd welcome my assistance."

Abby whistled. "You'd be surprised. Some of the best friends I've had through my life are currently locked away in institutions of one kind or another. I think they're the sane ones, and they're locked up for their own protection; not society's safety."

"So, was that everything you wanted to ask me?"

"No, there's one more thing. I think I've figured it out. You're not *possessed* by a demon; you *are* the demon."

Vollack beamed. "Very good."

"You're Cardinal Francis Russo, aren't you?"

Vollack smiled. "No, but he is the one who summoned me. I took over his body just before he died, but I am not him." His smile then vanished, and he sighed. "How unfortunate."

"What's unfortunate?"

"That you've learned the truth."

"Why's that so bad?"

"Because it means I'm going to need to slip away and start over somewhere else."

"Just like that?"

"Just like that." Vollack beamed. "Done it at least a dozen times already."

"Seriously?"

"Oh, sure. This body is getting too old and too sick, anyway, so I need to find a new willing host."

"Where will you find a willing host?"

"Out there," he gestured toward the nearest window. "There's addicts and ill people galore out there, who would welcome a controller who will set them on a better path."

"But how will you get out of here to slip away?"

"I know I can trust you, Abby, so I'll tell you one strategy I most recently used." He lowered his voice. "Over a period of weeks, I make a remarkable and steady recovery. I'll eventually be able to get day passes, and then one day I won't return from one of them. You forget that I've had more than three hundred years' practice with this sort of thing."

"Right, because you were born in 1701."

"No, I entered this world in 1701, but I guess that's close enough. It's so much nicer here than the Netherworld."

The two crossed the main foyer in silence until they were out of earshot of the security desk and beginning down the next hallway.

"Where will you go from here?"

"Are you really asking me that question?" Vollack gave Abby an incredulous look. "It would defeat the purpose of starting over if I let anyone know where I was going, wouldn't it?"

"I suppose it would," Abby admitted. "How do you disappear?"

"That's my little secret, but I'll tell you one of the ways I've done it in the past. I just slip into the masses of homeless people in the city, because people go out of their way to not notice them. Makes it really easy for me to disappear in plain sight in the least amount of time. From there, I can slip away and blend in pretty much anywhere until I'm ready to re-enter a different society under a different name."

"But why do you need to leave?"

"Because people don't take kindly to things they don't understand." Vollack coughed again. "I'd be hunted down and likely murdered by a mob of hysterical people, because that's how it always ends."

"Only if word gets out."

"Word has gotten out."

"Has it?" Abby smirked. "I know what you really are, but nobody else does, and nobody else needs to know."

"I appreciate that, Abby, but I am unwilling to take that chance, as the risks are too great. If anyone even suspects I'm not of this world, then things will inevitably get somewhat fiery and pitchfork-like."

"It doesn't have to."

He scoffed. "Tell that to the general public."

"You've been helping me to solve my first case, and it's because of you my maybe-still-girlfriend has a chance at a future outside of a locked cell. That buys a lot of loyalty and silence from me, so I'm not going to be the one to rat you out. As far as anyone needs to know, you're a delusional patient who needs to be here."

"I have very little faith in humanity as a whole, but occasionally, and very rarely, I meet someone like you who gives me a faint glimmer of hope."

"Thanks. Nobody's ever said that to me before. And you know what? I think I've figured out how it all works. The demon thing, I mean."

"Very well, then let me hear your theory."

"Angels and demons are the same things. Because people automatically sort stuff out into good and evil, the same beings got double-labeled. When the beings did things people liked, they were looked upon as angels, but when they did things that people didn't like, then they applied the demon label. As time went on, the story about what angels and demons are evolved into what we know today, even though it's no longer anything like how it started."

"Bravo, Abby."

"It was Santa Claus who gave me the idea."

"Then be sure to pass along my appreciation to him when Christmas comes around. I don't often say this to anyone, but I was wrong about you." Vollack pointed at her. "You're a bright young woman with an even brighter future."

"No, I don't have much of a future."

"Why not?"

"Because I'm dying." Abby scuffed at the floor with her foot. "The doctor I saw two years ago said I had from two to four years left to live, because of my damaged organs, so I could drop dead at any moment now."

"Nonsense," he roared. "You do need a liver transplant, that's true, but otherwise your organs are healthy."

"Are you sure?"

"I'm an angel and a demon rolled into one, so what do you think?"

"But he said there was damage to my organs."

"There certainly is, but they have been healing over those two years." Vollack winked. "The whole *four years to live* nonsense must have been based on how you were back then. Your liver is going to give out sooner rather than later, but otherwise, you're fine. Get your name on the transplant list immediately, because there's often a year's wait or longer."

"So, if I get a new liver and the transplant is successful, I'll live past thirty?"

"I don't know how long you'll live, but if you die young, it won't be from your other organs giving out." Vollack cleared his throat. "There's no reason you can't live to be seventy or eighty at least, assuming you stop scaling high rises, that is."

"That news really comes as a relief."

"Yes," he smiled, "I thought it might."

Monday: 1:07 p.m.

Abby was bringing Malcolm up to date on her recent findings.

"That was a good idea Jeff had, looking into Celia's family." He gave her a thumbs-up. "I'm surprised I didn't think of that right away myself. So, what did you discover?"

"Celia's sister runs an adult website."

"When you say adult website, what exactly do you mean? Is she like a porn star or something?"

"More or less. Well, more *more* and less *less*, if I'm being accurate. She has a private channel online where people can send her money to get a private X-rated video chat with her."

Malcolm blinked. "That's a thing?"

"Yeah, that's how some people make their money."

"Jesus. I had no idea." Malcolm looked horrified. "How would that even work?"

"The client electronically transfers funds to her, and then she sends them a link, and they engage in a steamy video call."

"Well, someone needs to question her, and I sure as hell am not going to be the one to do that. Mary'd have a fit if I submitted a porn receipt to the federal government as a tax deduction. Besides, at my age, *friends with benefits* means they'll help me move, or drive me to the airport."

"No, I'll question her tonight." Abby shrugged. "We need answers, and she has them, so leave her to me. I'll let Alyssa know the plan, too."

Monday: 7:27 p.m.

Abby sat in her small basement room, laptop computer open and connected. She had entered a video chat with Jenny Ocampo, who had just introduced herself. Jenny winked at Abby. "To be honest, I should add that you're the first woman client I've had so far, so

I'll need your help to get us started. What sorts of things are you into?"

"Women, obviously, but also men when I feel like it."

"I'm asking more about what you want me to do for you today."

Abby shrugged. "How about we start by you taking your clothes off, and we'll go from there."

"That's a good start."

"No, don't bother being all teasing-like. Just remove your clothes slowly, and drop them on the floor."

"Sure thing." She removed her clothes, one piece at a time, until there was nothing left. "What do you want me to do next?"

"I want you to just sit there in the chair and let me ask you some interesting questions."

"That could be fun," Jenny purred. "Go ahead and ask me anything."

"How did your sister come up with enough money to pay off everything she owed in the space of a month?"

"Wait, what is this? What kind of question is that to ask? Who are you, anyway?"

"You're asking way too many questions, and I've already forgotten the first one. You're the one who said I could ask you anything, and that's what I wanted to ask."

"But you can't ask about that, because it's out of bounds."

"You took off your clothes for a total stranger, but asking you an employment question was the thing that crossed a line for you?"

"Are you a cop?"

"Definitely not. Cops have all those boring rules and behaviour guidelines."

"If you're not a cop, how *exactly* did you know my sister?"

"We were colleagues," Abby lied. "We worked together at the clinic. Listen, I'm the one paying for this chat session, so I get to ask the questions. If you want to ask me questions, then you have to pay me for the answers."

"If you just wanted to ask me questions, why get me to strip?"

"I have three really good reasons. The first is I know from experience people are less likely to lie when they're naked."

"And the second reason?"

"I told you that when we first started." Abby shrugged. "I like women."

"I'm very uncomfortable now, so I don't want to do this anymore. I think we're done here, so I don't even want to hear the third reason."

"Actually, you will want to hear it, because it's the most important reason of all. I needed some time before I started asking you questions, and I couldn't risk you disconnecting too early. By getting you to remove your clothes slowly, I got the time I needed."

"The time you needed for what?"

"To trace your signal. So, you can answer all my questions right now for the money I sent you, or I can ask them at your private residence after I empty your bank account and leave you with nothing."

"You're really bad at lying. I'm going to take my chances and disconnect now."

"Fine, then I'll see you shortly, at 9760 Lougheed Highway, in apartment 2420. Looks like you're three blocks east of the mall. That's a convenient location, actually. You're close to shopping, transit, and necessities. Your bank account number is 5672–"

"Stop, stop, stop! How did you...?"

"I told you. I traced your IP address. It takes three minutes for me to get an accurate location, so as I said, I needed to buy some time. Literally, as it turns out. Also, I've been recording this session, so I'll be able to send it to anyone I want, including the *Canada Revenue Agency*. I'm betting you don't declare the income you make doing your weird video chats, so chances are good you're committing tax fraud; a felony the federal government tends to get really upset about."

"Stop recording, and I'll answer anything you ask."

"Deal."

"Can I put my clothes back on?"

Abby raised her eyebrow. "I paid for this session, so what do you think?"

* * * * *

"Okay," Abby prompted. "And then what?"

Jenny looked annoyed. "After my sister passed away, I was the one who had to pay off her debts."

Abby folded her arms. "No, her debts were completely paid off two weeks before she died, so try again."

Jenny shrugged. "Then God must have answered her prayers, what can I say?"

"I'm pretty sure gods don't do financial transactions, or all those preachers wouldn't need to keep praying for donations."

"I certainly hope you're not accusing me of stealing or anything. I'm not a vulture."

"I don't consider you a vulture at all. You're more like something a vulture would eat."

"I don't like you insulting me."

"And I don't like being lied to, so I guess that makes us even."

"Regardless," Jenny fumed, "my sister was a victim in this terrible tragedy, and it's sick that you'd try to smear her memory with this ugly accusation."

"I haven't accused her of anything yet, but this is where the money trail ends. Trying to deflect my questions just makes me more curious and convinced you're hiding something. None of this is personal, you know. These are just the facts."

"It's still immoral."

"You're the one who uses the online screen name of *HotVixen4U,* so you might want to skip the whole morality thing you're trying to guilt me with. So, last chance, or your next call will be from the government's tax department."

"Fine. Ugh. I'll tell you everything."

Tuesday: 8:05 a.m.

Malcolm had been waiting for Luis Garcia to begin his shift, and found him starting his daily site patrol.

"There you are. Hey, kid. Come here a second."

Luis tensed up as he approached Malcolm. "Yes?"

"Relax, will you? I come in peace."

"Okay."

"Can I ask you a few personal questions?"

Luis exhaled. "I... I guess that's okay."

"Good. Let's start with this one. Do you have any life ambitions?"

"Yes, I have a lot of ambition, but..."

After a couple of awkward seconds of silence, Malcolm prompted him. "But what?"

"Right now, everything in my life is on hold."

"No, if you want to be successful in life, you can't be putting things on hold." Malcolm frowned. "What made you wake up one day and think *my hopes and dreams are like everyone else's. I want to be a security guard in the most insignificant clinic in town*?"

"With my dad injured, my mom needs help with the bills." Luis stared at the floor. "So, around a year and a half ago, I suspended my studies, got the job at the hospital, and have been doing whatever I can to help her out."

"Jesus, I had no idea." Malcolm scuffed one of his feet on the floor. "What happened to your dad?"

"A workplace accident at a construction site left him with shattered legs. He was a private contractor, so he didn't have much in the way of extended health benefits. Disability payments help, but it's nowhere near enough to cover the expenses."

"So, you're just working as a guard to help your family until your dad is able to work again."

"Yes."

"And the reason you don't know what you're doing in five years is because you don't know how long your dad's injuries will take to fully heal."

"That's right." Luis nodded. "His bones have healed, but he needs more surgeries to repair the rest of his nerves, muscles, tendons, and stuff. Then, after all that, he'll need to learn how to walk again."

"And when he is fully healed and able to walk, you're going to go to college or something?"

"Yes, I'll be going back to continue my Business Administration courses in university, but I'll have to save money first. We spent my tuition funds on my dad."

Malcolm scowled. "I hate absolutely *everything* about that."

"Why?"

"Because it's sensible, responsible, noble, and other positive words ending in *B-L-E*, which means I've been acting like a total jerk toward you." Malcolm looked Luis in the eye. "I'm sorry."

"For what?"

"For thinking you were a slacker, and then acting like a total jackass toward you."

"You weren't being a jackass."

"Yeah, I was."

"Okay, yes, you were." Luis fidgeted. "So, what happens now?"

"Now? What happens now? I'll tell you what happens now." Malcolm put his hand on Luis' shoulder. "The first thing that happens is I apologize to you. And I'm truly sorry for insulting you, and for thinking the worst of you."

"Accepted."

"If you can put your own life on hold to help your family, then you're a better man than I thought you were, and that brings me to the second thing that happens. You're going to ask Alyssa out."

"And you're cool with that?"

"Hell no, but I'm going to have to learn how to be cool with it, damn it. With that in mind, can I offer you some advice?"

"That'd be great."

"Okay, I'm a very basic kind of guy, so I know there are lots of things I'll never understand, like can it ever be warm in a country called Chile? Is a million bigger than a Brazilian? And is a large man from Helsinki a big Finnish?" Malcolm removed his hand from Luis shoulder. "But those aren't the big questions in life. No, what I'm really good at understanding are the small but important parts, such as knowing who I can trust, because I happen to have the world's best-functioning built-in bastard detector."

"I can see how that would be a handy life skill to have."

"It really is. But you see, I'm not the sort of man who wastes time contemplating life's big questions. For example, I don't know why *tough* and *though* don't rhyme even though they're almost spelled the same. No, I'm the sort of guy who cares more about the things that can be addressed through outrage."

"Outrage?"

"Yeah, outrage." Malcolm punched the air with his fist. "Hot dog buns are sold twelve to a pack but the wieners are sold eight to a pack, and that won't change until people let their outrage spur those changes on."

"I don't think hot dogs are a big enough problem for people to be outraged over."

"No, but here's where I'm going with this." Malcolm locked eyes with him. "I don't know how life on earth began, but I have several ideas around how yours could end. So, don't do anything that will cause me to feel outrage."

"I won't."

Malcolm flashed a smile. "Good."

"Um, you look a little pale. Are you okay?"

"Yeah, I think so." Malcolm massaged his temples. "I just have so many mixed emotions right now."

"Do you need to sit down?"

"No, I think I'll be okay… eventually."

Luis gestured toward the hallway. "I guess I'd better…"

"Be on your best behavior?"

"Well, yes, but I was going to say I'd better get back to work." Luis stepped back. "But I'm glad we had this talk."

"Yeah, me too. I'm also glad we understand one another."

"We definitely do." Luis turned and retreated down the corridor.

Tuesday: 9:07 a.m.

Alyssa and Malcolm met Abby in the laundry area. Malcolm asked Abby how her meeting with Jenny Ocampo had gone, and Abby laid out everything she'd learned, though not the details as to how, seeing as both Malcolm and Alyssa had made it clear they didn't want any of those kinds of details.

"Jesus, Jenny Ocampo gave you a hell of a lot more information than she gave the cops." He shook his head. "We read all the stuff Neil Browne sent me, and she wasn't anywhere near as forthcoming. How did you manage that?"

"I can be very persuasive when I need to be."

"So, Jenny confirmed that Wing's wife set the plan in motion, and ended up taking home quite the insurance payout."

"Yeah, she did."

"But we only have Jenny's words as evidence. Wing's wife was in Taiwan when the fire broke out, so she has an iron-clad alibi." Malcolm looked at his pages of notes he'd spread out across the washer. "And as soon as she heard about the fire, she grabbed the next flight back here. How much was Wing Zhen insured for?"

"Just shy of two million dollars."

Malcolm whistled. "What made him worth so much?"

"He was some sort of import-export big shot."

"What was he importing and exporting?"

"Equipment, electronics, and parts for a lot of military stuff. Aircraft, ships, tanks, trucks, radar, and other stuff in acronyms I don't understand. He hadn't worked since his stroke, but his insurance policy hadn't been updated. He died before the insurance company could send an updated policy."

"And two million bucks can make a lot of short-term friends who are willing to do all kinds of things."

Abby nodded. "Yeah, but here's the weird thing. A week before the fire, Wing's soon-to-be-widow took out a bank draft for a quarter of a million dollars before she left for Taiwan."

"How do you know that?"

"I accessed her accounts. For your own peace of mind, don't ask me how."

"I won't. The bank draft... who was it made payable to?"

Abby shrugged. "It doesn't say, but it could have been to Celia. It would explain why her debts were suddenly cleared off, and for her to have eighty grand in her bank account."

Malcolm pondered this. "So, it could be she was simply taking the money to her family in Taiwan, or, at the other end of the spectrum, maybe she was paying somebody to do something flame-related here before leaving on her alibi vacation."

Alyssa spoke up. "She could be the one who set all this in motion, but nothing we've found so far can confirm that. Meaning it's a theory, but a bit of a stretch."

"No, popping my shoulder back into place is a bit of a stretch." Malcolm began pacing. "The idea of an honest politician is a bit of a stretch. This could very easily be something where no stretches are needed whatsoever, and as stretch-free as watching a movie in a recliner."

Abby sat on the edge of the dryer. "When I accessed Celia's financial records, I saw she'd had some serious money problems, and owed a lot of money. Her credit cards were maxed-out, and seven weeks before she died, her leased vehicle had been seized by a bailiff because she had defaulted on her payments."

Alyssa shrugged. "To be fair, a lot of people are experiencing financial hardship these days, so it's normal and doesn't necessarily mean anything."

Abby shook her head. "No, but a little over a month later, she died completely debt-free, and if you remember, I mentioned how she suddenly had eighty grand in her bank account."

"Okay," Alyssa exhaled, "it's considerably *less* normal when you remind me of that. Good point."

"But I don't get it." Abby frowned. "Why would she trade her life for money? It's not like debt follows you into the grave. It's almost better to die owing money."

Malcolm stopped pacing. "Not really, because then your beneficiaries have to deal with the money problems as they settle the estate. It's not like Celia had starving children or anything, so why trade her life for cash? It doesn't make sense."

"Then again, Jeff did say someone sabotaged the door." Abby wagged a finger in the air. "And if that's the case, then it does make sense."

"How?"

"What if…" Abby stared into the middle distance until she had the right words. "What if she'd been paid to kill Wing for the insurance money, got paid some or all of the cash up front, and then someone found out about the deal, and made sure the security door failed once the room filled up with smoke. Maybe that saboteur wanted to make sure Celia was deliberately silenced."

"Interesting theory." Malcolm gave an appreciative nod to her. "So, Celia might have been trying to make Wing's death look like Zee did it, but the plan went sideways, and she ended up dying along with the victim."

"Exactly." Abby looked into his eyes. "My guess is the soon-to-be widow made sure Celia died, too, in order for there to be one less loose end who could possibly blackmail her down the road."

"Meaning Mrs. Zhen could be our accomplice."

"Wait a second." Alyssa scrunched her face in confusion. "How is Mrs. Zhen connected to Celia?"

"I know that answer." Abby smiled. "Celia knew Wing's family, because Wing's wife came to visit him often and got to know Celia, as she was his primary caregiver. Wing wasn't going to recover and he was heavily insured, so maybe his wife decided to go for the insurance money. We already know Celia was deep in debt, so perhaps all it took for Celia to kill was a little nudge from the wife."

Malcolm nodded. "Yeah, I mean, as a working theory, it's all there."

"Not quite," Abby frowned. "Mrs. Zhen may be the one who organized everything, but she wasn't there the day of the fire. We know someone was helping Celia do what she did, but it couldn't be Mrs. Zhen."

"Which means," Malcolm held up his index finger, "we still have at least one more bastard to identify."

Tuesday: 10:06 a.m.

Abby stood inside the doorway of Zee's room. Despite Zee's offers, Abby declined to enter the room any further. She continued her discussion with Zee. "And Alyssa's cousin Tony will represent you for free when you make your next court appearance."

"Tell her I appreciate it."

"I will."

Zee buried her face in her hands. "This all sucks so much."

"What does?"

"Us. Me and you." Zee's finger points went back and forth between herself to Abby. "I can't believe I screwed up our relationship. I really want to make things right, because this is such a dumb situation."

"Yeah, it's as if it's straight out of one of those cheesy sitcoms."

"Or a bad novel." Zee reflected on that thought. "Wait, now that I think about it, a situation like this would never be in a novel. Fiction has to make sense, and nobody in their right mind would make up something as weird as what's been happening here these past few days."

"Yeah, that's a fair point."

"I need to say this."

Abby didn't respond. She just waited for Zee to continue.

"Abby, it doesn't matter to me if you're on the spectrum, off the charts, up the creek, or down in the mouth. I love you how you are."

"I know you do. And I think you're amazing, too. But I'm going to need some time. Trust is number one to me, and we don't have that right now."

"Can I earn that trust back?"

Abby stared at her own shoes. "I hope so. Let's take it a day at a time and see how it goes."

Tuesday: 10:18 a.m.

Robert groaned loudly enough that his voice echoed off the walls. "Oh, not you again."

Alyssa approached and exaggerated her smile. "And it's so nice to see you, too."

"You're now officially my favorite person, aside from every other person I've ever met in my life." He glared at her. "What the hell do you want now?"

"I just want to make a suggestion."

"I have a suggestion for you, as well, but it may not be physically possible." He sighed and rubbed his head. "What's the suggestion?"

"You should think about burying the hatchet with Luis Garcia."

"I have thought about it, but I can't decide."

"Decide what?"

"Whether to bury the hatchet in his head, neck, or spine."

Alyssa folded her arms. "So, violence is your go-to response whenever you're feeling threatened?"

"Don't be stupid. Violent thoughts aren't the same as violent actions, and you know it. I've never harmed anyone who hasn't harmed me first. Luis has earned my wrath and contempt, that back-stabbing little runt. He even looks like the kind of guy who'd betray someone."

"And you look like the kind of guy who could use up his entire vocabulary in a single sentence, but I don't hold that against you. Listen, Luis isn't a bad person, no matter what you think he looks like. I guess what I'm saying is, you can't judge a book by its cover."

"If I designed book covers, I'd be offended by that, but I'm not, so it's just a stupid saying."

Alyssa blinked at him. "Why?"

"Because you're comparing Luis to a book."

"And what's the problem with that?"

"Books are informative, useful, and don't stab you in the back."

Alyssa folded her arms. "Maybe we should take a moment to discuss the chip."

"What chip?"

"The giant one you've got on your shoulder."

"Great." Robert grunted with disgust. "Another wannabe comedian. Listen, kiddo, I've been passed over for promotion more times than you've had birthdays, so cut me some slack. Yeah, sure, I'm bitter, and maybe I do have a chip on my shoulder, and yeah, I'm not shy about letting the whole world know how I feel about getting shafted, but here's the interesting part. None of that shit is any of your goddamned business."

"If it's tied in any way to our inquiry, then it is my business."

"But it isn't tied to your inquiry."

"Oh, but it is."

He rubbed his face and shook his head. "What do you want from me? If I throw a stick, will you leave?"

Alyssa ignored the insult and pressed on. "Did you know Celia's phone was found?"

"No, because I didn't even know it was missing."

"Well, it was, and she has photos of you on it, plus text messages, emails, and more. You told me you viewed your relationship with her as purely transactional, but it's clear from what we saw that you were in love with her."

"Alright, sure. Maybe I was in love with her, so what? You going to call the cops and have me charged with *Being Attracted to a Sexy Woman with Intent* or some stupid shit like that?"

"No, but when she left you for the doctor, you didn't take it as well as you pretended."

"As I've said before, and I'll say one final time: none of this is any of your business."

"And, as I've said before, and will repeat again: if it pertains to the case, then it is very much my business. A jilted lover, dumped by his colleague in favour of another colleague sounds like a plausible motive for murder to me. Your messages to her after the breakup show that you didn't take the news well."

"Fine, sure, yeah, she broke my heart. I knew our relationship was temporary, I knew it would end, so it wasn't supposed to hurt, but it did anyway. Are you happy now? I tried to win her back and failed, so, yeah, I hated both her and the doctor because of it. And," he pointed at Alyssa, "just in case, this hasn't yet registered in your brain, you can hate someone without killing them."

"I know, and I'm not saying you killed anyone at this point, but your bitterness is affecting everyone else, too, including Luis Garcia. Why do you hate him?"

Robert stared at his computer screen for a moment, frowning. He then shrugged. "Luis is a good kid. Dumb as shit, but still a good kid. Look, I know he doesn't deserve to be on the receiving end of my anger, but life obviously doesn't give a shit about what I care about, or what's fair, so what goes around, comes around. Listen, I don't want to talk anymore, alright? I need you to leave."

Alyssa nodded and went back toward the hallway.

Tuesday: 10:44 a.m.

Abby knocked on Cenk Vollack's door and opened it. She peered inside. "Do you have a moment?"

Vollack, who was sitting up in bed, nodded. "Certainly."

Abby entered the room and closed the door. She leaned against the wall beside the door. "I need your help."

Vollack smiled and shook his head. "I've told you all I can, Abby Lunay. There is nothing left for me to tell you."

"Maybe there is. I've figured out who killed Celia, and I've also figured out how they did it, but I'm completely stuck when it comes to figuring out the why and the other why."

"Fascinating. First, who is your suspect?"

Abby locked eyes with him. "You are."

"Ah, how I do enjoy a good plot twist." He grunted as he swung his legs around so his feet could touch the floor. "You're wrong, of course, but how in heaven's name did the pieces I gave you point you to that conclusion?"

"It wasn't just the pieces you gave me; it was also the pieces the rest of us collected. If you want to know how I have you as my suspect, it comes down to you being the only person left."

"How so?"

"I didn't work here at the time, and Dr. Friesen was seen at another facility, miles away, so I know neither he nor I did it. The owner of the facility was in Winnipeg, so he's out. Celia's sister Jenny is a really awful person, but she was also elsewhere that entire day, and I was able to trace her phone's IP address and location for that entire morning. Wing Zhen's wife put the plan in motion, hired Celia, and paid her off to set the fire, but Mrs. Zhen couldn't have been the one who killed Celia, because she was in Taiwan. That leaves Gina, Jeffrey, you, Luis, and Robert. Before and during the fire, I was able to account for every move Robert made, so I know it wasn't him. Luis was at the other hospital across town visiting his dad that day, so I know it wasn't him either."

"Leaving myself, Gina, and Jeffrey."

"Right. I know it wasn't Jeffrey, because he hadn't moved the entire day, including the moment the fire started. Had Robert not gotten him out, he would have died in that same spot."

"Leaving Gina and myself."

"Right. I can't account for Gina's whereabouts, as she was off camera a lot of the time, but I do know she didn't make it down to the maintenance closet, but you did, while you were taking your daily walk."

"And why is that significant?"

"Because the closet is located inside one of several blind spots where the cameras can't see, so they don't film who goes in and out of that room."

"And?"

"And you were seen entering the hallway, and then leaving the hallway six minutes later. I know how fast you walk, and it should only have taken you forty-three seconds to get from one camera to the next. The alarms and wires for the door locks for that entire section pass through the maintenance closet, including the one for Wing Zhen's room."

"Continue."

"There's nothing more to say, really." Abby's fingers drummed against the wall. "The maintenance room door wasn't kept locked, so anyone who could follow a wire could figure out which one to pull out of the socket, so the electronic door release wouldn't activate when the alarms went off. You had more than five minutes in that closet."

"Interesting. Don't stop now, keep going."

"The maintenance room also has a line of sight to Wing's room, so you waited for Celia to go in and close the door, and then you went into the closet and yanked out the wire, meaning she'd be trapped inside once the fire started. It had to be you."

"Intriguing. And why do you keep looking at me after each thing you say?"

"Because if you really are an angel-demon, then I'm expecting you to sprout some sort of wings, or something, and then attack me."

"And interrupt your explanation?" Vollack laughed. "I wouldn't dream of it."

"But now we're at the part where I'm stuck." Abby pouted. "The why and the other why."

"Let us begin with the first why."

"The first *why* is around the motive for the murder. Why did you kill her?"

"You disappoint me, Abby. I gave you everything you needed to get Celia's wretched sister Jenny imprisoned, yet, instead, you point your finger at me."

"I just followed the evidence, and it led me to you."

Vollack grunted. "This is ridiculous."

"What is?"

"You," he snapped. "You're not a detective, and you've barely got a functioning brain. It is absurd to think you didn't arrive precisely where I directed you to be."

"I'm not the brightest person, you're right about that, but do you know what? I discovered that I'm actually quite a good detective anyway, and do you know why?"

"After all of this, I need you to enlighten me. Why do you think you're a good detective?"

"I'm good because I know there's a lot of stuff that I don't know and can't do, so I get others to help me. I know I'm a hopeless case, but I'm also smart enough to surround myself with people who know the things I don't. I didn't figure out it was you on my own. I mean, sure, I did a lot of things on my own, but I also had a lot of help. I know you killed Celia. And when I told you Zee was innocent, you saw it as an opportunity to put Celia's sister away, too. But I don't know why you hate her so much."

"Don't you believe in justice?"

"No, because it doesn't exist. You're the one who taught me that."

"I never taught you any such thing."

"Yes, you did. If good and evil are subjective, then so is justice, because it also doesn't exist anywhere except inside our heads, right? Everyone's going to have a different idea of what justice is."

"Well, then I shall endeavor to tell you what *my* idea of justice is. Celia was a contemptuous villain. She accepted money to kill an innocent person. She was always on that blasted phone of hers. If I pretended to be asleep, she'd just talk, and talk, and talk into the thing. I could hear her negotiating with someone, presumably

Wing's wife. I heard her talk about putting two bags of laundry in front of the vent, and setting the bags on fire."

"So, you decided to kill a person because they were going to kill another person?"

"No, I only killed her after she set her plan in motion. Had she not gone through with it, I would not have gone through with my plan, either."

"Which leads me to my second why. Why did you want me to go after Jenny?"

"She profited from Wing Zhen's murder. Such a foul person should never reap a reward for living the contemptuous life she does."

"Now that I think about it, I actually have a third *why* to ask you."

Vollack held up his hand. "Wait, I am keen to guess. Is your question about why I would help you solve a murder which I, myself, committed?"

"Yes."

"Oh, Abby. And you were doing so well."

"What do you mean?"

"I thought you told me you understood what a demon really was."

Abby reflected on this for a moment. "You said good and evil don't exist anywhere, except inside our heads."

Vollack nodded. "Meaning?"

"Meaning to you, all actions are neither good nor evil, they just are."

"Precisely."

"But that's completely wrong."

"Really." He cocked his head. "How so?"

"I think you're right that good and evil exist only in our minds, but that doesn't mean everything just is what it is. Maybe good and evil are restricted to our minds, but we're human beings, and we need guidelines because we're so dumb."

"But who gets to decide what's good and what's evil? It's a paradox, as different people will decide different things, and the good and evil labels will therefore have no meaning."

"They'll have meaning, they just won't be the same. I guess it's up to us to argue over what's right and what's not, but without guidelines of some kind, people won't be able to function. Societies won't exist."

"That is such a primitive way to think."

"That makes sense, because we're still a primitive species." Abby walked to the door and opened it. "And I've decided something else."

"What's that?"

"You're neither an angel nor a demon." She glared at him. "You're just a very sick man who needs a whole lot of help."

Abby closed and locked the door behind her. She walked down the hallway and then spoke into the hidden microphone down her shirt. "Did you get all of that?"

Tuesday: 11:30 a.m.

Luis approached the security desk and cleared his throat. Robert turned in his chair and glared at him.

"I'm here to cover your lunch break. Anything I need to know?"

"Yeah." Robert stood up and left the desk. "A police detective signed in an hour ago. He's working with Abby and her pack of freaks."

Luis nodded. "Thanks."

"You know what?" Robert approached him. "You're a good kid, Luis, and I'm sorry you have to work with an asshole like me. Listen… we'll never be friends, but I'll try to be a better colleague, alright?"

Luis gave his head a quick shake to get past the shock. "Yes, I'd like that. I'd like it a lot."

"Good. Then never mention I said that." Robert winked at him. "See you in thirty minutes."

Tuesday: 11:33 a.m.

Abby looked at Detective Browne. "You ready?"

"The arrest warrant is in my pocket and my badge is in my hand, so hell yes, I'm ready. Let's nail this bastard." He nodded. "Go ahead and open it."

Abby placed her access card on the reader and it turned green. Browne opened the door and marched inside Cenk Vollack's room with his badge held up, while Malcolm and Abby entered behind him.

Browne's eyes widened. "What the actual hell?"

Abby scanned the room. Vollack's bed had been made, but he wasn't in it. For that matter, he wasn't anywhere else in the room.

Browne put his badge away and began to search the room, inch by inch, foot by foot, looking for anything which could be part of a hidden door or escape hatch. Malcolm checked the window and the door, but nothing was altered, broken, or otherwise adjusted.

Browne looked at Abby. "Did you let him escape?"

"No, I locked him in here."

Malcolm nodded. "She's right. I was watching the video feed. Abby went into the room alone and came out alone. The computer shows the door and window were both locked at all times."

"Then how did he escape?"

They all looked at the ceiling at the same time, as though hoping something would present itself there as an answer, but the white concrete and plaster were undisturbed and still had cobwebs in the corners.

Browne sighed and sent a weary glance in Malcolm's direction. "Can anything with you ever be straightforward? I mean seriously, how does so much weird stuff just happen all around you every day?"

Abby grinned. "So, it was true after all. Cenk Vollack really was a demon."

Browne raised his eyebrows at Malcolm. "You sure she's not a patient here?"

"Yeah." Malcolm chuckled. "You should meet her colleague, Gina."

"I somehow don't believe I should do any such thing." Browne sighed again. "I'm leaving. And I'll be keeping the twenty-four doughnuts. Next time you need someone to arrest the Invisible Man, call 911."

"What about the…" Malcolm winked. "You know, the other matter?"

"If Wing Zhen's widow sets foot back in this country, she'll be arrested on sight. Her Canadian bank account's already frozen, and if I'm successful, the judge will seize her real estate holdings and liquidate them and confiscate her bank accounts. All going well, by this time next year, the Province's *Crime Victim Assistance Program* fund will be seven digits richer."

Tuesday: 12:48 p.m.

The doctor made some notes on the sheet attached to his clipboard. "I'm sorry to hear about your problems with Abby, Zee. I'd ask how you feel about it, but I can hazard a guess on my own."

Zee continued to stare at the floor.

"Perhaps I can come at this from a slightly different angle." Friesen put the pen behind his ear. "If you could do that day with Abby all over again, what would you change?"

Zee scoffed then glared at him. "I'd obviously not lie."

"That's wonderful."

"How is that wonderful?"

He beamed. "Just a couple of months ago, you would have blamed it all on Abby, or me, or any one of dozens of other people or factors. You actually owned the blame. That's growth."

Zee took a tissue and wiped her eyes. "Then it's weird how growth makes me feel smaller."

"Today, perhaps, but over time, you'll appreciate how far you've come."

"Then that's for future Zee to enjoy. Today's Zee feels terrible, so focus on her, if you want to be useful. I think you can be most helpful by avoiding discussing my relationship failings until it hurts less."

"I like that concept, how there's things for tomorrow's Zee, versus today's Zee. That's certainly food for thought."

"If there's a link between food and thinking, then I'd recommend the buffet for you."

"Oh, you flatter me so." Friesen placed his hand on his chest in a theatrical way. "Be still, my beating heart."

"I can arrange that through a variety of methods."

"Listen, Zee, I've been thinking…"

"That explains the grinding noise."

"If you recall, we'd been working on your empathy skills and the Golden Rule."

"I remember the empathy stuff, but what rule are you talking about?"

"You don't recall us discussing the Golden Rule? It states we should all do unto others as we would have them do unto us. That doesn't ring a bell?"

"No, there's no bell-ringing at all, because that's a really stupid rule. No wonder I forgot about it."

"And why do you think it's stupid?"

"Because not everyone has my pain threshold. I know this now. Thank goodness for safe words."

"The intention behind the statement is worth exploring."

"No, it's dumb no matter how you look at it."

Friesen's brows knitted. "Then explain to me why you feel that way."

"You shouldn't treat people the way you want to be treated; you should treat them the way *they* want to be treated."

"Is that really how you feel?"

"Yes. I didn't say I was any good at putting it into practice, but yes. That's what I believe. That's the point where I'm hoping to be some day."

"I'm delighted to hear you say that." Friesen beamed. "It confirms to me, beyond a shadow of a doubt, that you're neither a sociopath nor a psychopath. My report will be recommending you have daily medication and weekly mandatory check-ins with a licensed therapist, but otherwise, there's no reason to keep you confined here."

"You mean aside from two murder convictions."

"Well, yes indeed, but you don't need to be here for that. If you're guilty, then you'll be transferred to a correctional facility. However," he retrieved the pen from behind his ear and waved it, "if our mutual friend Abby finds success, and from what I hear, I believe she already has, then you'll be released from custody once the judicial panel reviews your case."

"Wait, so… you don't think I'm crazy?"

"You're mad as a hatter, but no more so than the rest of us." Friesen made a note on the page on his clipboard. "You do need some professional help, Zee, but if you take your medication, adhere to a strict code of behaviour, and agree to regularly see a therapist, then there's no reason at all for you to be confined anywhere."

Zee nodded and looked toward the floor. "Cool."

"I rather thought you'd be jubilant at the news." Friesen put the clipboard down and leaned forward. "Are you feeling alright, Zee?"

"No, I'm okay, I guess, it's just…" Zee sat motionless for a few moments. "I mean, I really did like hearing what you just said. You know very well that since I've been here, the only thing I ever wanted was to escape this hellhole, but I don't think I'm ready to be released just yet."

"Wait, you're serious, aren't you?"

"Yeah." Zee looked through her bangs at the doctor. "I think I need some more help before I can leave here. Will you be the one to help me?"

"Absolutely." Friesen smiled. "If you're serious about your healing journey, then I'd be happy to show you the ropes."

"I likely know ropes a lot better than you do, as well as a wide variety of knots." Zee looked at him. "And by the way, I know you feed me these dumb expressions on purpose. I think you just enjoy hearing me respond to them."

"You're only half right." Friesen winked. "I really do use those expressions as part of my every-day conversations, but yes; I make an extra effort to use them around you, just for the reaction."

Zee cracked a smile. "Then maybe you need therapy, too."

Friesen chuckled. "There is certainly no doubt about that."

Tuesday: 1:36 p.m.

Abby was folding the laundry while Gina made some sort of attempt to sweep the floor. Gina enjoyed sweeping, as the broom gave her something with which to help balance herself.

"I really admire you, girl. You're getting by each day without any DUDs."

Abby looked confused. "DUDs?"

"Yeah, you know. Drinks, uppers, or downers. D-U-D."

"The drinking was literally killing me, so it was easy for me to stop when the alternative was death."

"You're so brave, Abs. I mean that."

"How am I brave?"

"Like, since the fire last year, I've spent most of my days trying to forget about it. Like, I get nightmares, and panic attacks, and stuff, right? So, I started drinking to help me sleep, and it led to all kinds of recreational adventures."

"So, when you black out and forget where you are, it's because it's exactly what you set out to do?"

"You got it." Gina attempted finger-guns, but ended up dropping the broom. "Yeah. Hundred percent. But you've been through way worse stuff than that, and you're okay." Gina tried to pick up the broom, lost her balance, and ended up on the floor. She sat up. "Do you think you could help me get off the stuff?"

"I don't know. Are you still going to Dr. Friesen for help?"

"Yeah, but I'm going to become an official patient of his. I won't be, like, in a room with these other guys, but I'll, like, see him a couple times a week in a one-on-one kind of therapy thing."

"Yeah, then sure, I'll help. He can help you deal with the trauma stuff, and I can help you deal with the other stuff."

"Awesome. You rock."

"Once you're improving, I'll help you find a better distraction than drugs."

"Like what?"

"You ever consider taking up a hobby as an assistant detective?"

Gina's face lit up. "That would so rock."

Tuesday: 2:12 p.m.

Alyssa walked Abby across the street to the small coffee shop beside the deli. Abby followed Alyssa inside, but was completely confused. "Why are we here?"

"It's your break time, and I wanted to buy you a coffee to celebrate the end of the case." Alyssa waved toward the menu. "What would you like?"

"The quad thing looks good."

"That's four shots of espresso."

"I know, it's less than I usually have, but it's the strongest thing they have."

Alyssa got in line and Abby followed her.

"There's another reason I wanted to treat you to a coffee." Alyssa glanced at Abby to make sure she was paying attention. Alyssa was aware that at any given moment, there were at least a dozen things competing for Abby's attention, so it was worth checking. "It's a place we can talk about the case without any patients or colleagues overhearing anything."

"You realize they come here for coffee, right?"

"Okay, you're probably right, but I don't see any here now. Correct?"

Abby did a quick scan of the other patrons. "Correct."

Alyssa got to the front and placed the order for one quad and one tea, paid, and then moved to the end of the counter to wait for their drinks.

"So?" Abby held up her hands. "What did you want to tell me?"

"Mrs. Zhen did such a good job plotting her scheme, at first this whole thing just looked like a comedy of errors. If this were a detective show on TV, then that might be a good title for the episode."

"If this was a detective show, they'd make us change our names, because you're not supposed to have two main characters whose names start with the same letter."

"Well, just like any good show, this is all wrapped up, so I'd call that a happy ending."

"You know, Jenny Ocampo used that term in a completely different way."

"And I don't want to hear anything about that. Ever."

Their orders were ready, so they each grabbed their respective cardboard cups and walked to an empty table in the corner. Abby sat down, removed the lid from her cup, and took a slurp of her drink. "You're back to classes tomorrow, right?"

"Yes." Alyssa smiled. "You know, as much as I'm enjoying college, it was a fun break to help you with your case. I'm proud of you for doing this, Abby. Seriously, you did an amazing job."

"So, you'll help me with my next case?"

"Let's wait and see what you get first, and then I'll decide. Fair?"

"Fair."

"And chances are, even if I say no, I'll still end up helping you anyway. That seems to be the way it works with us."

"Apparently, that's also how the whole friend thing works, or so I've heard."

"Yes, I've heard the same. Let's face it, neither of us exactly have the problem of too many friends. We'd better hang on to one another, as nobody else wants us. Then again, it's their loss, right?"

Abby slurped down more of her quadruple espresso. "I don't know. Luis seems to want to be your friend slash boyfriend slash lover slash whatever."

"We'll see how that goes before putting any labels on it." Alyssa took a sip of her tea. "Speaking of relationships, it turned out Zee wasn't your client after all. You just wanted to help someone you cared about."

"Yeah, but I don't see why it can't be both."

"Because I'm pretty sure a person can only be considered a client if they're going to pay you, and I'm not sure helping your girlfriend counts toward your twenty-four-hundred hours."

Abby took a longer drink. "Maybe not, but I know Zee will repay me. It just won't be with money."

"And I want absolutely none of those details, thank you very much. I have to say, though, the two of you really seem to connect with one another. You're like kindred spirits."

"No, I haven't touched spirits in nearly two years."

"You know what? It doesn't matter. Let's just enjoy this moment."

"I'm not sure I can enjoy it, because I'm taking a break from seeing Zee."

"You're seriously not going to take her back? Why not?"

"No, we might get back, but it was a trust thing, so I take that seriously." Abby shrugged. "I don't know. I hope we'll move past this, but at the very least, I need some time apart from her before I decide what I want to do."

"I guess that makes sense."

"So, when's your hot date with Luis?"

"Tomorrow after class." Alyssa blushed. "And I'm so stoked."

"So you'll go on the date, have fun, and not get all weird?"

"Oh, I'm sure I'll be all weird, but I'm okay with that." Alyssa tried to smile. "I know I'm self-conscious. I know I tend to assume everyone is judging me, looking down on me, and shunning me."

"In other words, you're a teenager." Abby smirked. "There's a lot of stuff I don't know, but I do know this much. You're not at the top of other peoples' minds, as they're mostly too busy imagining their own rejections. Most people are so focused on themselves, they're not thinking about you, so you don't need to be so self-conscious."

"Easier said than done, I'm afraid. The only time I'm not self-conscious is when a good song comes on the car radio. And I know you're right, but at the same time, I also know I'm self-conscious, so until I can overcome it, it's just a trait I'll have to live with."

Abby smiled. "You're learning."

"Yeah." Alyssa smiled back. "I really am."

"I have one final loose end to tie up in this case."

Alyssa patted Abby's arm. "You mean *we* have one final loose end."

"I really like that you said that. Okay, then let's go do it together."

Alyssa paused mid-sip. "You know, it just occurred to me that I volunteered to help you with something, and I don't know what it is I've just agreed to do."

"I'm fixing up Jeff's room. I'm going to get Jeff a room with blacked-out windows and soundproofing."

Alyssa gave a slight nod of appreciation. "That's definitely worth helping you with. Where will you get soundproofing materials? Wait, do I even want to know?"

Abby's eyes met Alyssa's. "I don't think you'll disapprove, actually. I don't need to buy any materials, because I'm getting Jeff transferred to a facility that specializes in sensory deprivation."

Alyssa set down her cup. "How did you arrange that?"

"The facility owner has a really weak password on his corporate account, so I've done all the paperwork and added his electronic signature. In three days, they're sending someone to collect Jeff in a special van."

"The owner's going to find out there's a patient missing."

"I doubt it, because I've arranged for a patient to be transferred here from the main clinic instead. So, the headcount will be the same here, and I've edited the headcount at the clinic as well. It's all taken care of."

"I regret asking, but at the same time, I'm also prouder of you than I was a few seconds ago, and I didn't think that was possible."

"Do you realize how many times in the two years we've known each other that you've questioned what was possible, only to find out it totally was?"

Alyssa laughed. "No, but I'll bet it's a lot."

Abby nodded. "It's approaching triple digits. Just saying."

"So, what do we do about Cenk Vollack?"

"Nothing." Abby took a large mouthful and swallowed it. "He's gone now, and he won't be found."

"Why not?"

"Because he doesn't want to be found."

Alyssa studied Abby's face for a moment, looking for any hint, any clue she was withholding something. She finally gave up, and just asked. "Just between the two of us, did you help him escape?"

"No. I promise you I didn't."

"But you know what happened, right?"

Abby swirled the liquid in her cup. She didn't know for certain what happened to Mr. Vollack, but she had some renewed suspicions, none of which Alyssa would believe. Since meeting Abby, Alyssa had witnessed mercenary abductions, an actual haunted house, a blind astral-traveler, and been on more wild adventures than she thought possible, yet somehow, Abby was of the opinion that the theory she had about Mr. Vollack would be a bridge too far for Alyssa to handle. After a few more moments, Abby came up with an honest answer that her friend would believe. She looked deep into Alyssa's eyes. "No. I don't know what happened. I can only guess, and I know you're not a fan of people guessing."

"That's fair," Alyssa looked at her tea cup and smiled. "You know, turnabout is fair play. If you don't have an active case, how about you help me study once my classes resume?"

"I don't know anything about biology and chemistry."

"And I didn't know anything about detective work, either, but we seemed to manage."

"True."

Alyssa raised her cup. "Here's to doing what we can't do."

Abby smirked, raised her cup, and tapped it against Alyssa's. "I'll definitely drink to that. And I've made an appointment to see the doctor."

"What's up?"

"I've decided I want to live more than another year or two. I want to get a referral from my doctor to get on the organ transplant list for a new liver."

"That's great, Abby." Alyssa's smile nearly filled her entire face. "That makes me so happy to hear."

"Yeah, but there's a long wait."

"That's true." Alyssa looked away. "Um."

Abby blinked at her. "What?"

"Don't be mad at me, okay?"

"How can I promise something about the future if I'm not there yet?"

"Um, listen. I hope you're okay with this."

"Okay with what?"

Alyssa wrung her hands and began tapping her foot on the floor. "Okay, so you know how my mom is a big computer hacker nerd, right?"

"Yeah."

"And you know how we regard you as part of the family, right?"

"Wait a minute." Abby held up her hands. "I don't have to be a great detective to see where this is going. Let me ask you a question. How long ago did you mother put me on the transplant list?"

"This past Easter."

"And I was approved?"

"Yes, you just have to wait your turn, whenever a compatible liver shows up. I hope you're not angry she did that without telling you."

Abby blew a raspberry. "Yeah, as if I'd be furious at your mom for trying to save my life."

"She doesn't know how long it will take for one to be available, so she didn't want you to be disappointed. Sorry for keeping that from you. You're my best friend, so we should have full disclosure between us from now on. I won't keep things from you anymore."

"Thanks, I appreciate that." Abby took in a deep breath. "In that case, I believe Cenk Vollack is an actual demon, he used his demon powers to escape the facility, and he's currently hanging out with homeless people until he can find a willing host and slip into a new identity. I'm sorry for keeping things from you, too."

Alyssa grimaced. "Well, theories like that you definitely can keep from me, no problem. Demons don't really exist, so I think we're okay on that score."

Abby looked at the time on her phone. "I need to get back to work. I'll see you tonight after your date so I can get all the news, okay?"

Alyssa stood up. "There's no one I'd be happier to share the news with, no matter how it goes. See you later this evening."

Abby downed the last of her drink as she watched Alyssa leave. Abby then stood up and left the shop. The rain had let up, so there were more people mulling around on the sidewalk. Abby weaved around the throng until she got to the crosswalk at the corner.

When the light changed and the walk signal lit up, Abby crossed the street. As she stepped onto the opposite curb, a young, disheveled man approached her, holding out a metallic cup. "Spare change for some Lobster Thermador?"

Abby didn't recognize the man winking at her by his appearance, but there was no doubt in her mind as to whom she was speaking. "Tell you what." Abby fished around in her pockets. "Here's thirty bucks. I think you'll enjoy the sandwiches at the deli over there."

The man took the money. "Indeed, I shall, Abby Lunay, and mark my words. I shall repay you for this kindness."

"You want to repay me? Then promise me I'll never see you again, and we'll call it even."

The man nodded, then hurried across the street.

Abby just shook her head. "Alyssa's never going to believe this."

Titles by this author:

Murder Mysteries: The Baneridge Trilogy
The Baneride Murders
A Cruise to Die For
The Witness Who Wasn't There

Dark Comedy (18+)
Love by the Hour

Adventure Thriller
The Future Imperfect

Biography
Through the Woods: Dorothy's Story

Young Adult Trilogy
The Target
The Estate
The Suspect

Manufactured by Amazon.ca
Acheson, AB

11469298R00164